# A Bold Rescue

He kept his body between hers and the shooter as best he could until they came to a stop lying flat in the dust of the street . . .

"It might have been easier to get shot," the woman said from beneath him, her soft breasts pressing against his chest as she gasped for breath with every word. "You're a pretty rough rescuer."

A great confusion of feelings rose in him, flooding his veins to make his nerves tingle as if his whole body had been asleep. That silly remark made his jaw clench with anger, yet her sass, her very *breathing*, made him weak with relief that she hadn't been hurt or killed. Her voluptuous shape, her scent, and the fact that she lay pressed against his length with her legs twined with his and her arm clinging around his neck filled him with desire.

## Other AVON ROMANCES

THE DARKEST KNIGHT *by Gayle Callen*
THE FORBIDDEN LORD *by Sabrina Jeffries*
MY LORD STRANGER *by Eve Byron*
ONCE A MISTRESS *by Debra Mullins*
A SCOUNDREL'S KISS *by Margaret Moore*
TAMING RAFE *by Suzanne Enoch*
UNTAMED HEART *by Maureen McKade*

### Coming Soon

HIGHLAND BRIDES: HIGHLAND ENCHANTMENT
*by Lois Greiman*
THE PRICE OF INNOCENCE *by Susan Sizemore*

### And Don't Miss These
**ROMANTIC TREASURES**
*from Avon Books*

BECAUSE OF YOU *by Cathy Maxwell*
HOW TO MARRY A MARQUIS *by Julia Quinn*
SCANDAL'S BRIDE *by Stephanie Laurens*

# THE RENEGADES
## COLE

# GENELL DELLIN

AVON BOOKS ◆ NEW YORK

This is a work of fiction. Names, characters, places, and incidents either are the product of the author's imagination or are used fictitiously. Any resemblance to actual events, locales, organizations, or persons, living or dead, is entirely coincidental and beyond the intent of either the author or the publisher.

AVON BOOKS, INC.
1350 Avenue of the Americas
New York, New York 10019

Copyright © 1999 by Genell Smith Dellin
Inside cover author photo by Loy's Photography
Published by arrangement with the author
Library of Congress Catalog Card Number: 98-93788
ISBN: 0-380-80352-6
**www.avonbooks.com/romance**

First Avon Books Printing: April 1999

AVON TRADEMARK REG. U.S. PAT. OFF. AND IN OTHER COUNTRIES, MARCA REGIS-TRADA, HECHO EN U.S.A.

Printed in the U.S.A.

WCD   10   9   8   7   6   5   4   3   2   1

*To Artie, always*

# Chapter 1

He couldn't even get a good night's sleep and a hot breakfast anymore without somebody trying to kill him.

Cole McCord stopped at the door of Mattie's Diner and reluctantly turned away from the tantalizing smell of brewing coffee, toward the sound of his name being shouted in the street. He squinted against the midmorning sun to scan the crowded, dusty center of Pueblo City.

The rude summons rang out again. "Cole McCord! I'm callin' you out! I jist rode two hundred long, hard miles to prove you ain't the fastest draw there is."

Damn! Why had he ever come into Pueblo, anyhow? First, that ignorant tinhorn gambler who'd picked a fight last night before he'd heard Cole's name, leaving Cole bruised and sore—which had brought a scared apology—and now this stupid dare because some gun-happy waddy *did* know who he was. It was enough to make a man stay away from towns forever.

1

A creaking wagon loaded with logs rolled on past, and then he could see his challenger—a short, thin boy wearing two six-guns, scattering the good citizens of Colorado in front of him like chickens running from a hawk. Spread out across the street behind him, three rough-looking cohorts followed the would-be badman at the same, slow pace. Weary resignation flowed into Cole's bones—he'd probably have to kill them all.

He strolled to the edge of the sidewalk, taking deep breaths to loosen up for the draw. But before gunfire, he would try talking.

"After two hundred miles you need a cup of coffee instead of a bullet in your belly," he called back, his calm voice carrying easily across the rapidly emptying space between them. "Think about it, son."

"Think about it yourself, old man. You're the one who'll be eatin' lead. My name's Kid Dolby," his opponent yelled. "The next dime novel's gonna be about *me*." Cole waited, silent. Talking wasn't going to do the trick.

Cole stepped into the street, moving deliberately toward the center, raking his gaze over his adversaries, trying to judge them and their intentions. He decided that, most likely, the ruffians backing the kid would let the boy take the first shot: they were watching Kid Dolby more than they were watching him. Damn it all to hell and gone, he was going to have to kill this child.

Kid Dolby's eyes glinted with excitement and

fear—they shone bright as lights in the shadow of his battered hat. His face looked way too young for such shenanigans. He couldn't yet be called a man; his voice even cracked when he called out again.

"*Mister* McCord, your rep is a helluva lot faster than your hand."

The boy's own hands were shaking, hovering near his holsters, not quite steady enough to go for the guns. But he stopped walking when he reached the cross-street, and he just stood there, his chest heaving. With his next breath, or the next, he would grab his six-shooters and start firing, for he was in too deep to back out now, and his nerve was melting like snow in the sun. Cole got ready.

The circle of silence that always fell around two men ready to draw began to grow as people all up and down the street noticed what was happening. The town got so quiet that he could hear the flapping of a signboard in the wind and then, from off to his left, the sound of hooves and wheels pounding, rattling, coming closer. He needed to keep his gaze steady on the Kid's hands, but he had to risk a glance.

Dear God. A woman wearing a hat with a feather and a faraway look on her face was driving a big sorrel horse straight at him, headlong. He recognized the instant she noticed him and the Kid and realized what was happening, but it was too late for her to turn or stop. The rig rushed in between him and the boy as a glint of sunlight on metal flickered on the other side of the open cart where the woman sat. The kid had a gun out. She was rolling right into the line of fire.

Cole's brain went cold, his body moved on pure instinct, and he lunged for her, grabbing her out of the gig so swiftly that the momentum of her slight weight set him off balance. He hit the ground with a bone-crunching thud, but he managed to hold her tight in both arms and keep her from the Kid, who was firing round after wild round, making the shots echo from the brick buildings and ping off the metal watering trough, making horses whinny and people yell. He kept his body between hers and the shooter as best he could until they came to a stop, lying flat in the dust of the street.

Twisting his neck to try to watch his back, he jerked his right arm from beneath her and pulled his gun, but there was no need. Kid Dolby wasn't shooting any more, because Sheriff Bass was walking up to him with his gun drawn. Cole glimpsed other men holding guns on the Kid's buddies. Voices began rising from up and down the street.

"It might've been easier to get shot," the woman said from beneath him, her soft breasts pressing against his chest as she gasped for breath with every word. "You're a pretty rough rescuer."

A great confusion of feelings rose in him, flooding his veins to make his nerves tingle as if his whole body had been asleep for years. That silly remark made his jaw clench with anger, yet her sass, her very *breathing*, made him weak with relief that she hadn't been hurt or killed. Her voluptuous shape, her scent, and the fact that she lay pressed against his length with her legs twined with his and her arm clinging around his neck filled him with desire.

Anger he was accustomed to. He chose it.

"You ever *been* shot, lady? That's a damn-fool, featherbrained thing to say."

She did have the grace to blush.

"I was only teasing! Can't you take a joke and laugh a little?"

"You could've been killed if you'd been shot."

She gave an unladylike snort of disdain. "What a bit of wisdom. And *you* called *me* a featherbrain!"

He dropped his gun into his holster and started trying to untangle himself.

"Well, if you had the sense God gave an armadillo," he said as he managed to get to his knees, "you wouldn't have come galloping into the middle of a gunfight. What's the matter with you anyway, driving like a bat out of hell right in town?"

"I didn't know I was *in* town!"

He stared down into her heart-shaped face, surrounded by the cloud of curly, honey-colored hair. Her hat was long gone. She was beautiful. And, evidently, quite loco.

"Where else but in town do you see buildings and sidewalks?"

"You needn't be sarcastic. I mean I didn't

*look,*" she said, holding out her hand to him so he could help her. "I was thinking about something else."

She sat up and gave him a long, direct look. His hand engulfed her small one in its thin doeskin glove. Her eyes were wide and impossibly blue. Heat began to build beneath his skin.

Kid Dolby's sharp voice cut through all the other sounds swirling in the street.

"Cole McCord, you ain't rid of me. Be ready to draw when I git outta jail."

"Damn that boy, he's crazy," he muttered, looking over his shoulder for his tormentor. "He's gonna keep on until I'll have to kill him."

"Oh," she said, and closed her fingers tight around his. "Oh, my."

"Don't be scared," he said, turning back to her, "the sheriff's taken the Kid's gun away."

But she wasn't scared at all. She looked cool as fresh water sitting there in the middle of the dusty street.

"Cole McCord," she said, satisfaction filling her unusual, husky voice. "You're the man I came to town to see!"

Stunned, he stared at her.

"As a general rule, I don't like to hear that," he drawled. "You're not looking for a fast draw at sundown, are you?"

She smiled and tightened her grip.

"No. I'm here to offer you a job that you've just proved you can do—I want you to be my bodyguard while I trail twenty-two hundred head of cattle to Texas."

Oh, Lord, what next? The last thing he needed was another life in his hands.

"Trail drives're supposed to take cattle *out* of Texas," he said. "You're going backwards, miss, if you're moving 'em north to south."

"No, I'm not. I'm taking them to the last of the unsettled range—the Texas Panhandle."

He stood up, fast, and pulled his hand free, but one foot caught in her skirts. He jerked it and made a loud ripping sound.

"Wait!"

She grabbed his leg with both hands, and he felt the shape of her slender fingers through his pants and even the top of his boot.

"Let me," she said breathlessly. "Your spur's tearing my dress."

"Sorry. I had no idea . . ."

He bent double to try to help her, and suddenly their eyes were on a level, their faces close together, although his was upside down. They looked at each other for one long heartbeat. Then she dragged in a deep breath, and he straightened up to let her free him. He felt a fleeting sense of loss when she let go of his leg.

"I'm sorry about your skirt."

"Don't worry about it, it's not important. After all," she said, flashing him a devilish grin, "we could've both been killed."

He couldn't resist grinning back at her.

"We do have a law in this town," Sheriff Bass's voice boomed, "and you had best remember that, boy."

Cole turned to see a parade almost upon them, a crowd escorting his challengers to jail, with the sheriff and Kid Dolby in the lead. The Kid was glaring at Cole so fixedly that he ignored the sheriff's warning and everyone else around him. Various people were holding the Kid's compadres at gunpoint to follow him; some other concerned citizens—one, the doctor carrying his bag—were headed toward him and the woman. Cole waved them away.

"We're not hurt," he called, instantly wanting to be out of all the furor as quickly as possible.

"You're sure of that, Mr. McCord?" the doctor asked.

"Yes."

"Yes, I'm fine, thank you," the woman called, as she freed the spur and took Cole's offered hand to get to her feet.

The sheriff stopped in front of them, holding Kid Dolby by the arm. The Kid spoke before the sheriff could open his mouth.

"Cole McCord, I'll be famous yet for killing you. Next time I draw down on you you can't hide behind no woman."

People stood back immediately, especially those behind the Kid, watching Cole. He had to resist the urge to yell at them to stay where they were, that obviously he wouldn't shoot an unarmed man. He forced himself to take a long, deep breath and hold his tongue. Most people did give him a wide berth and plenty of respect, and if they overdid it that certainly was better than dealing with suicidal fools like the Kid.

"Next time you *see* me, you'd better be huntin' a hole to hide in," Cole said flatly. "Next time you draw down on me I'll kill you, Kid."

Didn't anybody in the world have any sense left? This boy couldn't be more than fifteen years old, and at least two of those no-good rascals riding with him were old enough to know how to keep him out of trouble.

"Get ready," the Kid said stubbornly, "I ain't lettin' you git away with this, McCord . . ."

The sheriff twisted his arm harder behind him, and he hushed.

"Sheriff," Cole said, "can you keep this boy locked in a cell until he grows up?"

"Reckon I might," Bass said. "Gunfightin' in the street's agin the law nowadays in Pu'blo City. Wanted to point that out, is all, Mr. McCord."

"He called me out. I had no choice."

"Of course," the sheriff said hastily, "of course. Not at all. I wasn't meaning that you done anything to break the law, Mr. McCord, not in any way."

"*He* wasn't fightin', that's right," Kid Dolby said, in a sarcastic singsong. "Don't arrest him, Sheriff. The great Cole McCord, the most *dangerous* man in Colorado, was tryin' to git away from Kid Dolby, that's all he was doin'."

"Shut up, you little smart aleck," said the sheriff.

He nodded apologetically to Cole and, trailed

by half the town, dragged the Kid on down the street toward the jail.

Cole turned to find the blonde woman still standing at his elbow. She held out her hand for him to shake as a man would do.

"Aurora Benton," she said, "of the Flying B."

He touched the brim of his hat, then shook her hand.

"Cole McCord, ma'am."

"Well, Mr. McCord, now that all the excitement is dying down, I can say thank you for saving me from a bullet and we can discuss my offer of employment to you."

"I'm not interested in a job but, out of curiosity, I'd like to know why you've chosen me for the offer, Miss Benton."

"You must know that people call you the most dangerous man in Colorado," she said. "You give no quarter, and you have the fastest draw of anyone, everyone says so. I take that to mean you could protect me from the most *obnoxious* man in Colorado."

"Has someone threatened you?"

He could've bitten his tongue if it would've stopped the words. He wasn't taking the job, so he didn't need to know that, didn't even want to know—why had he asked?

"He has told me, in his own jovial, avuncular way, that I'll never make it across the Texas line with my cattle, and I know him well enough to believe he'll stop at nothing to make his prediction come true."

Again, he spoke when he should've been walking away.

"Perhaps he's only trying to discourage you for your own good. Trailing cattle can be a dangerous undertaking, as I'm sure you know."

She narrowed her beautiful blue eyes and stuck out her chin. There was a definite streak of stubbornness there that she was using for a backbone.

"Obviously, I do know that, which is my reason for coming to you. I need someone to watch my back on the trail."

Then she suddenly gave him that blinding smile of hers.

"But Mr. Gates's threats aren't made with my welfare in mind. He claims the cattle are his, and since he can't prove it in a court of law he plans to kill me and take them. You, like most of Pueblo, may see Lloyd Gates as a charming, upstanding pillar of the community, but I know he's a vengeful, ruthless man."

She was so small and so clearly a very feminine young woman with her lace collar and a ribbon at her throat that it seemed ludicrous for her to be so set on talk of trail drives and ruthless men. Cole's old Rangering instincts immediately put a string of questions on his tongue, but he bit them back. Maybe she truly was in trouble, or maybe she was a little touched in the head. He didn't care, he didn't want to know, didn't need to know. He wasn't *going* to know. He had to get away from her.

"And Gates isn't the only one," she was saying in her husky voice, which had a little break in it now and then. "You know as well as I do that when word spreads that my herd is trailed by a woman, there'll be others who'll try to take it away from me."

He did know that—if she could actually manage to hold a herd together and start it south—but he closed his mind against the images springing to life in his imagination.

"It isn't a common thing for a woman to do," he said. "You might want to think again before you start out."

"I have no choice. I can do it if you'll come along to protect me."

The word "protect" sent a chill of the old guilt right through him.

"I'm sorry for your troubles, but I can't help you," he said. "I'm not the one to take responsibility for another person's life."

He turned on his heel and strode away.

"But you just did! You just did take responsibility for my life!"

He didn't even turn his head; he gave no sign that he had heard her.

She waited a moment and then called after him again.

"I didn't even ask you to, and you saved me from being shot. You said so yourself."

He kept walking.

Later, Aurora could not believe that she had called out after Cole McCord, had *yelled* at him in public, right out in the street like some kind of hoyden. And she could not believe that she couldn't think of anyone else for her bodyguard now that he had turned her down flat.

She had thought of nothing but Cole McCord from the moment he'd left her. When Tom Drury had caught her horse and brought him to her, she had been so immersed in watching Cole disappear around the corner that she'd hardly thanked the man. When she'd ordered the supplies to be sent to the ranch, she'd been remembering how secure she'd felt with Cole's arms around her, and she had had to go over the list three times before she got everything they would need for the drive. And when she'd bought the new dress to replace the dusty one his spur had ripped from thigh to hem, she had taken so long to make her choice because she'd been trying to guess how Cole would like each one. Mrs. Donathan, who owned the shop, had almost lost her patience, but money was so tight that she couldn't buy all three dresses she liked so much, as the woman kept suggesting. She really shouldn't have bought this one.

But she did carefully keep back the money she'd hoarded all winter for the bodyguard's pay, and she did get all the supplies that were on Cookie's list. The damage she'd done was to her emergency funds, which now were down to nearly nothing.

Sighing, she turned away from the window of her hotel room, where she constantly found herself lurking behind the curtains, hoping to see Cole out on the street. She crossed to the bed, where she stood and gazed down at the new dress she had finally chosen. It was worth its price, with its short jacket that showed off her waist and the divided skirt in which she could ride into a town along the trail, if need be.

But the deciding factor was its colors, the very blue of her eyes in the heavy twill of the jacket and skirt and, in the soft blouse, a honeyed fawn that matched her hair. She wasn't trying to attract Cole McCord, though. Not at all.

She was simply trying to look womanly and businesslike all at once, which was exactly how she needed to look to deal with Cole McCord. He had to realize that she was a woman who needed help so that his gallantry would demand that he hear her out. Plus he had to understand that she would pay him well and define his duties clearly. The fact that just looking at him made her want to grab his lapels and beg him to come with her was completely irrelevant. Any kind of personal relationship would weaken her authority on the trail.

Her pulse quickened with excitement and fear at the thought of the drive, and she fluffed her damp hair again with both hands before she bent over and shook it to let the air to all its layers. If she was going to take her five loyal cowboys and twenty-two hundred cattle safely down the trail, she *had* to have someone extra hired to watch out for trouble. And she had to hire him soon—after noon tomorrow she'd be forced to go back to the Flying B and finish preparations for the drive. At this moment, she really ought to be considering how to find some other prospects for the job if Cole McCord turned her down again.

But no one came to mind. She did try to think of someone, but her mind went blank.

Before she'd come to town, it had been merely an idea to hire Cole, based on his reputation. Now hiring him, and only him, to be her bodyguard had become an obsession.

It wasn't because he had muscles like steel and an unexpected, crooked grin like sunshine on a cloudy day. Or that he had dark, dark eyes the color of melted chocolate. It certainly was not.

It was because even the sheriff treated him with exaggerated courtesy, because people were afraid of his fast draw all around the country, and because everyone she had ever talked to who had had any dealings with him called him a square-dealer and a straight-talker who never went back on his word. God knew, she had to have someone she could trust.

Plus, he would be an interesting companion on the long trail to Texas, even if he wasn't quick to laugh and his smile was rare. There were mysteries in his eyes and a tension in him, and she wanted to know why. She was simply curious, that was all, and she was tired of having no one new to talk to for weeks at a time.

Restlessly, she walked to the window again.

A good many people were on the street, but Cole wasn't among them, at least not that she could see from here. He seemed to have disappeared.

A quick fear clutched at her heart. He couldn't have left town. When she had checked into the hotel a little after noon, a friendly visit with the desk clerk about her morning's adventure had elicited the information that Cole was, indeed, staying in Room 4 waiting to meet a man from Denver who, according to today's telegram, would be arriving tomorrow. That clerk had better be right.

Otherwise, she would've found Cole and followed him everywhere he went all day trying to convince him to take the job, even if her hair *had* been full of dust from rolling in the street and her dress dirty and torn. And the flirtatious old codger had better be right about Cole's taking all his meals at Mattie's Diner, too, because that was where she planned to waylay him at supper.

Swiftly, she turned away from the window and went to the mirror to begin putting up her hair. It was still damp, but she couldn't help that. The sun was starting down, and she wanted time to dress so she'd look her very best.

Lloyd Gates went straight to the Golden Nugget Saloon as soon as he finished his business at the bank.

"Bring me a whiskey, Nate, will you?" he

called to the bartender in passing. And then, before he thought, he added, "No, make it two."

His usual table in the corner was empty, so he took his position there with his back to the wall. A man couldn't be too careful when everybody in town was jealous of his success, never mind how they treated him to his face.

Nate brought the drinks.

"Expectin' somebody?"

"Nah. I'm just thirsty. Too tempting to get a bottle, though."

Too costly, too, but he didn't say that. People thought he was a generous man, and he was when it suited some purpose, but there was no sense throwing money away on a whole bottle of whiskey for Skeeter. He could get him to agree to the plan without an unnecessary expense like that.

He didn't want to admit that he was waiting for Skeeter, either. Everyone would see them talking, but that would appear to be happenstance. He made a habit of visiting with everybody who came down the pike, and the whole town knew he discussed everything with everybody. No, if he didn't mention Skeeter ahead of time, this little meeting wouldn't draw any special attention, not nearly so much as if they'd been spotted alone in a more private place.

Nate put both drinks in front of him.

"Was you around for the near-gunfight this mornin'?" he asked.

Damned if the man wasn't as nosy as an old,

gossipy woman. Ordinarily, Lloyd would enjoy picking his brain for news, but right now he needed some peace to think things out some more. However, he couldn't be rude without that being grist for Nate's mill, too.

"Yeah," he said. "Hard to believe there was that many rounds shot off and nobody killed."

"*Or* hurt," Nate said. " 'Specially Miss Benton, her driving in between the two shooters right at the wrong time."

"Yeah," Lloyd said. "She got there at the exact right . . . I mean wrong, time."

He managed to make his tone interested, yet impersonal, but the fire of frustration in his belly flared up again. He still couldn't believe that particular piece of rotten luck—if she'd been hit, as by all rights she should've been, he wouldn't have to be fooling with Skeeter at all.

Nate hung around for a minute, wiping at the table with a towel, chatting about a dozen inconsequential topics, but finally he went away. As Nate stepped behind the bar again, Lloyd watched him greet the two new arrivals walking up to it and thought about the fact that Nate knew all the cowboys for miles around and who worked for what outfit. But Nate would not think one thing about him talking to Skeeter, no matter what happened later far away from here.

He took another sip of whiskey and gave a big sigh of appreciation. It didn't matter what Nate saw or didn't see. Nobody still alive had a hint that he and Skeeter had known each other before.

He leaned back in his chair and watched the door, taking tiny sips of his drink, so as to save it as long as possible.

Aurora was still half a block from Mattie's Diner when the door opened and Cole McCord stepped out onto the sidewalk. Sheer surprise stopped her for a minute. He was coming her way.

The way he moved made her breath catch in her throat. He walked like no other man she'd ever seen, in a confident, unhurried manner that proclaimed he would go wherever he wanted and do as he pleased when he got there.

She watched him, trying not to let him see that she was. She needn't have bothered. He hadn't even noticed her.

His long, fluid strides covered the ground fast, but they looked lazy and slow, like a big cat's prowl. The long saddle muscles flexed in his thighs beneath his tight black pants, and his feet, even in boots, seemed to stroke the earth softly with each step. She couldn't take her eyes off him.

Without warning, she could feel his arms around her, could smell the starch of his shirt and the spicy scent of his skin through the dust of the street. Remembering sent an implacable desire pouring through her, the desire to be close to him again with her breasts pressed against his hard chest. She felt her face flame at the thought. Shameless. Not only was she becoming prodigiously bold but she was becoming shameless, too.

However, if bold and shameless were what it took to survive, then so be it. She'd already shouted at him on the street once today, so what would it matter if she initiated another public conversation with him? Living by society's rules wasn't going to get her a ranch in Texas or a safe passage to it.

"Mr. McCord," she said as he reached her, "how nice to see you again."

He tipped his hat. "Miss Benton."

But he intended to walk on past.

She swallowed hard and spoke quickly.

"May I have a moment of your time?"

He stopped, looking down at her with a quick, impatient stare that cut right through her. His remoteness made her heart lurch. What if she couldn't persuade him, after all?

"I ask you to please reconsider my offer of employment. This morning I neglected to say that I can pay you well."

"I thought I made it clear that I'm not interested."

His tone was a level louder than necessary—from irritation, no doubt—and a couple passing behind him on the sidewalk turned to glance at him, then looked at Aurora. She gave them only a passing glance so they wouldn't stop to talk, but they were Sid and Dolly Reichert, who owned the next ranch south of hers and who'd been kind to her when her father died. To her chagrin, instead of going on down the street, they strolled to the mercantile's window and stood looking in, staying within earshot of her conversation.

She stiffened her spine and concentrated on Cole McCord. It didn't matter what the Reicherts thought of her because they weren't helping her get her cattle to Texas.

"You may have heard in town today that I'm losing my ranch and am short of funds," she said, "but I can pay you. I can pay you very well."

She glanced at the Reicherts again, and he flicked the barest look in that direction, too. Understanding flashed in his eyes.

"Well, now, that makes me feel downright special," he drawled, just loud enough for them to hear. "If you're short of funds, what kind of compensation *do* you have in mind for me, Miss Benton?"

A lewd chuckle sounded behind her, and she whirled to see that they had an even bigger audience than she'd thought, for two old men sat on a bench placed against the wall of the mercantile, their beady eyes twinkling, their big ears straining for more. The Reicherts were still at the window, silently listening, too. Aurora turned her back on them all and gave Cole McCord a straight, hard look.

"I'll pay you money, of course."

"Money," he said thoughtfully. "To go down the Loving Trail with you?"

The way he said it, the name of the famous

trail took on an entirely different meaning, one that had nothing to do with geography. Her face burned with heat, and the old men cackled gleefully.

"Take 'er up on it, son," one of them said. "You'll regret it if'n' you don't!"

Cole McCord was looking her up and down, from head to toe, with open speculation in his eyes, as if he really believed that she had meant what he implied. Her temper flared. So he thought he could embarrass her enough to make her go away.

"Yes," she said briskly, in her most business-like tone, "I'll use the Loving Trail until we go through the Raton Pass and probably some farther—I'll decide after that where we should turn east."

"*You* will? You don't have a trail boss?"

"I *am* the trail boss."

He smiled at her, shaking his head as if she were a precocious child playing games of pretend.

"Then you must've bumped your head when we took our little tumble in the street," he said. "Don't you know it's easier to go to Texas through Kansas than the New Mexico mountains?"

One of the old men laughed out loud. Her blood went icy with anger.

"Mr. McCord," she said, "could we step into the diner there and perhaps talk about this over a cup of coffee? It's my treat, of course. I'd like to make you a specific offer."

She turned to start toward the door.

"No . . ."

She faced him again. He leaned back against a post and crossed his muscular arms, flashing a wry grin as he looked her over again, his dark, dark eyes lingering on her mouth.

". . . thank you, anyway, Miss Benton."

Lord, but he was enjoying this. And he thought he was winning. He thought because she was a woman behaving in an unconventional way he could intimidate her into giving up.

"Then we shall talk here," she said, willing her voice to stay cool, although her lips were warm from the heat of his gaze and her cheeks were hot from anger. "But if you think you can embarrass me into giving up my pursuit of you by making salacious innuendos that others can hear and rudely perusing my person, you're wrong, Mr. McCord."

He smiled.

"Mercy! I'll have to think on that a minute," he drawled, with infuriating insolence. "The only thing I caught for sure is that you are pursuing me and, ma'am . . ." he paused to tip his hat, ". . . I want you to know I'm truly flattered to hear that."

She felt her cheeks grow red again, she heard the old men laugh, and she knew the Reicherts had taken in every word. But what was a little bit of chagrin compared to what she'd face on the trail? And in Texas? Drought, outlaws, hard traveling, and maybe even Comanches. This teasing was nothing. If she wanted a ranch of her own, she had to ignore these little irritations and remember that from now on she was living by her own set of rules.

"My pursuit of you, as you well know, is purely business," she said briskly. "The compensation I have in mind is fifty dollars a month, but I'm willing to deal a little on that. Your only responsibility will be the safety of my person."

"*Will* be?" Cole McCord drawled in a low, intimate tone that made her feel as if he'd touched her. "You sound mighty sure of yourself, Miss Benton."

She smiled.

"I won't take 'no' for an answer."

He sighed and shook his head in mock sorrow. "You sound just like Kid Dolby."

The old men and the Reicherts waited, straining to hear her reply.

She tilted her head, crossed her arms, and looked Cole McCord slowly up and down in the same suggestive way he had looked at her.

"Why, Mr. McCord," she drawled, "all the Kid and I are after is a little satisfaction."

He tried but couldn't hide his surprise at her boldness, and that made her smile, even as she felt Mrs. Reichert's horrified gaze on her back. She could hardly keep from laughing out loud in spite of the fact that she'd slightly embarrassed herself. He deserved a dose of his own medicine.

"I'm not willing to satisfy the Kid by letting

him shoot me," he said with a wicked grin, "but to you, Miss Benton, I'd be happy to give a different kind of satisfaction . . . any time."

He let the words hang in the air between them for a long moment.

"At your pleasure, Miss Aurora."

He touched the brim of his hat with exaggerated politeness, then turned his back on her, stepped off the sidewalk, and started across the street with his prowling panther walk. The slanting beams of the setting sun made his white shirt burn orange like the heart of a fire.

Like the fearful anger inside her.

Not once, in two encounters, had he considered what she had to say or discussed it with her sensibly. He had dismissed her as demented or silly or impossibly foolish, as everyone else had when they'd heard she was planning to trail the cattle.

He stepped up onto the boarded walkway on the other side of the street, strolled across it, and pushed open the swinging doors of the saloon. Of course he would go there, where she couldn't follow.

# Chapter 2

**A**urora marched directly across the street to the entrance of the Golden Nugget. Let the Reicherts and the rest of Pueblo City gossip, it'd make no difference—she'd soon be gone to Texas, and anyway, from now on polite society might as well be on the moon. Any woman who carved a ranch out of the Panhandle would be living far beyond anybody's rules of behavior but her own.

She pushed the swinging doors back with both hands and burst into the saloon without changing her unladylike pace. How could she slow down with her blood beating in her head like a marching drum?

Cole McCord was leaning on the bar, his white shirt shining like a beacon in the dim, smoky room. As she started toward him, striding down the aisleway between tables with her skirts switching angrily back and forth about her ankles, conversation in the place began to lessen and then die. She didn't look at anyone, but she felt dozens of eyes on her. Soon, the tinny piano's lively version of "Buffalo Gals" became the only sound.

She ignored everyone around her and didn't miss a step on her direct path to the bar. The piano player started singing, then, and before she reached the place where Cole was standing, men's voices began to rumble again. A respectable woman in a saloon might be a novelty but not enough of one to stop gambling games and serious drinking. Or to make Cole McCord look her way. He hadn't glanced at her once.

At last, she walked up beside him and leaned on the bar, which was almost too tall for her. Cole wheeled on her then, with a hard look that held anger but no surprise.

"Good," she said, "that means you're alert at all times."

He stared at her as if she'd spoken in a foreign language.

"I wasn't sure that you saw me come in," she said briskly. "Now, from that irritated glare, I know that you did. Therefore, you'll make a good bodyguard."

"It was my understanding that you already believed I'd make the most amazing bodyguard on the face of the earth and that was the reason you're tormenting me."

"It was my understanding that you are enough of a gentleman to listen until I have finished talking with you. Instead, you ran away into this den of iniquity thinking it was the one place I couldn't follow you."

She marveled that her voice didn't shake
from the weight of her anger. Most of it
stemmed from the fact that she had very little
right to be angry at all, but she wasn't about to
admit that to him.

He cocked his head to one side and looked
her up and down again.

"But you did follow me," he said wryly. "Obviously, I can run but I can't hide."

Slight chagrin tinged her anger, and she
turned away so he wouldn't see it. Honestly, he
was being rather patient with her, since she was
following him around town accosting him at
every turn. Maybe women pursued him all the
time, since he was handsome enough to stop a
beating heart.

"Tell me, Miss Benton," he said, leaning close
to her as the din grew louder, "why me *again*?
I have refused your request. There must be fifty
other men, at least, right here in this one place.
Why don't you take 'no' for an answer and simply go find yourself another bodyguard?"

His breath felt warm on her ear. A thrill
passed through her, made her shiver. She
moved a bit away from him and lifted one hand
to signal the bartender, as she'd just seen someone else do.

"Lemonade, please."

"If you're man enough to come into a saloon,
you ought to be man enough to order whiskey," he snapped.

"I have to keep my wits about me."

She waited for her drink without looking at

him, but she could feel his eyes assessing her profile.

"Why not get someone else? Answer me, Aurora."

He had never called her by her given name before, but there was no thrill in it—the cold hardness in his voice could have cut wood.

She spun around.

"How many of these men in here are trustworthy, Cole? How many wouldn't leave me and my men tied to a tree or dead in a coulee somewhere, run new brands onto my cattle and start their *own* ranch in Texas? How could I know which one to trust?"

"You don't know me. I might do the same."

"Never. You're a Texas Ranger."

His full lips tightened, a sharp shadow passed through his eyes.

"Not any more."

"You still have honor, though. I've asked a lot of people about you."

"You wasted your time. Nobody knows me."

He held her gaze with a long, hard look. His eyes turned black, filled with thoughts she couldn't read, but she looked back at him steadily, not flinching, not giving an inch.

"Many men have honor," he said shortly. "You live around here. You know many who do."

The bartender brought a mug of lemonade. She sighed and leaned toward Cole, reaching for her glass with both hands, willing the few pieces of ice in it to cool the heat of rising anticipation building in her blood. A person couldn't make assumptions about Cole Mc-Cord, this much she had already learned about him, so the fact that he was actually testing her reasons for offering the job to him didn't mean anything. But maybe it did.

"Look, Mr. McCord, I know you think I'm crazy, I know you're sick of my annoying you, but I'm desperate. We're talking about my survival here. My only hope for a decent life is to try to get to Texas with twenty-two hundred head of cattle, five cowboys, and an old man and two youngsters, counting Skeeter, who's all crippled up from a horse wreck. I can't pay any more hands than that, so I have to ride scout myself, and I can't do that and keep constant watch."

"Sell something and hire some more men."

"I've sold all I can. And what money I've saved would be much better spent on you, considering your abilities and your reputation."

He shrugged. "Maybe."

"No maybes. I know it. Who better to protect me than the most dangerous man in Colorado?"

He gave a derisive snort.

"My reputation won't help you any—it'll just attract every would-be outlaw like Kid Dolby who can beg, borrow, or steal a horse to ride out to meet your herd."

She gripped the mug hard to steady her hands. Dear Lord, please let this discussion mean he was seriously thinking of agreeing to come with her.

"Your reputation will work the opposite way, too, though, remember that," she said, "especially on the man who's sworn to keep me from getting my cattle through. He'll be afraid of you, I know he will, so really, you'll have very little work to do."

"Just dealing with you every day would be a lot of work," he said dryly.

That annoyed her at first, but then it pleased her, too. This was personal, she was making progress! At least she'd pulled him out of that awful remoteness.

"I'll be too busy to give you any problems," she said. "I won't even talk to you—all you have to do is stay out of my way and keep an eye out for trouble."

He frowned fiercely.

"Stay out of your way?"

"While I boss the drive."

"Have some sense! I can't turn you loose . . . I mean, whoever you hire to be your bodyguard . . . can't let you make all the decisions when it's his job to keep you safe. What if you pick a stretch of quicksand as a place to ford a river and mire yourself up to your neck? Then it's his job to get you out."

"*You* have some sense! I know what I'm doing. How do you think I've held onto these cattle and my last few possessions for six months with half the thieves in Colorado riding out to my ranch, trying, legally or illegally, to strip me of everything?"

He raised his eyebrows.

"By threatening to put the greedy grabbers to work against their wills?" he said sarcastically. "By assigning a job to each one and badgering him until he either buckles down to it or runs screaming down the road?"

She laughed. "Right. But they've all run away, the cowards. I take you for a braver man than that."

His lips turned up at the corners. A little warmth ran through her. Good. If she could make him laugh and let down his guard, she could win him over.

They each took a sip of their drinks. He kept looking at her.

"This buzzard who threatened you," he said, "the one who told you he'd stop you from going down the trail. He must be a bad one."

"He thinks he is," she said, drinking from her glass again, suddenly dry-mouthed from too much hope, "and sometimes that's the most dangerous kind."

He shook his head.

"You think you're a trail boss, you think you know bad men, you think you can persuade me to come with you ... I think you're over-confident, Miss Benton, and that's a dangerous way to be."

Her spirits dropped into her shoes, but she made her expression as impassive as his.

"No," she said quietly, looking him straight

in the eye, "I *know* I can persuade you. I know I can be a trail boss, and I know a lot about people, bad ones and good ones. You're coming with me, Mr. McCord. You might as well finish your drink and go pack your warbag."

He stared at her for a moment more, then he threw back his head and laughed, really laughed. It was a wonderful, rippling sound, truly delightful.

"Aurora Benton," he said, "I've heard of mule-footed and mule-eared and mule-headed horses, but you're the most mule-*minded* human being I ever saw."

He was laughing at her, but there was admiration in his voice, too. She gritted her teeth and gave him a determinedly sweet smile.

"I'll take that as a compliment."

He looked into her eyes, searchingly, as if she were some kind of curiosity. "Don't you have any 'quit' in you?"

"Not anymore, I don't," she said. "If I quit on this drive, I'm lost."

"How so?"

"I'll have no freedom, ever again. If I don't save this one herd of cattle and find some free land to ranch, I'll have three unacceptable choices: move into town here and live in poverty as a teacher paid half what a man would make, marry a man I cannot abide, or go back East to live off the charity of relatives."

A warmth came into his eyes, a look she took to be admiration, a look that made her blood heat like a sudden stroke of the sun. She was going to win. He was going with her to Texas, and she'd better start learning right now not to let herself become too attracted to him.

But he only finished his drink, set the glass down, and pushed it away.

"I can't help you," he said. "But I wish you plenty of water, tall grass, and luck."

Stunned, she watched him fish a coin from the front pocket of his well-fitted pants and toss it onto the counter, indicating with a gesture that it took care of the lemonade also.

"Ride safe," he said, with a cursory tip of his hat.

Before she could think how best to reply, he was gone.

The smoke threatened to choke Cole with every breath he took, and his mind wandered so constantly that he couldn't keep in mind the cards he himself had been dealt, much less make a guess as to which ones his opponents might hold. No wonder he wasn't winning—it was pure luck that he was even breaking even. Before the next round of betting could start, he stood up and threw in his hand.

"I'm out," he said. "Thank you, gentlemen."

He was through the door and into the back corridor of the hotel in a heartbeat, striding toward the stairs at a feverish pace, but the air seemed just as thick there as in the Gentleman's Club. Worse, his thoughts continued to roil. He took the stairs two at a time. What he needed, all he needed, was sleep.

The thought twisted his lips into a bitter smile. Every night sleep was hard enough to come by, had been ever since Travis got killed, but tonight it'd be a true lost cause. He hadn't been this stirred up in years.

It must be because of how close he had come to having to kill the boy, or maybe because of the little whelp's insistence on not giving up until they drew on each other. Kid Dolby was even more of a greenhorn than Cole had been when he ran away from home to join the Rangers. At the rate he was going, he wouldn't live to become much older.

Cole reached his room, took out his key, unlocked the door, and went in, realizing as he closed it behind him that he was still moving as fast as if he were running from someone or something. Well, he was. All day long this emotional turmoil had been threatening to swamp him.

The latch clicked closed in the sudden silence of the room, but being alone gave him no peace: his thoughts kept racing, he still felt too hot, too confined. Maybe he ought to just turn around, go get his horse, ride on out, and take temptation away from the Kid. He could simply be gone when the boy got out of jail—and when the man he was supposed to meet tomorrow arrived from Denver. He didn't want a job with the Pinkertons, anyhow.

And he sure as hell didn't want any more days like this one.

He stripped to the waist, dunked his head in

the water bowl, went to the window, wrenched it open, and leaned out into the moonlight. The air bathed his skin—cold air—but in spite of the temperature it carried spring on its breath. A light breeze blew from the east, and he would swear it smelled of flowers and damp earth.

A sudden longing, a fierce, unnameable yearning, twisted inside him, and he searched the night as if he could see something that might assuage it. The sky stretched high and wide, clear and black, the full moon shone yellow, the stars gleamed white as the feathers they were said to be in the Chickasaw legends of his mother's people. A thousand more feelings surged, swirling, inside him, and, without warning, the truth rode to the surface.

Aurora Benton was the one who'd whipped up the maelstrom inside him. She had done it to him from the very first moment he had found himself lying in the middle of the street with her in his arms, while that terrible flood of relief and fury and desire roared in his blood.

The *life* in her, the way she'd taken him to task for being too serious, the way she'd smiled, the way she'd simply assumed he would be her bodyguard if she only asked had drawn him to her. The way she'd come marching into the saloon on his trail as no other respectable woman would ever do, hotly indignant because he hadn't stayed to hear her out, sharpened his curiosity even more. Dear God, the way she'd assumed she could trail a herd all the way to Texas and set out to do it was enough to make him root for her. Everything about her had pierced his hard shell.

How long had it been since he had laughed out loud the way he had today? How long, how many years, since he had taken delight in any trait in anybody the way he had in Aurora's stubbornness?

How long since he had even *noticed* anybody? People were part of the landscape to him, objects, good or bad, to be dealt with in the course of whatever job he was on. But Miss Aurora was different—*she* meant to be dealing with *him*—and she had put her trust completely in him never knowing how he'd destroyed Travis, who had trusted him, too.

Wearily, he drew his head back into the room and sagged against the window frame, dragging the cold air deeper and more slowly into his lungs while he faced the terrible fact he'd been keeping locked up out of sight for nearly eight months. He was merely existing, with no purpose. Running away from hell day in Texas to the cold mountains of Colorado hadn't helped him one bit.

It was Aurora Benton who had done this to him, she was the one who'd made him see that he was numb to the heart, no more than a walking dead man, and she'd done it by being so alive, so full of hope, so stubbornly determined to hire him. To Aurora, everything *mattered*. Most of the time, to him, nothing did.

And that was more comfortable, much more comfortable. Why did she ever have to cross his path, much less trail him everywhere like a bloodhound? Into the *saloon*, no less. Next thing he knew she'd be knocking on his door, ready to nag him for the rest of the night—he'd probably have to tie her to a lamppost and ride out of town at a flat gallop to ever get away from her.

As if the thought had conjured her, a rhythmic rapping sounded at his door. He turned and stared at it for a moment, picturing her on the other side of it all perky and stubborn, dressed in her stylish jacket that matched her eyes. Sudden anger swept through him. *Damn* it, why couldn't she take "no" for an answer? What did he have to do to make her leave him alone? He crossed to the door and flung it open.

A freckled boy about ten years old stood there, his russet-colored cowlick sticking straight up, his fist lifted to knock again. Stunned, Cole stared and, out of old habit, closed his hand around the butt of his six-gun. Dear God, what had he been thinking? Assuming the identity of the person on the other side of a door was a good way to get killed—the very fact that he had done such an idiotic thing made him mad all over again.

"*What?*"

The boy didn't shrink from his bark.

"Here," he said, thrusting a piece of paper at Cole. "Kid Dolby done give me a nickel to bring you this."

Cole took it.

"I reckoned you'd likely give me another nickel," the boy said hopefully.

Cole looked down into bold hazel-colored eyes that snapped and danced.

"Being that you're famous," he added.

"What does that have to do with anything?" Cole growled, putting on his fiercest glare.

The boy didn't budge.

"You wouldn't want the Kid to outdo you, would you?"

"You're the second toughest person I've been up against all day," Cole muttered, reaching into his pocket for a nickel.

"Who's the toughest?"

"Not the Kid," Cole said and dropped the payment into the dirty palm waiting for it.

The boy completely lost interest in the conversation. He unbuttoned his pocket, dropped the coin into it and turned and ran for the stairs. Cole opened the crumpled paper and read it by the light of the hallway lamps.

"I ain't quittin'," it said. "I aim to draw down on you if'n' I hafta foller you to Canady." KD

A slow, sick feeling ran deep through Cole's guts as he stepped back into his room, turning again toward the fresh night air for comfort.

He truly ought to get out of town before the boy got out of jail. He stared into the night again, but this time he saw only Kid Dolby's young face against the spangled sky. If he did leave now, nobody with a grain of sense would say that Cole McCord had run away from a fight, since it was with such a boy. Besides, he could live if some called him coward. The only way it'd hurt him was that it was bound to bring more of Kid Dolby's type out of the woods to try their luck.

And it would hurt his pride. Basically, his reputation was all he had left of his old life— which had been his only life.

Anger so swift it made him nauseous swept through him. *Why* had Travis had to die? Why had *he* lived, when the whole damn thing had been his fault? Now if he killed the boy he would always hate himself for that, too.

"Mr. McCord?"

He whirled on his heel and stepped out of the moonlight, at the same time drawing his gun in a reflex action that he couldn't stop, but he knew that voice from the first syllable. It startled him, how familiar it sounded.

Aurora Benton stood in the doorway, her small figure limned by the light in the hall behind her, and for an instant, just for that first moment he looked at her, a strange sense of himself came over his anger. He was as lonely as he'd ever been. Lonelier.

"I need to speak with you."

Here was another human being at his door, a beautiful woman who had eyes like the summer sky, a sweet-smelling woman who fit into his arms like a wonderful gift. A woman who could make him laugh.

He didn't need that. He didn't want a woman who could touch him in any way.

"I saw your door open," she said, and

stepped into the room without waiting for an invitation. "I've come to give you one last chance."

That made him grin.

"Mighty generous of you," he said wryly. "What this world needs most is one last chance."

He holstered his gun, went to pick up his shirt. She gave a little gasp of surprise as he passed through the wide shaft of moonlight and she saw that he was half-naked. He felt her gaze touch his skin, then she went to the window to look out while he slipped the shirt on and started buttoning it.

"I suppose I should get dressed," he muttered, "since I seem to have one visitor after another."

"Who else?"

"Is that any of your business?"

"No."

They laughed at the same moment, then let a silence fall. Finally, she spoke.

"This is my last chance, too," she said, and her voice trembled. "Lloyd Gates nearly scared me spitless a while ago."

He spun on his heel, took a step toward her. "What'd he do?"

"Came up to me at the bar right after you left and offered to escort me to my room. Asked if I'd been thanking you for saving my life this morning, then implied it wouldn't be saved for long once I hit the trail for Texas. All in the most charming, concerned way, of course."

"What'd you say to him?"

"Not one solitary word. I cut him dead, turned my back on him, and walked out the door. That son of a bitch was a big part of the reason my daddy killed himself."

The expletive sounded so surprising spoken in her soft, sad tones that it made him grin again. She might be sad and scared, but her spirit wasn't broken.

"I'll pay you seventy-five a month and twenty head of cattle," she said, whirling around to look at him. "Cole, it's as high as I can go."

Her eyes were huge and bright with hope, and they wouldn't leave him, wouldn't turn him loose. In the moonlight, she looked as delicate as the flowers he smelled on the breeze, so he crossed the room to the little table by the wall, struck a match, and lit the lamp.

"Do you know you're trying to settle in Comanche country?" he said, more harshly than he'd intended. "That there're still some remnants of free bands here and there?"

"Yes."

"Do you know it's dry land and a drought there can last seven or eight years?"

"Yes."

"Do you know that a woman trying to ranch alone will always be a target for thieves—both kinds, the ones with running irons and the ones with bankbooks and ledgers?"

"Yes."

"Do you know there'll never be a whole lot of top hands willing to work for a woman?"

"Yes."

A weight of worry for her came crashing down on him. She wasn't about to give up on this foolish, dangerous idea.

"You need to see reason," he said, pushing the words out of his throat, which had gone dry with fear for her.

"Nothing but a bullet can stop me," she said. "When Daddy died, I swore to love life and live every minute I have, so I will not sit and wither in some horrid situation. I'm taking those cattle to Texas."

For a long, solemn moment they looked at each other. He hated this, hated really caring what happened to her. She wasn't really as brave as she seemed—she was foolish.

"You sound like a child," he told her, "because you can't even imagine the obstacles you'll face."

To his surprise, she didn't respond with an angry retort. She only looked into his eyes and saw what he was thinking.

"Cole," she said, "will you come with me?"

He could barely hear the words for the roaring in his head. No. He ought to say no, he had to say no, because, at that moment, all he wanted was to keep her safe from danger and to break Lloyd Gates's face.

But that attitude wasn't personal, it couldn't be, because he didn't know her that well. No, it was the same he would feel for any woman, any weaker person who was being bullied.

And she would entertain him on the way to Texas. He might as well go back there; coming north hadn't helped him get rid of his demons. She would make the long trail much more tolerable than if he rode only with Trav's ghost for company. Also, if he did save her life, it might help balance things out for losing Trav's.

"I have my own reasons for going back to Texas," he said slowly, "and that's why I'm telling you 'yes.' It's not because you've badgered me all day. Don't think I can be nagged or manipulated into doing anything I don't want to do, Aurora."

She searched his face.

"I won't."

She came a step closer, and he caught her light, flowery scent.

"Thank you, Cole."

A wild urge to reach for her almost overcame him; he had to clench his hands into fists. No way was he starting anything like that, not on a long drive, and not with this woman. This ache of loneliness would pass when they started down the trail—watching for danger would keep him busy and keep his feelings at bay, as action always did.

"I can never tell you how right this feels to me," she said. "I've known since the moment we met that you're supposed to come with me."

He gave a bitter, little laugh. "And I've known you're deadlier than the Kid since the moment you took my eyes off him and his gun.

That never happened to me in the middle of a draw before."

She threw back her head and laughed, a joyous, robust sound that rippled through his blood like wine. Oh, Lord, what had he done? He never should've agreed to go with her.

Right then he wanted nothing so much as to kiss her. She smelled of perfume—lilac water or roses or some other flowers—and her eyes had gone so huge and dark blue that he couldn't look away from them. A man could get lost in her eyes.

"This is all on the condition that I'm boss, of course," he said.

She bristled furiously, as he had known she would.

"*I'm* the trail boss and *you're* the bodyguard. You knew that when you signed on."

She spoke in an infuriating, flat, I'll-give-no-quarter tone that set his teeth on edge. But no worry touched her eyes. She knew he wasn't going to go back on his word. She trusted him, she thought he had honor.

"We'll see," he said, just as flatly. "You'll be surprised what decisions belong to the bodyguard on a trail."

"Yes, we'll see," she said, stepping closer and sticking out her chin in that stubborn way of hers. "*You'll* be surprised what decisions belong to the trail boss, even if she is a woman. They are *my* cattle, this is *my* drive."

"Yet your life is *my* job. You'll have to learn reason, Aurora."

He was glad when the anger finally flared in his belly, relieved when all he wanted to do was grab her and shake some sense into her. This was the way it would have to be, all those miles and miles to Texas.

# Chapter 3

**A**urora sat straight up in bed the instant she woke, clutching the covers to her chest and trembling from the nightmare that had held her captive—an awful dream of Lloyd Gates laughing at her while he butchered one of her calves beside the trail. Pebbles clattered against her window, and she realized that was the sound she'd taken for his laughter.

Thank God it was Cookie instead, thank God Gates had been only a dream.

"I'm awake," she called, wrapping the blanket around her as she jumped out of bed and ran to throw the curtain back and the window, open. "Thanks, Cookie, I'm up."

The old man grinned at her in the waning light from the moon and shifted the bedroll he carried over his shoulder.

" 'Bout time you rolled outta them soogans, girl. I done saddled your horse and sent him with Skeeter like you wanted," he said. "Don't reckon there's nothin' more in the barn nor the bunkhouse that we can take with us."

The flat finality of his words struck her mute for a moment, sent a stream of sorrow running through her blood. This wasn't a regular, early morning job he was waking her for. This wasn't a usual drive from winter pasture to summer pasture. This was leaving for good, a drive of hundreds of miles.

Now, for sure, she had no home.

"All right," she said, at last. "I'll go through the house one last time and then I'll be down to the herd."

"No hurry. It'll be a little spell 'fore I can get the biscuits baked and the bacon fried."

The scent of the cowboys' campfire drifted to her on the night breeze, and she heard a faint lowing from the cattle. They were holding the gather within a quarter mile of the house.

"I wish I'd stayed in the camp last night," she blurted. "Maybe that would've made leaving easier this morning."

He didn't answer—there was too much raw emotion in her voice. He was afraid, no doubt, that she was about to burst into tears.

"But I thank you for sleeping at the bunkhouse," she said quickly, "so I could have one last night in my room before we go."

"Anything for you, Aury girl," the old man said, trying to comfort her with his childhood nickname for her. "And anything to spend one more night in a bed. Even that old shuck mattress spread on a board bunk is softer than the ground."

"I guess so," she said, smiling a little.

"By the time we get to Texas we won't even remember what a bed is," he said, his whole face wrinkling as he smiled. "By then we'll be tougher than whet-leather and rougher than a pair of Mexican spurs—why, we'll be able to bulldog any trouble that has the gall to come our way."

She laughed out loud. The old man knew her so well, knew just how to encourage her.

"And we'll know all about droving," she said. "Nobody'll be as good as we will at trailing a mixed herd of cattle with as few hands as humanly possible."

He threw back his head and laughed. Then, without another word, he turned and started for the herd. Aurora watched him go, smiling with affection, then frowning with worry. Cookie seemed to be limping worse than she'd ever seen him.

"Where's your horse, Cookie?" she called. "You should've ridden mine!"

His only reply was a wave of his hand over his head.

It wasn't far to the bedgrounds, true, and she herself would walk, because later in the day she'd be in the saddle for too many hours, but Cookie was an old cowboy who never walked a step if he could ride, either horseback or on the chuck wagon. His rheumatism must be acting up so much that he didn't want to make the effort to mount and dismount.

A new despair nagged at her. Cookie was in

worse shape than she'd thought. He'd have to drive the chuck wagon at all times because one of the thirteen-year-old neighbor twins she'd hired would have to trail the remuda while the other drove her household wagon. She couldn't spare a grown man for either job.

What was she *doing*? A third of her outfit for trailing twenty-two hundred head of cattle and a eighty-horse remuda was a crippled-up man old enough to be her grandfather and two little boys.

She gave a mighty sigh and turned back into the room, where her big dog, Bubba, was finally stretching and getting up from his bed in the corner to come to her.

"You're a lazy hound," she told him, bending over to hug his neck. "You sleepyhead, you didn't even growl. But you knew it was Cookie, didn't you?"

He would've growled if it'd been Lloyd Gates at her window. Bubba, who stood shoulder-high to her hip, and who many said looked half wolf, sometimes theatened to attack strangers. Yet she was getting ready to take him through a thousand miles of traveling where he would, no doubt, cross paths with quite a few strangers.

"We can do it, though, can't we, sugar?"

For a long minute she stayed still, holding her cheek against the dog's big head, taking comfort from his warmth and his soft fur. Today was the day she had to put up or shut up, the day she had to start doing what she'd been tell-

ing the world she could do, erratically vicious
dogs and broken-up old men notwithstanding.

"We've got an ace in the hole, though, don't
we boy?" she said, as Bubba leaned harder
against her, rumbling deep in his throat. "Cole
McCord's our secret weapon. He can handle
anything, I can just tell."

But she knew he would try to handle too
much of her affairs. And he was the strongest
man she'd ever met. Just his very presence ex-
uded power. People talked about someone
walking into a room and filling it with their personality, why Cole McCord had filled the whole
*street* in Pueblo City. He was the perfect example of the old Texas saying He covers the
ground he stands on.

She turned loose of the dog and went to take
her favorite quilt off the bed.

Cole McCord was a much more authoritative
man than her daddy had been. Stronger than
her uncles Jeremiah and Porter, whose house-
holds she had shuttled between during her
years in Philadelphia. None had been shy about
bossing other people around. But Cole would
find out, as they had, that she had her own
mind.

She smiled at Bubba, who was sitting on his
haunches, watching her with his head cocked
to one side in curiosity.

"The bigger they come, the harder they fall,
isn't that right, Bubba? You and I are going to
boss this drive, no two ways about it."

Bubba agreed, vocally, and came to lick her

hand. He could practically talk—he always made sounds nearly like words, with the intonation rising and falling in sentences. He howled like a wolf sometimes, too, and he growled at people he didn't like, but he rarely barked. He had appeared at the Flying B as a stray pup only a few days after Aurora had returned from the East, and they'd immediately loved each other with all their hearts.

"Come on, punkin," she said, burying her hand in the soft fur of his neck, "you have a little run while I get dressed."

She led him to the front door, let him out into the blackness that was coming on as the moon went down, then padded barefoot back through the dark, silent house. This was the day she had to leave this place. This was different from when she left to go east because this time she was never coming back.

*Now she had no home.*

She stood still in the hallway, her naked feet pressed hard against the cold wood floor, and she took a deep breath. The familiar smell of the house filled her nostrils. The smell of her family's house, which she would never smell anymore.

Now she had no family, either. Mama had been dead nearly five years, and Papa, six months. Cookie and her other hands were her only family now.

The thick dark of the time right before sunrise seeped in through the walls and blank windows, the cold of the early spring morning went straight to her bones. She shivered and wrapped her arms around herself. Everything suddenly looked different in the early, dark morning, but everything still was the same. This place belonged to the bank now, and she was going to make a new start for herself in Texas.

What she had to cling to was the freedom of being on her own. She could make her own decisions about the business instead of deferring to Papa's, even when she knew they were wrong. And wherever she was it would be *her* place instead of Papa's. Her time would be her own to do as she pleased instead of doing what someone else asked her to do or what society expected of her.

A fierce excitement began to thread its way through her trepidation. Hadn't she promised herself, on the day her daddy died, to live her life to the fullest? Every single moment of it? Well, then, she'd better get started.

Breaking into a run, she reentered her room and began throwing on the clothes she'd laid out the night before, began thinking about the business at hand. Was there anything else left in the house that she truly needed? Her few keepsakes that remained after she'd sold her mother's jewelry and the necessary household goods had been loaded into a wagon days ago. The bed she'd just slept in and the other pieces of furniture would just have to go to Banker McFadden, who'd foreclosed on the place. Both wagons were full to bursting.

She'd simply have to build up and furnish her new home a little at a time—the house wouldn't be all that important to her, anyway, because she'd be outside running the ranch. Only a few months from now she would be secure in a place all her own, and she would be free. No matter how small it might be, or how crude, it would be hers and hers alone, and no one could tell her what to do or foreclose on it and throw her out of it.

A sharp, hot surge of fury burned in her throat. Papa didn't have to be such a coward— if he hadn't killed himself the two of them could've held onto this place together and Banker McFadden couldn't have snatched it out from under them.

But that was water under the bridge, and it was nothing but a waste of her strength to think about it any more. She finished buttoning her blouse, then threw the stampede strings of her hat over her head and let it hang down her back. She stuffed her nightgown into the packed leather bag that had belonged to her mother, then took her belongings, and without even one last glance over her shoulder, she left the room.

In the hallway, she turned toward the staircase, then stopped. She wasn't going to take one last walk through the house, either. Everything that met her glance would hold a memory of her parents, of her childhood, of good times and bad ones, and all that was the past. It was gone.

So she pivoted on the heel of her boot, faced the front door, and marched toward it. Once through it, she pulled it closed and crossed the porch, whistling for Bubba, who came loping out of the shadows.

Oh, dear God, if only she could make the right decisions and not get them all killed or the cattle all lost! She couldn't bear for Cole McCord to say *I told you so.*

She reached for Bubba's head and rubbed it. He leaned against her and muttered some comfort. Aurora smiled, shifted the bag on her shoulder, and started walking fast toward the herd.

The sun was coming up now, bathing the whole world in pink and yellow light, coloring even the gray mist rising from the river. The cattle, strung out along the bank back upstream toward the house, were beginning to stir, a few heaving themselves to their feet to amble down to the water, bits of yellow sunlight flashing off their horns. Tom and Lonnie were taking their turn at watching them, riding slowly at the edge of the bedground.

The beautiful sight lifted Aurora's heart, and suddenly she didn't have a doubt in the world. She couldn't wait for the coming adventure. She ran the rest of the way.

When she arrived at the fire, Cookie was bending over it, frying bacon in a skillet while the aroma of sourdough biscuits wafted from a Dutch oven buried in coals at his feet. As usual, he told her what she could plainly see for herself when she looked past the wagons.

"Nate's done brought in the remuda and the boys ain't waitin' to eat before they pick their horses."

"That's good," she said, on her way to the household wagon to stash her things. "Did they say all was quiet last night?"

"Yep. Nobody come around 'til 'bout a hour ago when yore bodyguard rode in, Monte said."

She froze in the act of tossing her bag over the tailgate.

"He's already here?"

"Yeah. Monte's been here all night."

"You know I don't mean Monte!"

Her pulse and her mind both quickened. Cole had said he'd start from town at dawn, but he had come early. Suddenly, she realized that she needed a minute to prepare herself to see him again, which was a completely silly thought. She hurried back to the fire.

"Where is he now?"

"Who, Monte?"

"No! I mean . . ."

Then she caught Cookie's sly look and bit her tongue. He'd love nothing better than to tease her about Cole every step of the way to Texas.

"Mighty handsome man, that bodyguard o' yourn."

"I hadn't noticed," she lied. "I hired him for his reputation, not his looks."

"Mm, *hmm*."

"*Cookie*. Where is he now?"

"Lookin' over the remuda. He only brung one horse with him."

"That's all right. The one thing we have plenty of is horses."

Her heart was beating extra hard as she turned and went toward the chuck wagon. It was the whole excitement of this morning, that was all. This was the most significant day of her life so far. That and the surprise Cole was already here, that was all.

She took one of the tin cups from the fold-down table and carried it to the coffeepot hanging over the fire. Cookie tilted the pot with a long stick to fill it.

"This here's real six-shooter coffee," he said, as he said every time he ever made coffee. "I dropped mine into it awhile ago, and it floated just fine."

To please him, she chuckled at the old saw he'd repeated a hundred times. She started to say something else, while she watched him push the bacon aside and begin breaking eggs into the skillet and scrambling them, but she kept forgetting what it was. Cole McCord was already here.

"Come an' git it, boys, before I throw it out," Cookie yelled.

Aurora turned to see the men coming toward them. Cole was in the middle of the small bunch, and just a glimpse of him made her pulse quicken even more. That loose, sure set of his wide shoulders, that panther's prowl of his were both unmistakable, even though he was backlit by the rising sun so she couldn't see his face.

Monte and Frank flanked him while Skeeter hobbled along in front, and, as she watched, he said something that made them laugh—the low rumble of his voice and their appreciative chuckles floated to her on the northerly breeze. Well. Mr. Charming. Certainly different behavior than when he met *her* for the first time.

Unbidden, the feel of his hard-muscled arms around her and of the rock of his chest pressing against her breasts flooded through her. She must forget about that, must get it out of her system. He was a hired hand, she was his employer, no matter what he thought about making the decisions.

A sudden fear struck her.

Was he the sneaky kind? Here he was, at the herd before she was, looking over the remuda and picking his mount and becoming one of the boys. Buddying up to them. Was that to swing them to his side in case he and she ever had a serious difference of opinion?

She made herself take slow sips of her coffee and stood up very straight as befitted the boss of the outfit.

"I see you all have met," she said when they walked into the circle around the fire. "As he's probably told you, I've hired Mr. McCord to be my bodyguard on the trail."

"Yes'm," Frank said, and touched his hat brim.

"We met," Monte said, with the same gesture, and Skeeter nodded, briefly removing his battered felt.

"You men needn't tip your hats to me—we're on the trail now," she said awkwardly, knowing how sensitive they were to criticism but needing them to see her in her new role. "We'll be working too hard to worry about manners, so treat me as you would a man trail boss."

The three cowboys went to the chuck wagon for their coffee cups without replying. *Damn* it! Just having Cole watching was making her stiff and artificial with her own men. And her heart was still hammering.

He strolled toward her with that cavalier walk of his, looking her up and down with his hot, dark eyes.

"It'll be hard for them to see you as a man," he drawled. "I'd say downright impossible."

Her anger flared like a struck match.

"Nobody asked you," she snapped. "And don't look at me that way."

"How? As a man?"

"No!" she said, trying to keep her voice low so no one but him would hear. "As a *woman!* I told you on the street in Pueblo you couldn't intimidate me that way, and you can't."

"I don't have any intention of intimidating you, Aurora," he said.

His gaze wouldn't let hers go.

"Oh, yes, you do . . ."

The men came closer, drifting toward the fire for coffee.

"I'm just happy that you're here among us,

Miss Aurora," Cole said, loud enough for them and Cookie, too, to hear him, "and we've still got hot food and coffee."

He gave her that crooked grin of his.

"We've been about half-scared that you'd come flying in here in your buggy and drive right through the middle of the fire, scatter our bacon and biscuits from hell to breakfast."

All the cowboys burst out laughing, delighted as always with a bit of hoo-rawing, no matter who was the butt of the joke. They flashed quick, appraising glances at her.

That was one of the unwritten, unbreakable rules of the cowboy life. Anybody in their company had to be able to take teasing in good humor, as well as dish it out. If not, they rawhided the sensitive soul until he left the outfit or learned to laugh with them. And hadn't she just told them to treat her like a man?

Fury choked her, fed by fear. He was already starting it, already forming sides, boys against girl, trying to make her look silly and incompetent. She opened her mouth to give him a royal dressing-down, no matter what the men thought, but then she managed to bite her tongue.

"It *is* breakfast," she said, forcing a sarcastic sweetness into her tone, "so it can't be scattered from hell to breakfast. How about hell to *Texas?*"

That brought more laughter than it deserved and inspired the others to join in.

"We circled the wagons to protect the fire

and told Lonnie to whistle like a mockingbird to warn us when you passed the herd," Cookie said.

"Yeah, and we saddled our horses before we ate or even took a gulp of Arbuckle's, in case we'd need to jump on 'em to chase you down and stop a runaway," Skeeter said.

The laughter grew louder, and she felt the stiffness begin to leave her. The men were all right again, they were accepting her as one of them, the feeling in the outfit was relaxed and back to normal.

She took a long, deep breath and gave Cole a big smile, then turned to the others.

"That's why I came in here on foot instead of driving," she said to Skeeter. "I didn't want to cause a distraction that'd take you all away from your work."

They all laughed again, and Frank looked up from pouring his coffee.

"Yeah, I reckon she ain't gonna be no diff'rent from all the rest of the high saltys we ever rode for," he drawled. "I never seen a foreman or a trail boss yet that didn't worry from can-see to can't-see that we might git distracted from our work."

That brought the most laughter of all and sealed her place in their estimation. At least, until she had to pick the right crossing of the first river or decide where to bed down in dry country.

But the tension thrumming along her nerves

lessened a lot. At least Frank had said out loud that she was the boss.

Cookie winked at her and gestured for the men to get their plates and come to the fire to fill them.

"Sit down now and eat your breakfast, Miss Aurora," he said, holding out a plate he had filled for her. "Won't be no eggs on your plate tomorry mornin' or no other mornin' from here on out, so git 'em while you can."

She went to accept her food from the old man who had clucked over her since childhood. At noon she would make sure to serve herself like everyone else, but now was no time to make a point of that. Now she would quit while she was ahead.

But the minute they moved out and she was alone on scout with him, she would set Cole McCord straight. It wasn't his job to hoo-raw her in front of the men.

She turned her back on him then and walked to an upended bucket near the chuck wagon to sit down. For this moment, she needed to enjoy a little peace so she could eat—if that were possible, with her so excited and perturbed—what might be her only hot meal until supper, depending on how fractious the cattle were once they strung them out on the trail.

The cattle, the trail. That was what she should be thinking about, that and how to get a rein on Cole McCord. Once that was done, she ought to forget about him and anything he might say. She ought to forget the strange phenomenon that made her want him to hold her again and want to slap his face at the very same time.

An instant later he stood beside her with his breakfast in one hand and his coffee cup in the other. She glanced up and met his straight, dark look, and she felt that twinge again.

"You'll do," he said.

He sat on his haunches and put his coffee on the ground as the other men were doing near the fire. Heartily, he began to eat.

"I don't recall asking you to sit down," she said, "nor do I recall asking for your opinion of me."

"You don't have to," he said cheerfully. "The boss says we're on the trail now, we'll be working too hard to worry about manners."

She felt her cheeks flame as her anger came rushing back. It took every bit of control she had not to shout at him.

"Mocking everything I say and do is not part of your job," she said tightly.

"*Mocking?*"

He widened his eyes and arranged his face into an expression of purest innocence. "I'm not mocking you, Aurora. Not now and not before. I'm only trying to help."

"Well, you have a mighty strange way of going about it," she snapped, desperately trying to hold on to her temper. "I want to talk to you about that charming little performance you gave in front of the men."

He took a bite of biscuit and eyed her thoughtfully.

"It wasn't a performance, I was *sincerely* trying to stir up some fun," he said.

"Trying to stir up some support for yourself, you mean."

The deliberate puzzlement in his look became genuine.

"Aurora," he drawled, "you've got me buffaloed. Help me out a little."

"I'll put it to you straight as an arrow," she snapped. "You can stop trying to undermine my authority or ride out right now. Is that clear?"

"As mud."

He understood her, though. His eyes took on a glint of mischief.

"I've heard all my life about how women can change their minds fast as a pitching horse can shed a greenhorn," he said, thoughtfully sipping his coffee, "but you've gotta take the prize. I would've sworn you begged me on bended knee to take this job not much more than twenty-four hours ago."

"I never begged you for anything on bended knee and I never will," she said passionately.

He shrugged, shaking his head in disbelief.

"Came pretty close, in my estimation."

"Your estimation *and* your judgment are not the ones that run this drive," she said. "Mine are. So quit trying to buddy up with my hands so you'll have their support if you should start trying to do my job instead of your own."

He raised his eyebrows in the most infuriating, sardonic way imaginable.

"That's one of your pronouncements, like that one on the street in Pueblo City, that I'm gonna have to take under consideration," he drawled, " 'til I get it figured out."

He held her gaze with his while he ate another bite of bacon.

"Sounds like you're mighty distrustful, though, just on first impression, you understand. You're the same woman called me a man of honor, though—am I right?"

"You're a *man*," she said. "That means you *think* you're always right and you *think* you always have to control everything. I've never known one who didn't."

He raised his dark brows again.

"You must think all men are alike."

"In many ways—in *most* ways—they are. And I'll never be under the thumb of another one, so don't be trying to take control of this drive."

A flash of anger showed in his eyes. Good. It was about time he took her seriously.

But he stayed very cool, and that made her want to slap his face for sure.

"Aurora, Aurora," he said, shaking his head in mock sorrow, "I don't know how you can trust me with your life and still be so suspicious of my motives."

"All men want to run everything, no matter what," she said, through gritted teeth. "If Papa had listened to me about his investments, he might've kept his ranch and his life."

"You're a smart woman," Cole said, to her surprise. "Think. If you want to be anything more than Pretty Little Miss Flying B Ranch on this drive, you'll have to be accepted as the boss, which is what you were trying to tell them when they tipped their hats to the lady. Cowboys don't follow bosses who don't know what they're doing, it's just that simple, no matter what gender you are. A trail boss works his . . . or her . . . way up from riding drag, whether or not his daddy owns the cows."

She stared at him.

"*I* own them," she cried, furious, "not my daddy. *I* saved them and the horses when he was putting mortgages on everything in sight. And I know what I'm doing. I can figure out for myself how to trail them!"

"Good for you."

He began eating in earnest, as if there were nothing more to say.

She took a long, deep breath to cool down. If he could stay unruffled, so could she. If she didn't, he would always have the advantage over her.

Forcing some food down, she thought about it.

"So you're saying you weren't trying to take away my authority, that you were only hoorawing me to make me one of the boys?" she said, and drank some of her coffee.

He smiled beatifically.

"You did very well once you caught on," he

said. "It didn't assure your men that you know what you're doing but it did prove you could hold your head and your temper."

That remark made it flare again.

"Well, I'm just happy as a hog in acorns that you approve of at least one thing about me," she snapped.

"Oh, I approve of many, many things about you," he drawled, capturing her again with his dark chocolate eyes. "Want me to list them?"

His hot gaze roamed her whole person.

Desire flared in the core of her, made her lips tingle and her breasts go hard at his leisurely perusal.

"No! I don't!"

"Why not?"

She lifted her plate and stood up, stretching to her full height, squaring her shoulders.

"Because we both have jobs to do! Will you just keep your mind on yours? God knows, I have enough to worry about with you . . . and . . . the boys . . ."

He stood, too, so suddenly she took a step backward.

"Damn it, will you *stop* that?"

His tone was furious, disgusted, downright dangerous. He kept it low, bending over her so no one else could hear.

"If I have to take over this drive, I'll do it by a gun and a gag in your misguided mouth, *Miss* Benton, not by some sneaking childish conspiracy with your trail hands. Your suspicions are on the wrong man. You'd better put 'em on

Skeeter and realize *I'm* on *your* side."

"*What?* What are you talking about?"

"In Pueblo City I came across your old buddy, Lloyd Gates, a time or two—I wanted to know him by sight."

"Very professional of you," she said sardonically.

"I *am* a professional. You listen to me. Your man Skeeter's been powwowing with Gates. I saw 'em together twice, thick as thieves."

She frowned up at him, trying to think, trying to make that make sense.

"Gates is *always* in a powwow," she said. "He's got a flapping jaw. He talks to everybody."

Cole shook his head.

"This was more than that. Those boys know each other well, and they were making medicine."

Her anger came back, tinged with an eerie fear born of the surety in his tone.

"Look, Cole, you're imagining things. My men are loyal—why, they're my family—and I'd trust every one of them with my life."

"Don't. Watch your back."

"That's *your* job."

"Pleasant as it would be to have your charming company every minute of every day, there'll be times when, for privacy's sake, you're out of my sight. Watch your back."

"*You* watch your mouth. These men have ridden together for a lot of years and they

wouldn't take kindly to such talk about Skeeter."

He looked down at her with a pitying expression that told her how foolish, how naive
she was.

"If you don't know I have more sense than
that, then why the hell did you hire me?"

He turned on his heel and strode away, threw
his plate and cup in the wreck pan, and went
for his horse.

Aurora couldn't move from that spot because
of the cold chill in her blood.

Cole had been trying to size Skeeter up. He
hadn't been trying to get the men on his side
for some mythical future argument between her
and him. He'd been trying to protect her, nothing more. Even though she didn't believe Skeeter would be disloyal, she knew now that Cole
believed it.

He would also believe that her mind was un-
hinged, since she'd accused him of such a ridiculous thing so alien to every impression
she'd had of him. It was true she should've
known better. She *did* know better, and she had
since the moment they'd met. She had just let
her first-morning-on-the-trail jitters carry her
away—that was why she had temporarily lost
her judgment.

Now he'd think she was too stupid to come
in out of the rain, much less boss a trail drive.
Her mind twisted with chagrin.

But why should she care what he thought of her? She had hired him to protect her from Gates and that was it.

That was *all*.

# Chapter 4

⌒~⌒⌒⌒~

They got the cattle bunched, headed south, and moving well before the sun had risen very high above the horizon. By the time they crossed the boundary of the Flying B and officially started down the trail toward the little town of Rocky Springs, Aurora began to feel much better about everything. Especially Cole.

He had not made one sarcastic comment while she was directing the work, or uttered one personal remark when they were alone. In fact, he had ridden off in each of the four directions to check for trouble soon after they started, and he hadn't shown the slightest emotion when he was near her. No amazement at her insanity, no disgust at her decisions, no anger, no . . . desire. Well, to be perfectly honest, he'd *never* really shown *desire*—that look in his eyes when he'd said there were many things he approved about her had been only a leer meant to tease and embarrass her.

She jerked herself up straighter in the saddle

and looked around, as if someone could have seen the imaginings running through her head. Lord help her!

It was fine, it was *great* that he was behaving himself, and she hoped and prayed that he would keep it up. She could certainly do without the aggravation.

She picked Shy Boy up into a trot. Cole was doing his job this first morning, and she was sure he'd continue to do it. Since that was what she'd hired him for, she shouldn't waste any more thoughts on him. She had a trail drive to boss and a new home to find.

Then there he came, Cole McCord, riding back to her from scouting the next turn in the trail, and her heart just lifted right out of her chest. It was simply happiness that caused it, not the sight of him. She was happy because things were going so well, so far. That had to be the reason.

And because she felt really safe for the first time since Gates had first threatened her. Cole had scouted around, but he had never gone far, never let her out of his sight for very long.

She swung in her saddle to see the herd stretching out behind her. An old longhorn cow that her father had always called Brindle because of her roany, mottled hide had pushed her way to the front of the hundreds of cattle to trot beside a lanky young steer who'd been in the lead since the first day of the gather.

They made her smile. What a pair! But they would be the two main leaders for the whole drive, she could tell that much right now from the way they held their heads and the look in their eyes. Fine. Anywhere her men could get them to go, the others would follow, plus they were setting a good pace with no urging from the point riders, perfect for a herd on a road instead of on graze and an outfit trying to get them trail-broke in a hurry.

She turned to face south again, deliberately avoiding looking at Cole. Cookie in the chuck wagon and little Nate in the hoodlum one were rolling out to the side, picking up a little speed in front of the herd, so they'd reach the nooning place first and have hot food ready when the men arrived. The next thing she and Cole had to do was ride even faster than the wagons and pick that nooning place.

"Mmrhr, grrhr," Bubba said, trotting serenely beside her horse.

"That's right," she said, her eyes rebelliously fixing on Cole as he came closer. "Next, we have to find a good, shady spot by a creek to have our dinner. A picnic spot."

Her happiness grew, a feeling stronger by far than her apprehension of the early morning, and it swept all through her. She could do it, by thunder! With the help she had, she could get this herd to a new range and start a ranch of her own where no one, ever, could tell her to leave. The thought made her heart sing.

She rode through the warming sunlight to meet Cole.

"I suppose you and I might as well pull out

now and ride ahead to find the nooning," she said. "They seem to be trailing just fine."

He glanced back at the mostly peaceful herd.

"Not bad for the first morning," he said. "But I'd say we better stick with 'em until after Rocky Springs. I know this trail to below the New Mexico Territory line, and the only way through is right down the middle of Main Street."

"I forgot about Rocky Springs!" she cried and immediately wondered if she was really losing her mind after all. "I guess I thought we were halfway to Texas by now."

"Only a few hundred miles to go," he said dryly, swinging his horse around so he could ride beside her, heading back to the south.

The easy tone of his voice, low and rich, and the teasing grin he gave her made her want to ride closer, close enough that their legs might brush.

She *was* going insane. What had she just decided about keeping things all business?

"Thanks so much for reminding me," she said, mildly sarcastic.

"Any time."

Bubba lifted his big head and added what sounded like a whole sentence to the conversation.

"That's right," Aurora said to him. "But first we're going to get them through Rocky Springs. Then we'll eat."

Cole laughed.

"You didn't forget Rocky Springs because

you thought you were halfway to Texas," he said. "It was because you were deep in conversation with a dog."

She smiled at him.

"Bubba's a better companion than lots of people are," she said. "At least he agrees with me most of the time."

She looked up to meet Cole's slanting glance. "What?" she snapped.

"Listen to yourself," he said. "A good companion is somebody who agrees with you."

She shrugged, grinning a little at the teasing.

"That's right. Or . . . somebody who can put up a humdinger of an argument for the opposite point of view."

He raised his eyebrows.

"Well, now, then, we may have a right interesting ride from here to Texas."

"Meaning you disagree with everything I say?"

He cocked his head and looked at her, then nodded toward the wagons, which were almost out of sight ahead of them.

"No. Only with a few things you've done, such as trailing that second wagon. One would be plenty to keep repaired and rolling."

"No, it *wouldn't*. I *had* to bring two! I'm moving a household to a place where there are no stores and even if there were, I have no money and if I tried to put everything in the chuck wagon, we'd have no room for food!"

Bubba, responding to the defensiveness in her tone, added his vocal support.

Cole scowled down at him.

"And I'm not too sure about bringing that dog."

"Good heavens, Cole, you surely didn't expect me to go off and leave him! Haven't you ever had a pet?"

Even in the middle of the argument, she suddenly wanted very badly to know. What had Cole been like as a boy? Where had he grown up?

He ignored the question.

"If he gets footsore or hurt, you'll have to leave him. He's too big to carry in front of your saddle."

"We've left a spot in the back of the hood wagon in case we need it for new calves," she said coolly. "We'll put Bubba there if he needs to ride."

"What if there's already a calf in it?"

She scowled at him, her irritation rising fast.

"What if lightning strikes and burns us all to bits? Life's uncertain, Cole, in case you haven't noticed."

"I've noticed, O Wise Woman of Many Years," he said. "How old are you, anyhow, Aurora?"

The question surprised her into silence. Was *he* wanting to know about *her*, too? The thought was strangely intriguing.

"Never ask a woman her age," she said.

"I thought we were dispensing with manners on the trail."

She struck her saddle horn with her fist. But his quick wit also made her smile.

"Will you *never* stop it?"

"Stop what?"

"Throwing my own words back into my face. It doesn't become you, Cole, if you're supposed to be so good at taking the opposite point of view."

That made him grin.

"I *am* good at it and I'll prove it. I'll give you three irrefutable reasons that you ought to sell that wagon and its contents in Rocky Springs."

"*Sell* it?"

Horrified, she turned in the saddle to face him. His dark, amused eyes captured hers.

"One, selling it gets something out of it instead of wasting it and its contents when you have to leave it by the trail somewhere."

He lifted one long, brown forefinger to keep count.

"Two, it gives you another man on the herd. Or take the boy off the driving chores and put him with his brother on the remuda. It's a big remuda for one kid to trail."

"Eighty horses," she said, furiously biting off every syllable.

"Three, it saves you from having to worry about all that extra junk when you get to where you're going."

She glared at him.

"There's nothing *extra*. There's nothing *junk*. The contents of that wagon are the absolute, bare necessities. I can't do without any of them."

He shook his head."Gimcracks and gewgaws, I'd bet money."

"That remark just flies all over me," she snapped. "Bet your money and lose."

"We had better wager a kiss instead."

A surprised thrill seized her stomach and turned it over.

"A *kiss?*"

He gave her that impossibly innocent look he'd used at breakfast.

"A minute ago, you said you have no money," he said, in the voice of true reason. "I'm sorry. I forgot about that when I suggested a bet."

He smiled in such an infuriating way that her tongue tingled with the desire to tell him off roundly. Yet she couldn't stop thinking about a kiss.

"Of course," he said, with a shrug for emphasis, "if you're afraid you'll lose . . ."

"I won't lose," she said. "There's not a gimcrack or a gewgaw in the load."

His eyes looked deep into hers with the greatest of satisfaction, as if she had just fallen into a trap of his making.

"You needn't be so smug," she said. "You've already lost."

"No, darlin', *you* have," he drawled.

He gave her a look hot enough to melt her in her saddle.

Then he grinned that crooked, devilish grin

of his, and it and his dangerous, dark eyes told her he knew exactly what she was feeling.

"No, to tell the truth," he said, sure of himself as the sun in the sky, "I reckon we've both just won."

He turned away, faced forward, and loped on ahead, leaving her seething.

*Darlin'*. She'd show him darlin'. She'd show him wagers. It'd be a snowy summer day in hell before he ever collected a kiss from her, the arrogant sidewinder!

She smooched to Shy Boy to pick up the pace and started catching up with him to tell him so.

"The wagons are going into the cut," he called back. "We need to narrow the herd."

Aurora wheeled her horse, and they covered the quarter mile back to the front of the herd side by side. In a wordless agreement, they each headed for one of the point riders and rode with them to help start funneling the cattle into the winding gash between two mountains. Just before the leaders went in, Aurora beckoned to Cole, and they rode in front of them.

"The trail goes right through the middle of town," she called back to the point men. "We don't want to do any damage."

Monte raised one hand high to show he'd understood, and then she was following Cole into the narrow passageway with the herd coming on behind them. The horses held a long trot, and the cattle came on only a little slower.

The cut was about a half mile long, with the mountain on each side looming fifty feet or more over their heads. Then they reached the south end and came out of it into an only slightly wider valley still surrounded by mountains. They passed a farmhouse or two with the herd leaders only a stone's throw behind them, and entered the town. It was composed of only a dozen or so buildings, if that many, but three times that many people began stepping out of them to watch the herd passing through.

"Never seen a herd trailed by a woman before," a man's voice called.

"She ain't took 'em nowhere yet," someone answered, laughing. "Only brought 'em down from the Flyin' B."

Annoyed, Aurora looked at Cole.

"How do they know who I am?" she shouted over the noise of the oncoming hooves.

"Recognize your brand, probably."

"We're trailbranded Slash A. They don't appear to be fellow ranchers who'd know where the Flying B land is . . . or was."

He opened his mouth to answer. Then, as if he'd seen something in the corner of his eye, he turned abruptly. Aurora looked, too.

Three men, on muleback, were riding out from behind a building, the first of them already blocking the road. Two more appeared from the opposite side of the street. They all carried shotguns. In their hands, not in saddle boots. They looked poor and mean as snakes.

"Miss!" yelled the one in the middle. "Hey, Missy Benton! Hold it right there!"

A sudden, sharp fear raced through her. Had

the cattle damaged something? No. If that were
so these men couldn't know it, since they were
ahead of the whole herd. Who were they, anyhow?

She turned and held up her hand as a signal
for the point men, but they had seen and were
already slowing the herd. Worried, she stood in
the stirrups to try to see whether the flank men
had yet made it out of the cut, whether the cattle seemed likely to stay in the road or scatter.
She and Cole were almost upon the human and
mule blockade when she turned back around
again. Thank God she had hired Cole.

Shy Boy responded to her leg pressure and
moved her closer to him.

"I don't know them," she muttered, half under her breath. "*How* do they know me?"

He didn't answer. He didn't appear to even
hear her, he was watching the men so intently.

He didn't seem worried, though.

"Whaddya mean," shouted the man who had
called to her before, "comin' through this valley
with all them cattle? You reckon us folks got no
more sense than to stand here and let you
gather ourn in with 'em as you go? Yore a cow-
thievin' outfit, ain't you?"

For an instant, Aurora couldn't process the
harsh words.

Then they set fire to her temper. The only
worse insult was to be called a horse thief.

"I'm *not* stealing cattle! All I'm doing is taking my own down a public road."

"And I'm not a day over twenty-one," her

grizzled accuser said, drawing his mule to an arm's length in front of Shy Boy, where he could stare Aurora in the face.

"Around here, we hang cow thieves," called out one of the men riding with him.

Then the leader stood in his ratty wooden stirrups and looked all around them.

"Folks, listen up," he shouted. "This'n here thinks Rocky Springs is full o' greenhorns. She's aimin' to steal our cattle and throw 'em in with her herd. Mebbe she's already did such."

Astounded, Aurora stared at him, then turned to Cole as a buzz of excitement began all up and down the street. Cole kept his hard brown gaze trained on her accusers.

Her palms went cold. Was this coming to gunplay in a hurry? He couldn't take on five shotguns with his six-shooter, not with this madman holding the muzzle squarely on Cole's chest.

She waited for Cole to say something that would give her a hint of what to do, but he sat silent and stone-faced, his gun hand hanging at his side. Why didn't he do something, say something? *This* was the reason she'd hired him!

But all he did was make a quick gesture of his gun hand toward her, as if *she* should act.

"I don't know what you're talking about," she said loudly, drawing herself up to her full height in the saddle, glaring at the man who had accused her.

"You's mistaken about the public road," the old reprobate said.

So. *Damn* it. They were here to extract a toll. She'd never heard of such problems anywhere this near Pueblo City, but then she had hardly been off the place all winter.

"Virgil . . ." said one of his henchmen.

"Shut up, Buster," said another. "Virgil's in business now."

Five pairs of beady eyes were trained on her face, but Virgil's kept flicking back to Cole. He cocked his grizzled head to one side and squinted at him, then looked back at her.

"Wal?" he said. "You cain't depend on that curly hair and them big blue eyes t' move them cattle through here."

He fixed his beady eyes on Cole.

"Nor on yore gunslinger, *Mister* Cole McCord, neither," he said.

A cold hand gripped her stomach and squeezed. How did he know Cole? Maybe by sight? Or had word traveled ahead of them from Pueblo City?

Cole watched the men as if they were a contingent of rattlesnakes, but he was not going to open his mouth, she knew that now. Her temper flared, as much at him as at this snaggle-toothed rustler sitting in front of her.

"*You're* the cow thief, collecting a toll!" she said to Virgil's face.

He laughed at her. His men grinned at her.

"I'm missin' three yearling heifers and a

matched pair of black steers," Virgil said. "You got 'em."

Fury and fear raced through her blood, fighting for the control of her feelings, making her hands shake on the reins. She wanted to, desperately, but she wouldn't let herself turn to Cole again. He had to watch those shotguns and besides, hadn't she demanded to be trail boss?

And there was no other help. Most of her men couldn't even see her, had no way of knowing what the holdup was.

She tried to think. God only knew how many head they would demand as toll. But even if Cole took over, there wasn't anything he could do, either, and she knew it. It was two against five—although the point men might be able to avenge them once they fell. It wouldn't take many shotgun shells for these idiots to kill them all and get the *whole* herd.

Bubba began to growl, deep in his throat, and Virgil cut his eyes down at him without moving the muzzle of his gun. The one called Buster pointed his weapon at the dog.

Behind her, the point men were coming up on the horses blocking the street, trying to hold the herd's leaders without letting the cattle turn back when they saw there was no grazing here. The bawling was getting louder, and the ones trapped in the cut would be gouging each other trying to turn around or go on. The others, behind them, would be trying to scatter. This was enough of this.

"I don't want your cattle," she said, somehow keeping her voice steady, "which is more than you can say. You've made a mistake. I'm not paying a toll. Now get out of my way."

The tall man leaned from the saddle like a wooden puppet bending at the hip and spit a stream of brown tobacco juice. Then he straightened up and looked around him to make sure he had the attention of everyone within earshot.

"I'm missing three yearling heifers and a matched pair of black steers," he repeated. "I *ain't* aimin' to give them to ye."

A few mutterings rose from the bystanders. Cole was still silent as a tomb.

"I don't have your cattle. Get out of my way."

"Oh, but ye do. And I've got friends here. We'll sort through yore herd ourselves, if'n' you don't."

That's all she needed. Talk about scattering the herd. She was going to get them moving again if she had to run right over dear Virgil and his crew.

"All right," she said tightly, "we'll see who's right about this. Let's get them moving again, ride alongside, and *look* for your five head."

She turned away haughtily and wheeled Shy Boy, goose bumps springing up on the skin between her shoulder blades, every nerve tingling in expectation of a blast from the shotgun or a shot from Cole's gun. But none came.

Aurora rode to the side of the road, all the while signaling the point men to start the cattle walking again. For one heart-stopping instant, she thought Virgil and his friends were staying behind to shoot Cole if they weren't going to shoot her, but finally they started moving their mules.

"Buster! Toady! You two search the herd on that side of the road fer my stock," Virgil yelled, loud enough for the whole street to hear. "The rest of ye come with me and keep an eye on this here fast-draw fool, McCord, an' the thievin' girl."

So they moved toward her, Cole in front of Virgil, who kept the gun on him. The other two had one trained on him, the other on her.

It seemed only seconds before the stick man bellowed in her ear.

"Now tell me again you ain't got none o' my stock," he yelled. "Do you see yore brand on them cattle right there?"

A paralyzing shock went through her. He was nodding his head and his friends were pointing, from both sides of the street.

She stood in her own stirrups to see better. Sure enough, the cattle he had described were bunched on the edge of her herd, trotting along with them, a dozen yards or more behind the brindle lead cow.

Her knees gave way, and she dropped back into the saddle. Now the whole town would be after her for a cow thief.

She ignored Virgil and looked at Cole.

"How can that be?" she called to him over the noises of the cattle and the men's voices urging them along. "How'd they get in with ours?"

He shrugged.

"They must've had some help."

Virgil laughed.

"Must have," he said, and spat another stream of tobacco juice.

He glared at Aurora with a triumphant gleam in his eye. Then he stood up in his oxbow stirrups.

"Cut 'em outta there, boys!" he yelled. "Them's mine an' she ain't gittin' away with 'em!"

Aurora was relieved to see Frank move in smoothly to separate the tight little knot of strange cattle from the herd. He could do it without scattering any.

"She's a cattle thief, I tell you, and no tellin' what else!" Virgil yelled. "If'n' she ain't up to somethin' underhanded, how come she's hired a shooter to side her? This here famous man my boys have got their sights set on is none other than Cole McCord!"

Interested murmurs came from the townspeople, and they stretched their necks to see better. Virgil waved one bony arm in the air for them to draw in closer.

"This 'ere is how come a petticoated pretty little thing is atrailin' a herd," he yelled, looking all around, into one face and then another. "She's a-figurin' she can build up her stock on the way t' Texas and if'n' she gets caught won't nobody have the stomach fer hangin' a woman."

Hanging! The word rang in her ears. Now he was threatening to *hang* her if she didn't give him some of her stock? A rustler given to blackmail?

"This is nothing but a plot to make me look bad," she said loudly to the varied faces looking up at her. "I did *not* steal his cattle. He put them in my herd himself."

No one answered, no one expressed an opinion one way or the other. That silence made her nervous.

"I say we hold this herd and hang this little vixen!" Virgil shouted.

His shotgun still trained on Cole made her even more nervous. It was wobbling as Virgil warmed to his speech—he might even fire it without intending to.

The townspeople's curious eyes were staring holes in her, and her face began to burn in spite of the cold seeping through her insides. She felt a terrible need to move her horse closer to Cole's, but she was frozen in place. Oh, *why* didn't he do something? But what could he do without getting himself killed before her eyes?

The cattle kept shuffling by, moving more quickly now, pushed from behind by the ones that had been bottled up in the cut. The riders were urging them on, too, anxious to get them out of the town.

Panic threatened, Aurora's heart raced, and her strained nerves made her arms tingle. Was

Virgil letting the whole herd go? Did he not want several head for toll, after all? Was the whole purpose of this ridiculous charade to jail her or *hang* her and Cole?

"What say?" Virgil shouted. "I reckon we oughtta save the folks down the road some cattle and some trouble and take these two off'n' the trail."

His companions shouted agreement, and Aurora thought some of the townspeople did, too. She searched their faces, trying to read them.

"She's rich," Virgil yelled. "And she's out to rob and steal from the poor! I'm tellin' ye . . ."

His raspy voice shut off abruptly, then a shot cracked, followed instantly by the shattering roar of a shotgun blast.

Shy Boy half-reared, but Aurora jerked him around anyway, frantically trying to find Cole, already weak in the knees from what she might see.

He was locked with Virgil in a one-armed struggle for the shotgun, which he immediately won by kicking the skinny man out of the saddle. His other arm wasn't wounded, either, she saw with relief; it held his six-shooter, which he was firing at Virgil's man behind him.

"Aurora!" he yelled.

He was wheeling his horse toward her as he called, using only his legs because he had a gun in each hand, leveling Virgil's shotgun and his six-shooter in front of him. For the first time she glimpsed Virgil's man who had been holding the gun on her—he was still behind her, but he no longer held a weapon and he sat slumped in his saddle holding onto one arm, his face a mask of pain.

That was the last thing clear. Cole fired the six-shooter at Virgil's other henchman, holstered it, and grabbed for her reins all in one move. Shy Boy plunged toward him, and in a blur that was made up of cattle and dust on one side of her and a long, steep sweeping of pine trees on the other, she leaned over her horse's neck and rode.

# Chapter 5

They raced up and up the side of a stony, tree-dotted hill. When they'd reached the cover of the thicker trees, they slowed to a long trot slanting across the side of the slope, always heading south, away from Rocky Springs. Aurora reclaimed her reins then, but the terrain still kept them riding single file.

She was happy to let Cole lead, in case there were any more mule-riding hostiles around, but she wanted to talk. She was bursting with relief and gratitude and excitement and frustration and questions, not to mention theories about Virgil and his men. But Cole had signaled for quiet when he'd returned her reins, so she kept quiet as they rode and he only muttered, "Heads down, there's a low limb coming up," then, after a long pause to listen, "I don't hear a thing. I reckon Virgil must be having trouble raising a posse."

Another mile, and finally he called a halt.

"Catch your breath," he said to her in his

91

normal voice. "You're pale as milk."

"I am *not!* I'm not even scared anymore."

She took a long breath and unwound her stiff fingers from Shy Boy's mane.

He watched her.

"If you're not scared anymore, why're you still pulling out your poor horse's hair?" he said, laughing a little.

Drawing in another, deeper breath, she tried to will her heart to slow down.

"Thank goodness, he still has a little bit of mane left," she said, smoothing the crumpled handful. "I didn't even know what I was doing."

Then she looked at Cole and couldn't think of a single one of the things she'd been so eager to say before they stopped. He gave her a sympathetic smile.

"You had a right to be a little bit rattled," he said. "Ol' Virgil and crew was enough to spook you right out of your skin."

She nodded.

"To the point I was thinking of trying to ride right over them or through them, screaming my head off," she said, with a shaky laugh, "and shotguns be damned."

"I'm glad you decided against *that* course of action," he drawled, with that slow grin that always made her helpless to take her eyes off his mouth. "It could've left me in a troublesome spot."

They both laughed, and she felt better.

"You took care of the whole sticky situation

in fine fashion. You probably saved our lives."

He shrugged. "Who knows? Could be Virgil couldn't have talked up a lynching, after all."

"He'd have done *something* to us—insisted on the lawman jailing us for stealing his cows, most likely. You know that."

He gave that little abrupt half-nod that cowboys used to show hearty agreement.

"Looked like it."

As calm and unruffled as if they were out for a pleasure ride, he started them moving south again, this time side by side.

"Anyhow, Cole, thanks for getting us out of it."

"That's what you hired me for."

"Speaking of *that*—what took you so long? There for *ages* I thought you never were going to do anything because you kept putting it all on me."

"Whoa," he said.

Border Crossing stopped in his tracks.

"Situation like that's why the trail boss draws a little extra pay," he said, scowling.

Shy Boy stopped too.

"But the bodyguard starts earning *his* pay when there's shotguns pointed at the trail boss."

"I'm not hired to do your palaverin' for you. You're plenty capable of doing *that* for yourself."

"Well, thank you very much!"

"Now, don't get all flustered. We just misjudged their intentions taking them for toll-takers, that's all."

She put her hands on her hips.

"Well, even so, weren't you planning to do anything to save my cattle?"

He grinned that grin again.

"I'm guardin' *your* body. Not your cows'." He smooched to Border and started them south again. "And I must admit that I'd sure rather watch yours than theirs."

"Don't you try to change the subject," she said, and dragged her gaze from his sensual mouth to look him in the eye. "I wanted you to tell Virgil that they should get out of the way of my herd that minute or you would shoot them all."

He threw back his head and laughed, really laughed.

"You're not paying me enough for that kind of action, Miss Aurora," he said. "And, even if you were, I'm not quite *that* fast."

"I think you are," she said. "I think you were just waiting to see what I would do about the toll."

That made him laugh even more.

"My curiosity don't run *quite* that strong," he said. "Although I'll tell you straight that you do rouse it some."

She felt a blush warm her cheeks.

"Well, you rouse mine a *lot*," she blurted, before she thought. "I mean you *did* . . . back there in the road . . . wondering if you had any idea what we should do."

"I've been in worse jams."

He made a gesture of disgust and turned suddenly somber. "I deserve to be horsewhipped, letting them get the drop on me like that. I'm gonna have to do more scouting ahead, and behind us, too. Can't take a chance on another ambush."

A new, fretful fear chilled her. It was too frightening not to have him riding beside her; she didn't even want to think of it. What would've happened to her if he hadn't been there to come to her rescue?

"No," she said tightly, "stay with me. You can't be everywhere and see everything."

He appeared not to even hear.

"My gut should've told me," he said, more to himself than to her. "I must be losin' my handle all of a sudden."

He spoke in a calm, careless tone, but it held an edge of hardness that told her he didn't intend to let such a thing happen again. Oh, Lord, he'd be going out scouting around all the time and leaving her alone.

"You're only human," she said, more sharply than she'd intended. "You couldn't have known they were waiting for us. You can't see everything for miles around."

Her voice came out sounding like a stranger's, even shaking a little bit. He finally looked at her, gave her a long, searching look.

She wanted to cry, suddenly, with relief at their narrow escape and frustration that he was even *thinking* of not being constantly at her side every minute from now on.

"Aw, come on, now," he drawled, "we're taking all this way too serious. I don't see a scratch on us, do you?"

She forced a smile onto her stiff lips.

"You're just like all the rest of the men—can't stand to see a woman cry," she said.

He raised his brows.

"All the rest of the men? . . ." he said, in a teasing singsong meant to distract her.

She ignored that.

"Well, you needn't worry," she said, and was thankful that she sounded much more like herself. "I'm not going to put you through any tears. I'm not going to worry about what's down the road, I'm just going to be happy right now because you got us out of a really dangerous situation."

"Me, too," he said. "Don't get me wrong about this second-guessing of my tactics. I *am* plenty glad not to be swinging from a tree right now."

She smiled back at him and relaxed inside for the first time since she'd seen Virgil on his mule.

"Well, you're the one who saved us," she said, "even if you did take your time about doing it. All *I* could think to do was try to *talk* the good people of Rocky Springs out of hanging us."

He raised his eyebrows, and his eyes twinkled with glee.

"See? What'd I tell you about the power of your palavering? Now I wish I'd held off a few minutes more to hear you. Most likely you could've talked 'em into hanging Virgil instead."

"Just because I talked *you* into coming on this pleasant little jaunt with me and my cows."

It pleased her that that made him laugh. Then he fixed her with a long, serious look, as if he were sizing her up all over again from a new perspective.

"We *both* got it done," he said. "I wouldn't've had my chance at ol' Virge if you hadn't ridden to the side of the road and split the rubes into two bunches."

She stared at him in surprise.

"I never thought of it that way."

"You should."

"Ol' Virge himself did that for us," she said, trying to be as nonchalant as he had been in accepting praise. "He sent the others to the opposite side of the street."

"You made it happen," he said generously.

The warmth from his praise began to melt the cold knot lingering in her stomach. Maybe she *hadn't* been so helpless, after all. Oh, yes, she had. Her riding away from the bad men had been desperation, not craftiness or courage.

"Good ol' Virge," Cole said, lifting his horse into a trot again.

By unspoken agreement, they began angling down and down out of the trees toward the valley floor and the herd.

"Good ol' snaky Virge," she said. "Gates hired him, don't you think?"

Cole shot her a quick, approving glance.

"Yep, glad you noticed. And I'd call him good ol' *simple* Virge. Gates probably would've paid him just as much for shooting us but he thought he had to throw a necktie party."

"I don't know. If they'd hanged us, then the responsibility would've been spread around to the whole town. And that's more Gates's way. He's an upstanding citizen, you know, one who doesn't like to take responsibility for his crimes."

Cole nodded.

"At least now we know Gates is serious."

"*I've* known it all along—didn't you believe me?" she said indignantly.

"I took the job, didn't I?"

That silenced her as they made their way downward to take the trail again. Did he mean he'd signed on to protect her from Gates and not for the money? Not to get out of town and keep from killing Kid Dolby? Not to go back to his home state of Texas?

No. It was silly to even let herself think something like that.

It was silly to be thinking so much about Cole McCord, even if he *had* just become her hero of the day. She must get her mind on her business and keep it there.

"How far do you think the herd is by now?"

"We're ahead of 'em," he said. "We covered some ground back there."

"Our horses covered it, you mean."

She leaned over and gave Shy Boy's neck a hug.

"You did great," she told him. "Good Boy."

Cole cleared his throat ostentatiously.

She turned and saw mischief in his eyes.

"What?"

"I reckon I deserve a hug, too," he drawled. "I was the one kicked ol' Shy Boy loose so's he *could* carry you out of there."

"Cole McCord, you're impossible," she said lightly, entering into the fun, glad to get her mind off the future. "First trying to bet a kiss, now shamelessly asking for a hug . . ."

"There's no *try* about that bet," he said, holding her gaze fast with his hot brown one. "It's a done deal."

Her heart began suddenly beating faster. Why did the idea of kissing him do this to her? No, of him kissing *her*. She had no intention of kissing him back if such an unlikely thing should occur. She had been kissed before, several times, and it certainly was nothing to get all wrought up about.

"You *are* impossible," she said.

"That's what they all tell me."

"Who all?" she said boldly, eager to know something about his past, something that might help her understand why he had taken the job with her.

But he changed the subject.

"You've got more sand than most, though, Aurora, you've got to know that. It took a lot of guts to turn your back on those shotguns the way you did."

That pleased her inordinately, but she tried not to show it.

"No, it was pure frustration," she said. "Worry about the herd. I couldn't bear to just sit there until the cattle scattered or ran over each other to get out of the cut."

"Spoken like a true trail boss," he said, as they trotted off the slope and onto the flatter ground of the narrow valley. "Let's go see about your cows and their nursemaids."

"While keeping a lookout for ol' Virge," she said.

"You got it. But I doubt he'll come after us now if he didn't follow right then. Not without new orders."

"Maybe he'll run off and hide in the mountains as a failure. Lloyd Gates has a rep as a pretty hard boss."

"Maybe. But if it's not Virgil, be ready for somebody else to give it another try on down the trail."

"Thanks for reminding me," she said dryly.

"That's what I'm here for."

"No, what you're here for is for *you* to be ready," she said, and gave silent thanks again that he'd accepted her offer of a job for *whatever* reason.

They picked up the pace and didn't talk any more. Aurora was glad, because her relief at their escape and her pleasure at Cole's praise were sinking now, beneath some other feelings she couldn't quite name.

Or perhaps she was only still scared. That surge of stark fear when those shabby men had materialized in the middle of the road, three shotguns at the ready, would stay with her for a long, long time.

They met the herd within a mile, pushing on a little bit faster than before they'd come through Rocky Springs, with the flank men riding back and forth between their own positions and the drag to help watch for attackers from the rear. The wagons had gone forward without knowing anything of what had happened.

"We won't stop for nooning," Aurora told Monte, whom she had chosen as her segundo. "Tell the men Cole and I will be back after awhile with cold food from the wagon to keep them going until dark. I want to bed them down as far away from Rocky Springs as we can."

"You got it," Monte said. "Them plowboys is liable to follow and try to give us a stampede for a good-bye present."

"I'll pick a spot where they'll be hard to scatter," she promised, and, waving to the men farther back, turned her horse to head south.

What if there was no such spot? What if Gates did arrange a stampede the first night on the trail? What if she didn't know what to do about it, what orders to give? What if she froze with fear and couldn't come out of it?

Dear God, please help her learn to be trail

boss. Cole and her crew could take care of everything else.

Cookie was in one of his famous snits when they reached the wagons. He had gone so far as to pick his own nooning spot and have Nate build a fire, and he was gunning for Aurora the minute he walked around the wagon and saw her and Cole riding up.

"Where in tarnation have you been, Missy?"

"I'm sorry you've already had Nate build a fire, Cookie, because we're going to have to keep moving all day. I want to be as far from Rocky Springs as we can get before dark."

He glared at her.

"Somethin' wrong with the town?"

"Its citizens," she said, reining to a stop. "They want to hang me and Cole."

"I ain't in no mood fer tall tales. I've got dinner to cook and a late start on it—"

"She's telling you the truth," Cole said, stepping down from his horse. "I had to shoot two men and kick another in the teeth, so their brothers and cousins may come after our hides."

The expression that came over Cookie's face as he absorbed the news made them both laugh.

Aurora ordered the cold food for the men, and she and Nate climbed into the chuck wagon to pack it into cloth flour sacks while Cole told Cookie the whole story. She heard the cook shout Gates's name furiously before Cole had gotten halfway through. The story ended as she finished her chore.

"Thank ye for gettin' her outta there safe!" Cookie cried as she climbed down over the wheel.

He grabbed Cole's hand and began to shake it.

"I'd shore like to've been there to protect that girl but you done as good as I could've, Mc-Cord."

"Thanks, Cookie," Cole said. "She helped me—she set it up so I could get a swipe at them. I don't think we have to worry too much about Miss Aurora."

*Oh yes, you do. Without you, I'd still be back there in Rocky Springs facing an uncertain future, to say the least.*

The feeling of sharp relief came over her again. If Cole hadn't been so fast with his gun—and his boot—there was no telling what might've happened.

He took half the food sacks and she took the other to go back to the herd. Nate and Cookie began breaking up camp even before she and Cole had left them.

"Let's get everybody fed and then head out to find the bedgrounds for tonight," she said. "I want a river or a mountain at our backs if we can find one."

"We can. And we can welcome anybody Gates sends to visit us, so there's no need to run your horse like a Nueces steer."

She realized for the first time that she was holding them at a high lope, so she slowed Shy Boy and tried to relax a little. Her gaze kept sweeping the horizon ahead, though, looking for the dust of the herd.

When they saw it and drew closer, Monte rode ahead to meet them and took the food to distribute, then Aurora and Cole took off to the south at a long trot. Mostly they rode in silence, because he suddenly seemed as remotely distant as he had the day they'd met.

And she was too exhausted to talk. The reaction was setting in, and all she wanted was to fall off her horse into the thick grass beneath their feet and stare up at the sky. She didn't want to ever think about Lloyd Gates again.

Yet her mind was whirling like a dust devil that would never stop, and her nerves were strumming, her emotions swirling in confusion. She resisted the urge to keep looking back over her shoulder. Cole was quietly keeping a sharp lookout, even though he seemed lost in thought. Cole was with her, so everything was all right.

But she hated depending on him!

Finally, when they'd covered what she judged to be the most miles the herd could travel before dark, she began scanning the horizon for the best bedgrounds. They were coming out into a more open valley, and ahead, running a little to the west of the trail, ran a curving line of trees.

"Let's go see if that's a river over there," she said.

He nodded, and they headed in that direction. When they rode through the trees and out onto the bank of a wide, meandering creek, they could see the rocky bottom through the water.

"Well, at least our first river crossing won't require us to swim," she said, laughing a little. "Do you think it's too shallow to hold them if somebody tries a stampede tonight?"

"It'll do," he said. "They'll try to break out into the valley before they'll take to the water."

"The bank's fairly high, on downstream, there," she said.

They rode up and down the north bank for half a mile in each direction, but the bend Aurora had pointed out seemed to be the best spot, so she chose it for the night camp.

"Don't you think we should bed them here?" she said.

It was the third time she'd brought them back to that spot.

"I truly do," he said, "but you're the trail boss and I'm the bodyguard, remember?"

She made a face at him.

"That's it," she said, as much to herself as to Cole, for she had to make a decision, and make it now. "Let's go back and get Cookie."

Shy Boy moved forward at her command, but then she stopped and turned. Her blue eyes questioned Cole sharply from beneath the brim of her hat.

A dozen different feelings grabbed at his gut. The strongest, by far, was the most recognizable: he wanted to pull her off that horse and into his arms, he wanted to kiss her until those pieces of sky eyes of hers glazed over with desire.

He wasn't going to be able to stay angry with her all the way to Texas as he had hoped. This was only the first day on the trail, and her beauty, her bravery, even her confusion was drawing his interest. No wonder he had let those ignorant yahoos ambush him back there— all his instincts were pulling him toward Aurora instead of feeling for danger.

To keep her from saying whatever was making her look at him that way, he said the first thing that popped onto his tongue.

"It's fine," he said. "You've done fine picking your first bedground. You're gonna make a trail boss that'll lay old Charlie Goodnight himself in the shade."

He intended to ride on, then, but she wouldn't let him look away.

"I never took you for a flatterer," she said, with a faint, suspicious smile curving her luscious mouth. "How come you've turned so encouraging, Cole?"

Her amusement *and* her distrust stung him a little.

"What do you mean? I'm . . ."

She interrupted.

"Two days ago your freely stated opinion was that I couldn't trail a herd of turtles across a hardpan yard," she said, "and now I'm better than Goodnight and Loving all rolled into one. How come?"

He folded his arms across his saddle horn

and smiled. That was another thing he liked about her: everything up front and on the table.

"I've gotta make you feel confident now that my life is in your hands."

"How do you figure that?" she demanded. "From my point of view it looks like that'd be the other way around."

"You're telling me where to sleep and where to wade the rivers," he said.

"And you're telling me that I can take care of myself and Cookie not to worry about me. Are you getting ready to go off on some big scouting expedition and leave me to fend for myself?"

A sharp sympathy tugged at him. Virgil and crew had shaken her up pretty bad.

He tried to shut off the compassion. He hadn't taken this job to worry about her feelings or what she might be thinking. All he intended to do was keep her safe until he deposited her on some ranch in Texas.

"No, I'll not leave you for very long at a time," he said, irritated that he felt so much for her. "But when I do, you'd better be on guard and able to watch out for yourself."

That seemed to satisfy her for the moment, and she said no more about it as they rode out to find Cookie and guide him and Nate in. But still his mind kept trying to think of other ways to reassure her, and that didn't improve his mood any.

Finally, as they pulled the wagons onto the campsite and Nate began to gather more wood for the fire, he left her with the boy and Cookie and rode up onto the next ridge to the south. He wanted to look for riders and also, to get an idea of the lay of the land. But sitting there staring off into the distance didn't help him much— he kept seeing Aurora's pale face when Virgil had appeared and then the shocked satisfaction in her eyes when he'd knocked the man off his mule and got them out of there.

He could still hear her husky voice, too, saying, *You saved us, Cole.*

At that moment, too, he had ached to drag her into his arms and kiss her senseless.

He shook his head, finally, and turned Border back toward camp. The horse deserved to be unsaddled and grained, deserved to get some rest. The remuda was catching up to them, coming on at a steady pace, and the dust from the herd announced they would be bedded down before dark.

Even the word "bedded" made him think of Aurora.

Giving a great sigh, he lifted Border into a long trot. What he ought to do was seduce her, bed her, and get it over with. That would restore his instincts for danger and his balance, that hardly ever failed to dull the fascination any woman held for him.

What was it she had said that night in his room? Something about having experiences and living life to its fullest. Well, being seduced by him was an experience she definitely should not miss.

He reached the bedgrounds and unsaddled Border, grained him, and turned him over to the boy in charge of the remuda. Then he washed up, all without so much as a glimpse of Aurora, and as he came back toward the fire he was wondering edgily where she might have gone. He was headed for Cookie to ask if she'd gone out to meet the herd—which, knowing her, she might've done simply to try to conquer her new worry of riding without him—when the sudden music filled the night air.

The sound stopped him in his tracks.

Piano music, there was nothing else it could be. It was coming from the wagon he had told her to sell in Rocky Springs.

A *piano*, for the love of all that was holy! What was it she had said?

*There's nothing extra. The contents of that wagon are the absolute, bare necessities.*

Surely it was Aurora playing, for the ravishing melody held as much turmoil as they had gone through all day and the whole confusion of feelings that he'd seen in her eyes that afternoon. He stood still for a long moment, listening.

Well, there was one thing he could set straight for her.

He turned on his heel and strode toward the sound. He was going to collect on that bet.

# Chapter 6

Cole was in the wagon at her shoulder, before she knew it. She startled, then glanced up into his hawk brown eyes and immediately lost the thread of her music.

He dropped onto the bench beside her, facing her, refusing to let her look away. She kept on playing, but not very well now.

"Not one unnecessary item in this wagon, hm?"

The purposeful look in his eyes sent a thrill through her.

"Not one single thing," she said, and played louder.

Those four words used up all her breath, took all the air out of the crowded wagon. Even so, she continued to play.

"I disagree," he growled, "and we had a wager on that."

His *closeness*, the incredible heat and bulk of his thigh touching hers weakened her wrists, caused her fingers to falter. She tried to speak but could only shake her head.

"It's dangerous to welsh on a bet," he whispered, and took her mouth with his. She played only one note more.

His lips tasted of hot, molten honey, and they knew her already. They devoured her, they made her mouth open to him, in pure instinct, the shock of their power erasing any resistance she might have offered.

It was too late for pushing him away, too late, even, for holding back her own response to him. She knew that in her bones and in her flesh. And in her soul, which felt a sudden, sweet peace. Yet he also stirred her like a storm, carried her off on the wind of desire and then she was lost, lost forever, offering her tongue, entwining it with his.

The amazing magic of his kiss took the strength from her body but not from her mouth. She stayed still as midnight in his arms, telling him, *begging* him with long, stroking caresses of her tongue and tiny pleading sounds deep in her throat, never to stop. She wanted him to kiss her forever.

He promised that he would, swore it with his lips and his tongue, pledged it with the way he sat so close to her. But he wasn't holding her.

*You can get up and go away from me any time you want.*

That was what he was saying with his one hand resting securely at the small of her back. Only it and his mouth were touching her.

And that marvelous mouth wasn't letting her

go unless she could find the will to move it away.

The smallness of her waist beneath his hand, the sweetness of her hair brushing his face should have moved him, but the marvel of the kiss made him powerless to want more, much less to take it.

There had never been another woman like this, not in his experience. Her lips burned against his, her tongue stirred in him a new desire, a craving beyond hunger he had never felt before, a wanting that burst to life as a conflagration in his blood.

He took her in both his hands, his thumbs just beneath her breasts, almost spanning her body with his fingers, feeling the wild beating of her heart. Absorbing the heat of her through the thin fabric of her blouse, he moaned a little, and her tongue pushed deeper into his mouth, teasing his, stroking it, and then pulling away. Calling him to her.

He moved one hand higher to cradle the perfect roundness of her breast. Her mouth went still on his.

With his thumb, he brushed the hard, firm tip, standing waiting for his hand, caressed it through the fabric of her blouse. Once. Twice.

She broke the kiss to give a little, helpless gasp, as if she had no more breath and never would. Then, after a moment, she melted more completely into the palm of his hand and pushed the nipple against his thumb in a mute demand for more.

He gave it. And he kissed her again at the same instant, branding her lips and her tongue as belonging to him with a stormy passion he had never felt before.

She responded with wild, unbridled desire for one heartbeat, then she tore her mouth away.

"Oh," she said, gasping for air. "No, Cole."

He had scared her. He'd lost all control, he was losing his mind.

But still he couldn't help himself. He kissed her cheek, her nose, then her chin and her slender, arching throat, dropping pleading kisses lower and lower on it, pressing *begging* kisses to her hot, sweet skin until she tore herself away from him.

"Stop," she whispered. "Stop, Cole. We must stop."

"We can't."

His own voice was so hoarse he didn't even recognize it.

"We have to. I . . . I . . ."

"Did I scare you? I'm sorry."

"No. I mean . . . yes. Yes, you scared me bad."

But he hadn't. Her voice and her eyes and her swollen, bruised lips told him that.

Her gaze kept going to his mouth and lingering there.

"You didn't *act* scared," he drawled.

She looked up and stared at him, her eyes huge in the dimming light that filtered in through the canvas.

"Go," she said. "Get out, Cole. You shouldn't have come in here like this."

The dismissal sparked his anger, it was so unexpected, so abrupt, after all they'd just shared. He didn't move.

"*You* shouldn't have hauled a goddamned piano down the trail in a hoodlum wagon."

"Stay away from me."

"How the hell can I stay away from you when I'm your bodyguard? Are you firing me off this job? For a *kiss?*"

Her hands flew to his arm, clutched it, then let it go. He could still feel the long, slender shapes of her fingers as he had the day they'd met.

"A kiss. And you can't say I held you down and forced it on you."

"No, I'm not firing you. Just go."

He stood up, took the two steps toward the door, then turned to look at her again.

"We don't want to stay away from each other, Aurora. You know that now."

"Yes, we do," she cried. "Don't you ever kiss me again."

"Suit yourself."

He stepped outside and jumped down from the tailgate. She appeared in the doorway, color high in her cheeks.

"Don't kiss me," she repeated, her voice breaking a little on the last word.

An edge of steel came into it.

"And don't ever grab my reins away from me again!"

She closed the canvas flap between them with a fast, sharp snap.

Cole strode off into the growing gloom of the evening as fast as his feet could move. The woman was *loco*. He had thought so the first time he saw her.

Aurora's plan had been to change and sleep in the hoodlum wagon after the cowboys had taken out their bedrolls at night. She intended to dress and undress in there and unroll her bed in the aisleway between the boxes and barrels each night so that she could maintain a modicum of privacy.

But tonight, the very first night out on the trail, she thought she would smother in there. She barely had room to spread out her quilts between the piano and the wooden boxes that held her grandmother's silver and china.

But what was most disturbing was that Cole's scent hung in the air. A scent made up of horse, leather, and his own renegade self, some cedary *man* scent that belonged only to him. She had to get away from it or she'd never be able to sleep. It had been on her, too, on her skin, and she had deliberately washed it off when she changed her clothes for bed.

A cold pain twisted her heart. She couldn't sleep because she couldn't stop thinking about him.

She pressed the tips of her fingers against her swollen lips, tasted the flavor of his mouth on her tongue again. Tears stung her eyes.

He was staying away from her, all right. From the time he'd walked away from her wagon, he had not shown up at the fire all evening.

Thank God, Cookie had sent Nate out with a plate and some coffee to find him. The boy had come back empty-handed, saying that Cole was keeping watch, and she had felt a little bit better—it would've been terrible if Cole had eaten nothing after the horrendous day they had had.

The thought made her throw her arm over her eyes. For the first day on the trail, this one had held enough adventure and excitement for the whole trip. It had worn her out completely, and she had to make decisions in the morning— like exactly where they should cross the creek. And there might be a river to cross before the day was over. That or some of Gates's minions to fight or a runaway wagon or no telling what else.

She had to get some sleep or she wouldn't be able to think.

But, although pure exhaustion held her body limp on her quilts, her mind went back over and over the day, and her memory wouldn't let her rest.

Never, ever, would she have believed that a kiss could rock her whole world, that it could shatter her bones. She thought she'd been kissed before, but she hadn't.

Cole McCord. She'd had no idea what she was doing in hiring him.

But the whole thing was scarier, even, than

the desire he roused in her. He had touched her
deepest self, she was coming to depend on him.
Already. On the very first day.

When Virgil and his crew had had them under their guns, she hadn't been able to think of
what to do because deep down she'd kept on
expecting Cole to take care of her. Which he
had.

Then she hadn't even been able to make a
decision about a bedground without asking his
opinion, and his praise had warmed and reas-
sured her. *Her*, Aurora Benton, who never re-
lied on anyone but herself!

She was relying on him, not just for her physical safety but emotionally, too. Already. On the
very first day.

Worst of all, so frightening she could barely
bring herself to think of it again, was the way
she had felt at the first instant of his kiss. That
weird calm, that sense that this was so *right*,
their mouths melded together, their flesh delivered up into flame in a heartbeat. That harmony
was stronger than the heat and desire. *That* was
the danger, far more than the pleasure.

She had wanted to be with Cole forever, to
kiss him from now on, to feel she was with him
for the rest of her life.

That in itself was far scarier than Virgil and
five shotguns.

The next morning she stayed busy giving orders while Cole rode out ahead, even before the
wagons started, to scout for enemies. He came

back when the herd began to move and then rode three or four lengths ahead of her south down the trail.

By the time the sun was halfway up, the silence between them was too heavy to bear. They had hundreds more miles to ride, after all, and there was no reason they couldn't behave like civilized persons.

"Cole!" she called. "Wait!"

He greeted her with a scowl as she loped up beside him.

"What?"

"I just wondered how you like your mount so far."

Both of them were riding different horses to let their personal favorites rest and travel with the remuda.

"How can I know a thing like that? This is the only one I've tried."

Each of the hands had approximately ten horses in his mount, and the same was true of her and Cole.

"You don't have to be so grouchy," she said in a teasing tone. "I wish you could see your sulky face."

He didn't take it well—he looked surprised and then fighting mad. No doubt he was the handsomest man ever born, with his dark, mysterious eyes and the hard, uncompromising line of his jaw that fairly begged her to run her fingertip along it. She wouldn't, though, and she wouldn't think such things. She'd look at him dispassionately from now on.

"You're getting mighty personal with your remarks," he growled.

"My *remarks?* Plural? I haven't said a word to you before now and you talk as if all I've done since sunrise is talk your ears off!"

He threw her a wry glance.

"That wouldn't take you from sunrise to the middle of the morning. That'd be about an hour's job for a medicine tongue like you."

His tone was still gripy, but a bit of amusement had crept into it, too, and she decided to try to make him smile. They might as well be pleasant as well as polite.

"That's not fair," she said, pretending great indignation. "Yesterday there were long stretches of silence in our scouting."

"Hmpf! About half an hour, as I recall, and that was only when we were riding at a high lope to save our necks from a hanging tree."

Her irritation became a little more real.

"I'm perfectly capable of maintaining a companionable silence," she said. "I do *not* talk all the time, Cole. You have to admit that."

"You promised me that night in the saloon in Pueblo City when I foolishly signed on with this piano-toting trail drive that you wouldn't talk to me at all."

"Did I?"

"Yes. You did. Remember that and abide by it."

"But you would get too lonesome," she said, unable to resist teasing him some more. "I'm only thinking of you."

That did make the corners of his mouth turn up in the tiniest hint of a smile.

Then his face filled with thunder again.

"Yesterday you weren't thinking of me," he said, "throwing me out, telling me to stay away from you, ordering me never to grab your reins again. You've turned through yourself since then, Aurora. How come?"

All of it came rushing back to her—the passion and fear that his kiss had inspired, the desire that had threatened to take her over. Those feelings had been there all night long and all morning while she'd been trying to deny them. When would they go away?

"I was thinking of both of us," she said to her saddle horn, so quietly that he had to lean toward her to hear. "Such a . . . an association would be impossible."

He didn't answer, but his silence seemed to contradict her.

She turned to look at him.

"I meant it," she blurted, fighting through the images in her mind to find a new topic of conversation. "Don't ever grab my reins away from me again. I hate that. It makes me feel like I have no control over where I'm going."

"Because you don't. And I'll grab them again if I have to."

Then he just sat there, riding his horse at a slow trot, watching her. He nodded, slowly, while he searched her face.

"What else? And don't ever kiss you again?

Don't you want to repeat *that* order, too, Miss Trail Boss?"

Her lips parted, but no sound came out.

He was looking at her with his eyes hot enough to burn her skin.

"I thought so," he drawled.

She *couldn't* see him dispassionately. She wanted to taste his mouth again, *yearned* for it with such a savage intensity that she trembled all over. It made her furious that she couldn't either make the feeling go away or ignore it.

*And* that she couldn't repeat the command to stay away from her.

"You're just like all the men," she snapped. "You think one kiss from you will have a woman on her knees begging for more."

"All the men? You're in the habit of kissing a lot of men?"

His arrogant tone fueled her anger.

"That's not what I said."

"Sounded like it to me."

"Then you must think I'm pretty loose with my favors."

"That's not what I said."

"Sounded like it to me!" she cried.

They both laughed in spite of their ire, but their laughter sounded more bitter than amused. Aurora took a deep breath, hoping it would calm her.

"This conversation's going around in circles," she said.

Cole wanted to grab her by the shoulders and shake some sense into her. And kiss her, damn it. How had he let her get them talking about kisses? How had he let her get him talking at all?

"I'll put it on a straight line," he said. "If you aren't in the habit of kissing all the men, then what *have* you been doing with them?"

He could've bitten off his tongue. Where in the hell had that come from? He'd no more intended to keep on prying into her life than he'd intended to listen to her prattle again today.

She shot him a startled look, angry at first, and then haughtily defiant.

"I don't appreciate your tone one bit," she said. "I hired you to be my bodyguard, not my father."

"You've got a known enemy hiring idiots and laying plots with your own men, trying to get you killed," he said coldly. "And you mentioned some suitors who told you you'd never make it to the end of this trail. Seems to me I'm asking for information that affects my job as your bodyguard."

He hadn't meant to pursue this line of inquiry like a dog on a trail. This was as bad as when they'd barely met and he had quizzed her about her enemies although he'd had no intention of becoming her bodyguard. What was it about her that made him as loco as she was?

"Well, back East, I went to socials and lectures with several different escorts," she said, "and I had other gentleman callers come courting as well. But then I don't suppose *they* would have any connection with your job, do you?"

Did he detect a teasing tone in her voice? What had happened to her haughtiness?

"No, they wouldn't," he said, feeling a little foolish.

But flashes of fashionably dressed, dandified dudes bowing to kiss Aurora's hand—or maybe her lips—crossed his mind. Dandies offering her a supporting arm and escorting her into her parlor. Or out of it. Aurora responding to them with that incredible, magical smile that could blind an eagle.

"Since I returned home to Colorado, I have accepted three of my bachelor neighbors as gentleman callers," she said. "Terrence Peck, Darius Martin, and Harvey Thorne. But then, their names may not help you much, since I'm assuming you don't know any of them."

There definitely was amusement in her tone. Was she making fun of him? Well, she probably was. She probably was thinking that he was wanting to know all this because he was jealous. She was deluding herself that she'd hurt some feelings more delicate than his pride last night.

"Never heard of any of the three," he said.

"Terrence is my favorite of my Colorado men," she said thoughtfully.

*Her* Colorado men.

"That doesn't sound too good," he said. "Sounds like you worked as a saloon girl before you started down the trail."

"Do you want to hear this or not?" she cried, suddenly completely exasperated.

He grinned. That was the thing about her that interested him—she was so alive, every minute, so completely caught up in whatever was going on, whatever she was feeling. To her, everything mattered.

And to him, dead in spirit as he was, nothing had mattered that much for a long time, at least not since Travis was killed. He pushed the thought of his old partner away, pronto, and fastened his gaze on Aurora's blue eyes.

"Maybe I ought not," he said. "This may be too risqué of a tale for my young ears."

She gave an unladylike snort that made him smile again.

"You are so delicate," she said. "I'll be careful what language I use."

"Thanks."

She rolled her eyes at him.

"Terrence Peck. He's a true gentleman and a scholar, a writer and photographer and I could sit and listen to him recite poetry all day long. He loves animals, too. Especially Bubba."

She shot him a significant look.

"Where is ol' Bubba today, by the way?"

"Nate wanted him to ride on the wagon seat with him so he wouldn't get so lonesome. He's used to always being with Newt, since they're twins, you know."

"Can't baby him too much, Aurora. Young'uns who go down the trail have to grow up in a hurry."

She gave him a long, straight look.

"I'll baby whomever I please," she said.

"Sometime I'll tell you about how fast *I* had to grow up. Now, do you want to hear about Terrence or not?"

He shrugged.

"Can't see that I have any choice since now you're threatening me with your whole life story."

That time, he made her smile.

"Terrence saved my sanity this winter," she said. "He came to see me as often as he could with the snow so deep so much of the time."

He gave a skeptical grunt.

"How far did he have to ride?"

"Twenty miles."

"He must not be too tough nor too serious about you if he let a little snow and twenty miles get in his way."

She threw him an irritated look.

"Oh, he's serious, all right."

"Let me get this straight," he said, wishing fruitlessly that he could jerk his mind away from this petty subject, which was none of his business anyway, no matter what he'd told her, "this poet fellow saved your sanity and hugged your big wolf-dog but you can't abide him."

She gave him the blankest look.

"Those were your very words that night in my hotel room," he said, locking his eyes on hers. "One of your unacceptable choices for your life was to marry a man you can't abide."

"I didn't mean *Terrence*."

"Then *who?*"

The expression on her face made him vaguely

aware that his tone was the one he always used to intimidate outlaws and bandits and other long-riders, and he tried to add something more kindly, but he was powerless to speak another word until he heard her answer. Hell. Now she'd probably start to cry or something.

But no. She sat up as straight as if she had a poker down her back and raked him with an icy stare.

"*Who* is none of your concern. I don't know why we're talking about this, anyhow."

"Neither do I," he snapped.

However, before they'd ridden one length farther, his mouth fell open again and, nosy as an old camp cook, he had to pry. He even used a falsely careless, softer tone.

"Terrence hasn't asked you to marry him?"

She relaxed, mollified by the change in his manner, but she didn't reply right away. Finally, a little stiffly, she did. But it didn't answer the question.

"Darius Martin and Harvey Thorne are the ones I referred to that night in your room," she said. "I never did want to marry either of them, but now I cannot *abide* them because after I refused them, they each made the long ride out to my place for the specific purpose of telling me that I should stay and marry him because there's no way on earth I'll ever get these cattle to Texas."

She slowed her horse more and gave Cole a long, searching look.

"Wouldn't you think they'd have sense

enough to know that that was no way to persuade me?"

In the morning rays of the sun, her finely boned face looked as fragile as a porcelain doll's, her tiny wrists incredibly delicate where they showed at the edges of her leather gloves. Those men *had* been talking sense to her.

"The sensible thing for you to have done would've been to marry one of them and drive your cattle to his place instead of halfway across the West," he said softly.

She let go of her reins to set her fists on her hips.

"Don't tell me you're agreeing with them! Where's that encouragement you've been handing out trying to build my confidence since your life is in my hands?"

He grinned.

"I was just giving you a hard time, Aurora. They're a couple of selfish, overbearing bastards who would've broken your heart without a qualm."

She grinned back.

"That's better."

"I can tell 'em right now there's not a doubt you're gonna get this herd to Texas," he said. "What I'm not too sure about is the piano."

He'd meant that to be funny, and she started to smile, but both their thoughts immediately went to the evening before and the kiss. He could see his own memory reflected in her eyes.

It took all the strength God gave him to hold himself back and not reach for her.

"You were talkin' sense last night, Miss Aurora," he said. "I had damn well *better* not ever kiss you again."

She couldn't look away from him. She couldn't move. She couldn't stop hearing the nuances in his voice, even though he didn't say another word. Hurt was in it, way down deep, and anger, and impatience and the iron hardness that edged everything he said and did.

Danger lurked in it, too.

Because it sounded as if he *would* kiss her again, when she least expected it, and that he wouldn't stop there.

God help her, then she'd be lost.

"I didn't intend to be mean to you last night," she blurted, "I'm just not used to . . . it, that's all."

His eyes took on a glint of mischief.

"I thought we just established that you're accustomed to kissing and carrying on with men scattered from the East Coast to the Rockies."

She tried to smile.

"I'm not used to depending on somebody else is what I mean," she said hastily.

"And you don't want to depend on me for kisses."

"No. Depending on you for my life is hard enough."

Cole looked straight into her heart and right on through it to her soul.

"I hear you talkin'," he said. "I'm an old lone wolf, myself."

He wheeled his horse and rode on ahead.

*   *   *

Aurora heaved a great sigh and flopped over onto her back, pushed the covers down to her waist so she could feel the cool night air on her body as well as breathe it in. She filled her lungs with it and slowly expelled it, willing it to calm her while she listened to the night.

Everything was quiet, so quiet she could hear the occasional popping of the fire that Cookie kept burning all the time for the hot coffee which was the one constant besides biscuits and beans in the cowboys' diet. An occasional low bawl came from the cattle, but they had bedded down fairly easily after their long day on the trail, and they lay basically quiet. Monte was singing to them—among her cowboys he had the only voice so pleasant it could soothe people as well as restless cattle—and for a short while she concentrated on the sound of his song. It almost put her to sleep.

But she couldn't let go of her thoughts of the day; she felt so wrought up she could sit up and scream.

Gritting her teeth in frustration, she scooted down closer to the end of the wagon and propped her shoulders against the stacked boxes, stuffing her pillow into the space at the small of her back. She was tired—exhausted, actually—by the three days they'd been on the trail. *Why* couldn't she slip off into oblivion?

Maybe she was too tired to sleep.

Or maybe she kept thinking about Cole.

All yesterday afternoon and all of today he'd

ridden somewhere near her, but it had been almost as if he weren't there. He had become the lone wolf he'd called himself—in fact, watching him ride a little bit ahead of her, she thought of stories she'd heard about the Plains Indians who sometimes pulled a wolf pelt up over their heads to wear into battle or to disguise themselves to creep up on an enemy.

He had pulled his aloneness, his oneness, up over his head and left her to hers.

Wasn't that what she'd wanted? What she'd told him to do?

Now that was what was driving her crazy.

She missed him terribly. They were already connected in some strange fashion—she'd been too late in sending him away.

No, it had been too late from the very beginning. Hadn't she felt connected to him the minute she found herself in the middle of the dusty street, wrapped in his arms?

Now, every fiber of her body was urging her to move, to just *see* him. She crept to the end of the wagon, reached for the canvas flap, and pulled it aside enough to peek out.

He was there, just where he had said he would be, with his bedroll laid out on the ground across the end of her wagon. Anyone coming to get her would have to go through or over him, he was so close to the tailboard.

He slept on his side with his back to her, cocooned in the covers pulled up over his shoulders. The wash of moonlight drew all the color out of the fabric and made it look white, but even the moon was powerless against the black of his thick, tumbled hair. There it could only add silver, like tracings of frost, to the pure blackness.

She couldn't stop looking at him, couldn't quit measuring the breadth of his shoulders with her eyes, and the lithe length of him, couldn't help remembering, with all of her body and soul, their kiss.

If she were snuggled into that bedroll with him, then she could sleep. She'd be wrapped in his arms, her head cradled in the hollow of his shoulder . . . No, she *wouldn't* be able to sleep, she would never sleep then. The hard muscles of his chest would be pressed against her breasts . . . oh, Lord, that very first touch of his had sent such a trembling thrill right through her even though she'd been shocked out of her mind when he'd snatched her from her gig, even though she'd been filled with fear that she'd be shot any minute.

Then his kiss, his unforgettable kiss . . .

Her whole body began to melt at the memory, and she pressed her knuckles to her mouth to keep from making a sound.

And then she thought maybe she had already done so without realizing, because suddenly Cole had gone perfectly still, the soft rise and fall of his shoulder had stopped. She didn't see him move, but he was lying on his back when she took the next breath, his head turned toward her.

She couldn't let him see her! Her hand dropped, the flap fell into place.

But she couldn't bear to stay there, all alone. She reached behind her for her bedroll and started dragging it behind her as she moved out onto the tailgate without letting herself stop to think. Outside. Out there with Cole. She would sleep outside tonight because she'd smother if she stayed cramped up in that wagon.

# Chapter 7

The moon was bright enough to let her see her way, but the light from the fire didn't reach her wagon. That was good—she didn't want the men to see her as they came and went on their guards and think she was being immodest to sleep out, one woman in a camp full of men. Cookie's breakfast call would wake her before dawn.

Quickly she spread out her bed again, lay down, and pulled the covers over her. She dared a glance toward Cole. He hadn't moved.

Her heart beat faster. There he was, only a short stone's throw away, his long body a vague shape beneath his blanket.

Again she felt that overwhelming urge to touch him, to stroke his moon-silvered hair, just to feel his skin beneath her fingertips. And, oh, dear God, his mouth on hers.

She turned her face to the sky and tried not to remember, tried not to think about him at all. Sleep had to come, had to take her away. Tomorrow she'd be too tired to sit in the saddle, much less make a quick decision if she had to, unless she could get some sleep. She would not look at him again. She would *not*.

There were only a few stars in sight among the shifting clouds that would drift across the moon any minute. She watched them, willing them to blot out the light so she could sleep. If the whole night, and not just the shadow she lay in, was completely dark, she could sleep. Surely she could.

The fresh, slightly damp air rolling down from the mountains caressed her cheeks, and she drew in great, deep breaths of it and snuggled deeper into her bed. Deliberately, she turned her head away from Cole. Her tight muscles began to relax a little.

"Aurora."

The whisper was no more than a breath in her ear; she might have imagined it except that it came less than a heartbeat before a hand covered her mouth.

Instinct brought a scream to her throat, made her struggle in vain to sit up. She didn't panic, though, because the hand was Cole's. Instinct told her that, too.

"If I let you go, can you be quiet? You know these cowboys of yours will string us up if we start a stampede."

After an instant to absorb that, she nodded.

He took his hand from her mouth, but he kept the other one cupped around her shoulder. His fingers imprinted her skin and filled her blood with warmth. She didn't even need covers anymore.

Oh, yes, she did! He was lying beside her, his whole length right next to hers.

It sent such a sensual shock through her that it made her furious. She wanted to yell at him, but she managed to attack in a hoarse whisper.

"*What* are you doing sneaking up on me like this? You scared me so, I could kill you."

"Not yet," he whispered back, his breath tickling her ear, his hand poised to cover her mouth again. "First let me see who's skulking around out there in the dark."

She froze in place, then tried again to sit up, but he held her down effortlessly.

"Somebody's out there?"

A desperate desire to simply turn into the haven of his arms and hide her face came over her.

"Don't sit up," he said, with almost no sound at all. "Even after I leave you. Keep down."

*No. Don't leave me. I'm going with you.*

She wanted to scream the words at him, but even then she knew he had to go alone. He could move like a shadow. Even this close, she hadn't had a glimmer that he was even out of his bedroll, much less right upon her.

"I was fixing to go see who and how many when you came crashing and banging out of the wagon."

"I wasn't *that* noisy!"

"Like a dozen drunk bandidos crashing through the brasada."

In that minute she blessed him in her heart for trying to lighten her fear. What if Virgil and even more of his cronies had followed them? What if Gates had hired someone smarter and faster than Virgil?

"Be careful," she whispered.

He gave his short nod of agreement and let his hand fall from her shoulder. He started to move away, then stopped.

"Keep flat on the ground," he said into her ear again. "And stay here so I'll know where you are."

Those words made no more noise than sighings on the night breeze, and his going made even less. One moment he was there, his hot flesh touching hers, the next he was gone, and so was her breath.

She lay, every muscle in her body stiff, her blood chill, listening to try to follow his progress. She heard nothing.

Cole was fast, she thought. When he'd kicked Virgil in the teeth nobody had seen it coming. And he was just as fast or faster with the gun he wore—that word was on everybody's lips who'd seen him shoot, that was what had made her hire him.

And he was so quiet that she hadn't heard him get out of his bedroll, although he'd been so close she could've touched him.

He had the advantage, too, because he knew the enemy was out there and whoever it was didn't know he knew. She strained her ears even harder to try to hear something.

After what seemed an age came a faint sound, then another. She couldn't identify either.

"I tell you, I'm trying not to wake the whole camp, that's all!"

The mellow, well-modulated male voice floated quietly on the night air. It wasn't Gates's, was her first thought. The next was that she knew it but at that instant couldn't quite place it.

"Then shut up," Cole growled. "And quit dragging your feet."

Aurora sat up as he hauled his prey into the light of the fire—a tall, thin man who was stubbornly pulling back against Cole's irresistible strength, digging in his heels hard enough to raise a dust.

"Now," Cole said, keeping his voice low so as not to wake the whole camp, "sit right there in the light with your hands in front of you and tell me who you are and where you came from. If your story suits me you can ride out all in one piece."

"Too late for that! You've already broken both my wrists!"

"Just be glad I didn't break your arms."

Aurora's thoughts fell back into place, her fear vanished.

"Don't hurt him, Cole!"

She threw back the covers and scrambled to her feet.

"Let him go," she cried and ran toward the circle of firelight.

"Cole McCord," she said, "I'd like you to meet Terrence Peck."

Cole stared at her, then at his captive, until finally he regained sense enough to open his hand and turn the idiot loose. Then he had to reach out and catch the clumsy scalawag because he stumbled backward and nearly fell.

Aurora caught him on the other side.

"Terrence!"

The surprise and joy in her voice ran through Cole like a sharp blade and rooted him to the spot as if a thrown lance had nailed him there. Aurora was leading the fool visitor to the log beside the fire.

Good God, she was wearing her *nightgown*, of all things, and that was *all*, because when she was between him and the fire he could see through the cloth. Then, mercifully, she passed by the light.

"What the *hell* do you think you're doing skulking around a camp in the dark?" Cole said, advancing on the two of them as they sank down to sit much too close together.

Even though he'd put all his menace into the tone of the question, the man barely glanced up at him, he had such eyes for Aurora.

"I didn't want to wake Aurora up suddenly," he said, grinning at her like an absolute fool. "I know what a bear that makes her."

That bit of news fueled Cole's anger like a dash of kerosene on a fire.

Then she added more.

"Oh, Cole, did you have to be so rough?" she

said, reaching for the skinny fellow's hands. "Terry, are your wrists really broken?"

"Rough?" Cole roared, forgetting the tired crew completely. "He can thank whatever God he worships that I didn't shoot him through the heart."

He set one foot on the log on the other side of Aurora and glared down at them.

"I'm afraid I may have exaggerated a bit," Terry said, smiling at her.

"At least that's one honest remark out of your mouth," Cole said. "Were you aiming to creep into Aurora's wagon or what?"

"I was *aiming* to sleep out near the camp and come in in the morning," Terrence snapped back, still without taking his gaze off Aurora. "If you hadn't attacked me and made such a scene!"

He glared up at Cole then, and Cole thought he might get up and hit him.

"Come on," Cole said viciously, not even bothering to step back and put both feet on the ground. "I'd love nothing better."

"What are you *saying*?" Aurora cried.

Then she started talking to *him* as if *he* was the one who was loco.

"Cole, get hold of yourself. It's all right. It wasn't Gates or any other enemy out there. Terrence is an old friend come for a visit. Remember I told you about him?"

"I know who the man is," he said, biting off every word. "I'm only trying to impress on him that he's damn lucky to be alive after skulking

around through the dark like a murdering
horse thief."

"My horses!" Terrence said. "I must see to
them."

He got up, and so did Aurora. Cole stepped
back and turned to see Cookie and a couple of
other men sitting up in their soogans, staring at
the little group by the fire. Damn! They'd heard
Aurora's remarks that had made him out to be
crazy.

"Everything all right, Missy?" Cookie called,
when he could see perfectly well that it was.
"You all make enough noise to wake the dead.
For a minute there I thought we was havin' a
Comanche attack."

"Cole's only doing his job, Cookie," Terrence
called back. "I foolishly thought I was far
enough away to spend the rest of the night, but
he heard me."

Shocked, Cole stared at the skinny man.

"McCord's got ears like a deer," Frank put
in. "He heard me muttering to Monte in the
middle of the remuda yesterday."

"Well, he heard *me*, too," Terrence said, and
started toward his horses, "and I must've been
half a mile away."

The sleepy men lay down again.

Terrence turned back and lifted his hand to
Cole.

"Pleased to make your acquaintance, Mc-
Cord," he said. "Thanks for protecting Aurora."

And then, smooth as you please, he was leaving the firelight to see to his animals.

Stunned, Cole looked down at Aurora, who was standing beside him.

"What was *that?*"

"Terrence didn't want you to be embarrassed about waking the camp," she said. "He's a thoughtful fellow, which is more than I can say for some people!"

Cole snorted. "That sounds a little ungrateful considering I was only looking out for your skin."

"Well, you didn't have to keep on *bullying* him after you knew who he was."

"Well, you didn't have to run over here in your nightclothes and display your whole shape in front of the fire."

"Oh!"

She clapped both hands over her mouth in dismay, turned, and ran for her wagon.

He followed on her heels at a long, fast stride.

"You ought not be wearing that anyhow," he said. "Only a greenhorn takes off his clothes at night on the trail."

In the shadow of her wagon, she whipped around to defend herself. The soft white cloth swirled back and forth at her bare feet.

"*I* am no greenhorn!"

"Would that lace thing hold up to a wild ride to turn a stampede?"

She looked down at the garment, put a hand to her throat.

"It's only lace across the top, so yes, it probably would but that's beside the point," she said fiercely, keeping her voice just above a whisper. "You needn't worry about me. I can ride buck naked if I have to."

"Sounds good to me," he whispered back, with an almost soundless chuckle, "but it might get a little breezy for you."

"You are possessed of such an incredible wit I'm splitting my sides laughing."

"I'm glad you appreciate *something* about me, since you don't approve of my bodyguarding tactics."

Even in the faint moonlight he could see the stubborn set of her chin as she drew herself up even straighter.

"It's not bodyguarding to pick on someone after you know they're a friend."

"Your friend. And where does he come in *thanking* me for protecting you? He doesn't own you."

"He's ..."

"I know. Thoughtful. Well, before that thoughtful fellow comes back, you need to get some more clothes on. Or better yet, crawl into your bedroll. This's no time to be sitting up visiting half the night."

"I'll sit up *all* night any night I please," she snapped. "And when I want orders from you, I'll ask for them."

"Suit yourself.

He turned and started to his own bed. Then he stopped, turned, and walked back.

"And *how* the hell did that yahoo know

you're a bear when you get waked up suddenly? *I* didn't even know that."

She had jumped up onto the tailgate of the wagon. She looked down her nose at him.

"Terrence has known me a lot longer than *you* have."

Then she turned and lifted the canvas door, disappeared inside, and brought it closed behind her with a quick, angry slap.

He strode to his bed and gave it a kick with the toe of his boot. It'd be a useless effort to even try to sleep again tonight, for he felt wire-edged as a snaky bronc run into a corral for the first time.

But he made himself toe off his boots and stretch his body out on top of the roll. If he didn't, he'd be watching for Aurora to come out of her wagon, keeping an eye on her and Thoughtful Terrence, straining his famous hearing to find out what they were saying.

God help him, was this *jealousy* driving him? What was the matter with him?

He'd been too long without a woman, that was all. Even on the few occasions he'd been in a town and not embroiled in some job, no woman had looked good to him for months and months, and Aurora did. It was as simple as that.

Stretching his legs straighter, he crossed his ankles, folded his hands behind his head, and stared up at the stars. They were shining brighter now, those white feathers. They would calm him.

But in his guts, the turmoil raged. He made himself ignore it and think.

He had overreacted to someone nearing the camp unannounced, that was all. He hadn't even had a prickling along his scalp or a chill down his spine before Virgil and his mule-back brigade had appeared, so now he was making too much out of this.

She came out of her wagon; he heard the scrape of her feet on the tailboard and the soft thud when she hit the ground. He turned his head so he could see her as she went toward the fire.

Aha! She had dressed. At least, perhaps, he'd gotten one commonsense lesson through her head.

He needed to follow through on his plan to seduce her soon, very soon, so he could quit thinking of her so much. However, since this was Aurora, she'd probably interest him even more, instead of boring him, after he'd had her in his bed. He could not think of one woman he'd ever known who could affect his emotions the way she could, who could have him acting crazy in a heartbeat and thinking about her all the time.

But desire was all it was. That Aurora was the most intriguing, as well as the most beautiful, woman he'd ever been around for any length of time had nothing to do with the way he felt.

Terrence led his horses in close, and Aurora went to him. They talked in low tones Cole couldn't hear. Then he unloaded what seemed a ton of stuff off the one horse and his saddle off the other.

Dear Lord, was he moving in? Surely he hadn't come with the idea of staying with the drive to the end? From the description Aurora had given of him, he didn't sound like the trail hand kind. But maybe he wanted to write poems about the drive.

That preposterous thought made him flop over onto his stomach so he couldn't see them any more. Terrence obviously had *thoughtfully* ridden all the way out here to press his suit and beg Aurora to change her mind about marrying him. And she had said that she liked him, that he wasn't one of the men she couldn't abide.

So that's what she ought to do: marry Terrence. Give up this insane drive and marry the man, go home with him and turn the cattle loose on his ranch and have a dozen babies.

He forced himself to think about that as long as he could. To try to visualize it.

No, that wouldn't work, after all. Little spitfire Aurora would clobber thoughtful Terrence, and that would be that. Terrence might know that she was a bear when waked up suddenly in the middle of the night, but he, Cole, knew that she had to have this trail drive of her own, had to run that new ranch at the end of it, no matter what she had to go through to get it.

*Because* of what she had to go through to get it. Aurora had been determined to get her herd through Virgil's blockade. No matter how scared she'd been, her stubbornness was greater. She'd hidden her fear, she had stayed cool and quick, and next time she'd be much more confident about what to do. He grinned, remembering.

*Don't ever snatch my reins from me again.*

Yes, poor Terrence had risked his life sneaking up on Aurora's camp for nothing. No matter how thoughtful he was, he didn't have a chance.

The next afternoon, however, by the time the sun had climbed down toward two o'clock, Cole was beginning to think that he might be wrong about Aurora's response to her old beau. Terrence and Aurora had ridden off to the west at sunrise to make some photographs, promising that they would be back to the wagons by noon. They had not appeared.

Most of the packs Terrence had taken off his horses the previous night were filled with cameras and all sorts of equipment and supplies to go with them, that and books, but he and Aurora had been gone long enough to use every bit of it and take pictures of the scenery for miles around. Perhaps they were doing something else entirely.

The thought made him grouchier, even, than his scanty sleep of the night before had done. Where the hell had they got to? It wasn't like Aurora to let someone else choose the nooning site and now, by golly, he'd be choosing the night's bedgrounds if she didn't hurry up and come back. He had scouted alone all day.

"Whoa," he said, and Border Crossing stopped.

He wasn't going on down the trail another step. He was going to find Aurora, and if he rode up on the two of them in a private moment, that was just too bad.

Turning the horse, he headed straight west. They would work their way southeast as they made the pictures, Aurora had said, and, by noon would catch up with the wagons or, at the very least, with the herd.

Peck wore a six-shooter, but he'd been slow as Christmas trying to draw when Cole had crept up on him in the dark. What if Gates had some men prowling around out there west of the trail?

The picture *that* thought brought to his mind twisted his gut for sure. He stopped the horse at the top of a rise and stood in the stirrups to scan the country ahead.

Patches of wildflowers—purple and yellow and a deep, deep blue that reminded him of Aurora's eyes—grew in great patches spreading through the greening grass, but he saw no sign of two horses with riders in spite of the fact that this was probably the highest rise for fifteen or twenty miles. His heart gave a lurch, and he reached back to take his binoculars from his saddlebag without taking his gaze from the land. If that idiot Peck had gotten them off somewhere trapped in a box canyon or lost . . .

but Aurora had a good sense of direction, even if he didn't . . .

He raised the glasses and looked through them, adjusted them, looked again. Two horses broke out of a stand of trees at the base of the next hill and started east at a short lope. They were a long way away, too far for him to have seen with the naked eye.

His heart plummeted. One was a tall, rangy sorrel, sure to be Shy Boy, and the other was a gray like Peck's. The only bad thing was that both saddles were empty.

He saw no one in the trees behind them. Dropping the binoculars into the bag again, but keeping it open against his leg, he loosened his gun in its holster and started toward them. That act, for some reason, reminded him of Travis.

Travis would have loved this, he'd always loved riding into the unknown—until that last time.

Then the guilt sliced him right through. Last night he hadn't thought about Travis, not once during all those sleepless hours. Aurora had driven Travis right out of his head. Somehow, that made him feel guiltier than ever.

The loose horses came to his own and they let him catch them, so he set out on their back-trail, leading them. He'd noticed before they met that Shy Boy was limping from a swollen hock, but he didn't take time to get off and see about it. He circled toward the edge of the meadow, trying to get closer to cover, but he wasn't moving too fast for the horse to keep up. If need be, he'd leave him behind.

Silently praying that Gates wasn't behind the trouble that had set Aurora and Peck both afoot, he smooched to Border Crossing and finally rode alongside the trees until he came to the place where the horses had come out. He entered, rode through the trees and out onto the bank of a rushing creek. The track the horses had beaten down in the grass showed on both sides of the water.

Then he lifted his gaze and saw them, Peck and Aurora, trudging down the hill and toward the creek, Terrence's arms filled with camera equipment and Aurora's with two fat books. Cole took a deep, full breath of relief.

"If you'd only told us you wanted to walk to Texas, we would've let you do that on the trail," he called, sending Border into the creek with the other horses at his heels to splash across and meet them. "Looks like we need to get you two some pushcarts to put your plunder in."

"It's not funny!" Aurora yelled back at him.

"I wish you could see your sulky face," he said.

That made her laugh. The treacherous feeling of fascination bloomed full-grown in Cole's gut again.

"I'm glad you caught the horses," she said, stopping to put her burden down on the grass. "Shadow can carry these books from here on out."

"Yes, thank you, Cole," Peck said. "We knew you'd find us, but we were afraid the horses would go the wrong way to try to find the remuda."

Cole threw Peck the reins to the gray and stood in the stirrup to dismount.

"Your horse has hurt his hock, Aurora, so you'll have to ride with me."

Shut his mouth, he was getting as bad as Cookie to say what didn't need saying! That was perfectly obvious, since Peck had bags of every size hanging off his saddle and enough junk to put in them to weigh down a pack mule.

Aurora ran to Shy Boy and hugged his neck, then went around him to examine his hocks. Cole went to her.

"I think he cut it on a rock coming down off the hill," she said. "He made me so mad taking off like that—just because Terry's horse spooked, Shy Boy had to run off, too, and he never does that."

"What spooked them?"

Aurora didn't answer.

"I shot at a rattlesnake," Peck said, busily filling the bags on his saddle. "My horse likes any excuse."

"Shot *at* it?"

"Yes."

"Slow as they are this time of year, you might've got 'im on the second try."

"I was afraid of hitting Aurora," he said. "It slithered right at her."

Cole stared at him incredulously.

"Tell me," he said, from between clenched teeth. "What happened?"

"I jumped up and got out of there," Aurora said. "I'm fast, so no harm done."

She touched Cole's arm to make him look at her. He tore his gaze from Peck's worried face.

"He feels bad enough already," she whispered. "And I'm fine.

"Let's get this hock into the creek for a few minutes," she said, loud enough for Peck to hear. "The cold water'll take the swelling down, and then we'll not push him on the way back to the herd."

"It'll take us 'til dark to *catch* the herd," Cole muttered sourly.

Aurora flashed him a warning look.

"I'll be down to the creek in just a minute," Peck said. "I want to get this load balanced, although I shouldn't do one nice thing for this obnoxious animal."

He was stroking the horse's neck as he spoke.

"Terry, you spoil all your animals, and that's why they don't obey you," Aurora said.

Cole bit back the same sentiment that he'd been about to put into much stronger words.

"Terry's good as gold," Aurora said quietly as they led Shy Boy to the creek. "I cannot bear to see him with hurt feelings—he takes everything so to heart."

Cole rolled his eyes.

"I mean it," she said, and gave him a little jab in the side for emphasis.

"All right, all right! Haven't I been biting my tongue?"

"Yes, and I thank you for it."

"How come you never worry about *my* tender feelings?" he said. "Not only do you not protect me from anyone else, your own tongue has been known to flay the skin off me in long, thin strips."

She laughed.

"Because you are tough as whit-leather."

They soaked the hock for as long as it took Peck to get his stuff packed, which was about fifteen minutes. Then, when Peck mounted and started toward them, Cole set his hands on Aurora's waist. He could span it with his two hands.

She felt light as air as he set her up into his saddle, still clinging to her horse's reins. She gave a small scream of surprise.

"You could've just told me to mount up!"

"Not with the way you follow orders," he said, letting his hands stay there, clasping her warm body far longer than was necessary. "I don't have time to argue."

"You just have to be the boss every chance you get."

He ignored that.

"You lead him," he said dryly, pushing Shy Boy over to follow on Border's off side so **he** could mount. "That way I'll have my gun hand free in case of a snake attack."

She glanced over her shoulder at Peck to see if he had heard that.

"You be nice," she hissed.

He stuck the toe of his boot into the stirrup and swung up to sit behind her.

The sweet curve of her hip pressed against his crotch, and the perfect shape of her breast brushed the inside of his arm as he picked up his reins. A deep thrill of desire rose in his blood.

He bent his head and pressed his cheek against her fragrant hair, smelled her soap and the light sweat on her skin. He wanted to turn her face and kiss her more than he'd ever wanted anything in his life.

Instead, he set his lips against her ear and growled into it.

"Don't be running off alone with that ignorant tenderfoot again if you want me to stay hooked as your bodyguard."

"The devil you say," she snapped, quick and fierce as some hardened old trail driver. "I don't have to get your permission to go *anywhere* I want."

She tried to turn her head, but he kept his face against hers. She gritted her teeth.

"Terrence is no danger to me, Mr. *Bodyguard*," she said, her stubborn chin stuck out in front of her. "He would never snatch me off my feet and throw me onto his horse like a side of beef, for example."

"No," he drawled. "*Terrence* wouldn't, would he?"

Her skin smelled like flowers, too, but he lifted his head then, and let hers fit into the hollow at the base of his throat. She sat up straight and leaned away from him.

"You've squished my hat," she said, and pulled it up from where it hung on her back to jam it onto her head.

The breeze picked up a strand of her hair anyway, and blew it across Cole's lips. She wasn't thinking about the hat, he knew that from the absent tone of her voice. She was thinking about what he'd just said, and well she might.

In a moment, she twisted in his arms to look back at Terrence.

"Slow down, Cole," she said. "That horse is really loaded, and we're being rude to leave him behind."

All he really heard was the sound of his name on her lips. Even in that tart tone she'd used, it struck him like taking a step out of the shadows into sunlight. Inside, he felt a surging sensation like a river on a rampage.

The next instant she changed it into a torrent.

"Cole, will you teach me to shoot? I've decided I really need to wear a gun."

"What the *hell?*" he said. "Aurora, that's an insult as long as I'm in your employ."

"What were you telling me not two days ago? To be able to take care of myself when you're not around."

Or when Terrence was around. Was that it? Were things between them going the opposite way from what he'd guessed, and she was trying to get at least one shooter in the family?

One thing he did know about women for sure: they were protective of the people they loved. And, six ways to Sunday, Aurora was out to protect Terrence Peck.

"And don't be calling Terry a tenderfoot," she said. "He was born in the West and grew up in Colorado. His father started his ranch there not long after we moved up here and Papa started ours."

"You don't say," Cole drawled, glancing over his shoulder to see the heavily laden Terrence closing in on them. "Well, one thing's for *damn* sure: he ain't no Texan."

To his surprise, instead of rushing to Terry's defense, she laughed.

"But *I* am, I was born in Nacogdoches. That's why I have to learn to shoot," she said lightly, "so I won't disgrace you and the whole state of Texas in a fight."

"All right," he said, though his jaw was stiff with aggravation. "We'll start as soon as we pick the bedgrounds tonight."

"No, no. Wait until Terry's gone!"

At least she didn't expect to be going *with* Terrence. Something inside him relaxed a little.

"Terry needs shooting lessons worse than anybody I know," he said.

She giggled.

"Maybe so. But I don't want to make him feel bad."

He pretended to be shocked.

"You think you'd show him up that much, huh?"

"I *know* I would."

That warm feeling about her spread through Cole again. She wouldn't be bragging and joking like this with anybody else, and she wasn't going home with Peck.

"Spoken like a true Texan," he said, and held back to let Terrence catch up.

# Chapter 8

⌒◯◯⌒

Cole watched Aurora set the boxes of extra ammunition on a rock to keep them out of the dew-wet grass. She didn't seem sad now, but she had looked after Terrence Peck until he and his horse had turned to a tiny black speck and then disappeared over a hill.

"I'm going to run over there and check Shy Boy's rope and stake one more time," she called to him. "It may be that he'll always spook at gunfire now."

"Border Crossing won't turn a hair," he called back. "That'll help."

Then, as she was running toward her horse, he shouted to her again.

"Check all you want but don't touch anything. I locked him down pretty good a minute ago when the wagons pulled out."

She stopped in her tracks and turned back, her hands on her hips. He grinned. She'd get riled up now and forget Peck entirely.

"Because you thought I couldn't even stake a

horse by myself?" she yelled at him.

He deliberately turned away and arranged two more empty airtights on the length of the dead tree that had supplied their firewood the night before. He was *not* going to cross the space between them in two strides, pull her into his arms, and kiss her. Peck's departure was making him a little light-headed with relief, about to make him lose control.

"No," he called back in his most reasonable tone, "because your boy, Nate, hit the stake with a wheel when he followed Cookie out of camp. He was too busy teaching ol' Bubba to sit beside him on the seat to watch where he was going."

Slowly, she turned around and walked back toward him. He looked away and set another airtight into the line.

"In a way I'm jealous Bubba's taken up with Nate so much," she said, "but I'm glad, too. It keeps him from wearing out his poor paws walking all day, and Nate needs him."

"Well, I need you to get your mind off your children and dogs and onto your shooting," Cole said. "Your horse can't get loose, and Peck's isn't here to agitate him."

"I can't believe Terry came all the way out here to find us and then rode four more days down the trail. It'll take him a week to get back home."

He set the last tin can into place and turned, came to meet her.

"I don't care *how* long it takes, I'm just glad that he's goin' home," he said.

She looked startled when he said it, as if he had surprised her as well as himself by blurting that out. Surprise made her look very endearing.

"Why, Cole, I'll declare, if I didn't know better, I'd say you might be jealous."

She gave him a flirtatious smile.

But he managed not to smile back, managed not to stand too close.

"Nope. And nothin' against him, either," he said. "I'm tired of poetry with every meal, that's all."

"Now that's an exaggeration if ever I heard one," she said, going to pick up the ammunition.

"Leave it," he said. "We'll start you out shooting from there."

He followed her, trying to stop looking at her, trying to figure out exactly why he *was* so happy about their guest's departure. It was none of his business who came and went, as long as they didn't threaten Aurora's physical well-being. And Peck certainly didn't—at least not directly.

"Well, maybe only dinner and supper," he said, wrenching his mind back to the conversation. "I'll have to hand you that the old boy was generally too busy rubbing his eyes and gulping coffee to spout poems to us during breakfast."

"Terry's not used to getting up early or to

working," she said. "His father has always hired everything done."

"Well, Terry better hope they never lose their money," he said. "I'm not sure he could trade those poems for food. The pictures, maybe."

"What did he say to you when he told you good-bye?" she said.

Ah. So that was which way the wind blew. Maybe she just wasn't letting him see how she really felt about seeing the back of Terry. Although, again, she might just be curious. She truly was a curious one.

*He told me to take good care of you and said it in a way that sounded like he was giving you to me.*

"Told me to keep a sharp lookout," he said, "whenever you have a gun in your hand."

"He did *not!*"

Cole motioned for her to start handing him bullets to fill the loops in his gunbelt.

"Better get your mind on your shooting instead of your old beaux," he said. "Every time you pick up a gun, don't be thinking about *anything* else. You're the one responsible for where your bullet goes."

"Aren't you going to let me wear that holster?"

She reached for the buckle, but he took a step back. This was no time for her to touch him, not with her eyes sparkling so blue and searching his with that secret little smile on her lips.

And she knew that, too. As usual, she was reading his mind.

"You're the one wanted shooting lessons," he snapped. "Now pay attention."

"Yes, sir."

She waited one significant beat.

"*You* pay attention, too, Cole."

That made them both laugh, finally, as they stood looking into each other's eyes. Then, still holding her gaze, he grew deadly serious, forced his thoughts off her looks and her teasing. He made his voice completely solemn.

"Learning to use a gun could save your life sometime, Aurora," he said, "but it could also get you killed."

"I know that. I've carried a rifle all the time since Papa died, after I went through all the papers and saw what a treacherous back-shooter Gates really is."

"How good are you with the long gun?"

"Not bad. I've done a fair amount of practice."

"This will be entirely different, so start getting the feel."

He lifted the Colt from the holster and gave it to her.

"Use both hands," he said, "one to brace the other."

He stepped around behind her as she took the six-shooter and immediately had to restrain himself from putting his arms around her in order to place his hands over hers. Words. He could do all this with words.

"Lock your elbows," he said, as the muzzle wavered in a widening circle.

"This thing is heavier than it looks," she said.

"You can do it. Now, pick out an airtight and look along the top of the barrel through the sights."

She did as he said, held the gun level for an instant, then wavered again.

Instinctively, he grabbed her hands and steadied it.

That was his first mistake. The curves of her breasts lay against the insides of his arms.

"Have you picked your target?"

His own voice sounded so rough he hardly recognized it.

"The peach on the one in the middle," she said, very low, in her husky, breaking voice.

So she felt it, too, this nearly unbearable force pulling them to each other.

He could do nothing except reholster the gun and fold her into his arms, take her down beneath him right here in the sweet-smelling grass.

Instead, he set his feet farther apart and dug the heels of his boots deeper into the ground.

"Might widen your stance a little," he croaked, and she did.

That was his second mistake. She threw him a blue-eyed glance over her shoulder.

"Far enough?"

*No. Step back one pace. Come closer to me so I'll have no choice. So we can make love and the responsibility won't be all on my renegade soul.*

"Fine."

Damn it all, he had to get a grip on himself.

Had to get this over with so they could walk away from each other and get on their separate horses and stay on them, God willing, until they were too exhausted to move when they dismounted way after dark. So long after dark that he couldn't see her beautiful heart-shaped face.

Except that he would always see it when he closed his eyes.

"Now when you get ready to take your shot," he said, helping her cock the gun, "squeeze the trigger. Slowly. Don't jerk it fast."

Then he peeled his hands away from hers and hooked his thumbs, as hard as he could, into his front pockets. His whole body ached from wanting to put them on her, instead.

She did as he said, she even took in a long, steadying breath and let it slowly escape as she squeezed. The shot cracked through the early morning stillness. The empty airtight with the tomato on the label, two over from the peach one in the middle, went flying.

"*Dang* it," she said through clenched teeth, rocked back by the recoil.

He caught her by the shoulders.

"Mustn't let it drive you into using profanity," he said, teasing her, laughing a little. "At least you hit *something* on your first try."

She grinned at him, faced front, narrowed her eyes, and sighted again.

"This time I'm not telling you which one I'm aiming for," she said.

"Deception and lies lead to a wide, straight

road downhill," he chided. "Best be honest with your teacher."

She chuckled, a low, ragged sound that heated his blood.

"I'm taking a better stance, too," she said, "and you can prop me up for when this thing kicks me back."

She set her boots just inside his, and her pert, round hips brushed against his thigh.

To hell with virtue. He was no saint, and he'd be the first to admit it.

Coolly, deliberately, he placed his hands on her hipbones.

That brought a sharp little gasp from her, and she turned her head to look at him. He captured her gaze with his own and held it, pressed his palms flat against her and slid them slowly, firmly, over onto her flat belly, circled them on it deliberately, boldly, while he looked into her eyes. They widened with pleasure. They devoured his face.

The real sin in this deal would be *not* to kiss her.

The heavy gun dropped to her side, her arm sagged with its weight. He lifted one hand to cup her delicate shoulder, slid it slowly all the way down her arm, savoring the shape and the feel of her soft flesh, her small bones, took the six-shooter from her and holstered it.

That done, he pressed her belly with the one hand to bring her back against him, to rock her small, rounded hips against him, to bury his face, just for an instant, in her cloud of fragrant hair. But his mouth was starving for the taste of her, and he soon had to cradle her cheek in one hand and turn her to face him with the other.

"Aurora."

He said her name, very low and against her mouth in his dark velvet voice. She melted even more against his warm hardness, her very bones giving way, her whole being aching to surround him. To kiss him.

God had better protect her, because she was long since past protecting herself. She had to have Cole's mouth on hers again or die.

But more than the kiss she wanted her skin against his skin, every inch of her demanded to feel every inch of him, while her mouth begged to kiss him. She slid her palms up his chest to cup his face in her hands, but he was already devastating her mouth, drawing the air from her body never to put it back again.

Yet he did. He became the source of every breath she took, every sensation she knew.

Her very womanhood wept for his touch, her breasts strained for the feel of his hot, hard hands, her arms flew around his waist to hold him tight to her. Her mouth had to say his name, had to feel the shape of it.

"Cole," she whispered, against his lips, "Cole."

He took her face in his big hands and made her fall into the hot, honeyed world of his mouth once again, kissed every thought right out of her head and every shred of strength from her body. She would have fallen if he hadn't been holding her up.

When he tore his mouth from hers and stood stroking her back, her arm, the curve of her shoulder as gently as if she were something precious made of glass, she clung to him, looking up into his deep, dark eyes.

"We're alone," he said. "All the others have gone."

She was in danger of losing her sanity, right here, right now. She had hungered for his kiss all those endless days since the first one until she couldn't even think. If they did more, much more than kiss, she'd be in a fit of wanting him forever.

"I know," she said, tracing the intriguing slant of his strong cheekbone with the tip of her finger as she had longed to do from the first moment she saw him, "but we have to go on, too, and soon."

He found her breast and cupped it in the hollow of his palm.

"Not *that* soon."

Longing washed through her in such a powerful wave that she swayed toward him, deeper into his hand. He flicked his thumb across her hard, yearning nipple. Even through her shirt she could feel its strength, its calluses. Its skill.

Cole McCord obviously knew what he was doing when it came to women. How could she ever hope to be his only one?

Somehow she took a step back from him even

though her feet felt rooted in the ground all the way to China.

"Cole, we have to finish my lesson! And we have to catch the wagons and go past, way past, to find the nooning place."

His face filled with thunder. He let his hands fall away from her.

"Still thinking about *Terry*? That's it, isn't it? Well, why didn't you accept his offer and go back with him? I really thought you might do that."

He turned on his heel and strode away fast. For the first time since she'd met him, she couldn't even see the loose-hipped, prowling way he walked. All she could see was a red blur of hot anger which, at bottom, was cold as white ice. He didn't know her. He didn't know the first thing about her. He wasn't even *trying* to know her, or he would have seen her true feelings for Terry.

And for *him*, bless goodness! Could he not *see* the difference in her feelings for the two of them? Did he think she'd kiss him the way she'd just done if she were thinking of Terry?

No, because he hadn't even thought, hadn't looked, hadn't even tried to see it—Mr. Cole McCord, bodyguard and scout extraordinaire who never missed a scrap of sign on a trail. She was not an individual to him, not a real person, she was just another woman to him and that was all. Thank God she hadn't made love with him. Now, knowing this, she never would.

\* \* \*

She *had* actually been thinking of it, she realized, as they rode along south in an uncomfortable silence. Ever since he'd kissed her the first time, no, to be brutally honest, ever since she'd opened her eyes and seen him looking down at her, holding her in his arms in the middle of the street in Pueblo City, she had wondered what it would be like to be in his arms in a bed with something on their minds besides dodging bullets. She had kept that wondering a sort of secret from herself, she supposed, because it *was* quite bold and shocking.

But wouldn't such an experience fit right into her plan to really *live* every moment of every day . . . and night?

"Cat got your tongue?"

She flicked him a disdainful glance.

"Well, pardon me for asking," he drawled in his most irritating way, "but for somebody who's always dead set on stirring up a little confab to pass the time, you've surely held your peace too long."

He made a great, dramatic show of pulling his watch out of his pocket.

"I'd say for a whole hour or more."

Frowning at the watch, he shook it and then held it to his ear.

"Yeah, it's running. I reckon it's right. Why, Aurora, it's been nigh onto two hours since you have said one word."

"I've decided to keep my promise not to talk to you. You know: the promise that gave you so much hope."

"Too late," he said. "You've talked so much in the past you've got my curiosity all stirred up."

She turned on him.

"Don't try to tell me that! You have not cared to learn the first thing about me, and you haven't'!"

He raised his black eyebrows.

"Well, now, I wouldn't say that. I know you've got a dickens of a temper and a heart of stone."

She narrowed her eyes and flashed him a vicious look.

"Just because I wouldn't let you have your way with me. What a selfish thing to say."

He raised one hand in the air between them.

"No, no, now I'm not thinking only of myself. There's poor old Terry, too, you have to admit. By the time he gets home, we'll have to say that he rode for a solid week on a horse that may have run off and left him every other night for all we know—in fact, Terry may have to walk home, which will take considerably longer than a week . . ."

She interrupted abruptly.

"Does this rambling diatribe have a point?"

He gave her that *aggravating* grin he used so well.

"The point is that you treated him downright heartlessly after he went through so much just to see you and recite poetry to you and give you one more chance to marry him."

"No," she said sarcastically, "*as usual*, you

have got it wrong. Terry knew when he rode out here that my refusal of his proposal was final, that my feelings for him were not of that kind. He wanted more pictures to remember me by and to say another farewell."

"Sounds foolish to me," Cole said conversationally, glancing around at the land that lay ahead. "Looks like he'd either bust a gut trying to persuade you to change your mind or stay home and tend to business. This's a busy time of year on a ranch."

"I *told* you, he doesn't work at anything but his poetry and photography. Besides their ranch, his family owns the Colorado Queen gold mine and most of three counties."

"Well, then," he said, nodding judiciously, "how come you're letting him get away?"

Her anger grew.

"That is *precisely* what I would expect from you," she said, furious now. "So I strike you as a greedy, insincere, shallow person who can be *bought*?"

Her obvious rage didn't cause him to turn a hair.

"Now, now, no need to get yourself in a lather. I wasn't necessarily talking about *you*, personally."

"It certainly sounded as if you were when you used the phrase 'I don't know why *you* let him get away.' "

"More accurately, I was speaking of women in general."

"Ah!" she cried. "Just as I thought!"

"Then why did you take it as personal?"

"Never mind," she said, flapping her hand at him impatiently. "I'd be curious to know why you have such a low opinion of women in general."

"Experience."

"You think most women are so mercenary they'd use money as a reason to marry?"

He shrugged. "I don't think it—I've *seen* it. I've seen many a good man shot out of the saddle when that saddle's about all he owned."

"You don't know what really happened with any man and woman if you weren't there."

"I *was* there."

She stared at him, amazed.

"You were in love? You asked a woman to marry you?"

He frowned at her.

"How come you look so surprised?"

"You . . . well, you don't seem the domestic type to me."

"Back then I was too young to know better."

She knew she was still staring rudely, but she couldn't help herself.

"Who was she?"

"Heck of it is," he said, laughing a little, "she was a rich girl. She didn't *need* my money."

"Maybe she broke it off because you were a Ranger and she wouldn't let herself love you because you might get killed."

He eyed her suspiciously.

"How'd you know I was a Ranger then?"

She smiled.

"I guessed."

"You're right. But Mary knew that and we were all set to tie the knot and her folks were askin' me over to supper right along until they ran into somebody who set 'em straight about which family of McCords I was from."

"Were the other McCords wealthy?"

He gave that definite little nod.

"Yep. The Circle M McCords owned the biggest part of the county we lived in. Once the Lassiters learned they'd jumped to the wrong conclusion about who was my daddy—and my mother—I never saw Mary again."

"Well, then!" Aurora said triumphantly. "Your sweetheart wasn't a gold digger, her family was a bunch of snobs."

"My mother being Chickasaw likely had something to do with it, too," he said, "but from what I knew of her papa, he would never have let that worry him any if I'd been heir to the Circle M Land and Cattle Company."

"But that's her *papa*, don't you see? You've taken a low opinion of all women when the real greedy one in this deal is a *man*."

"She let him get away with it, didn't she? She could've run away and come to me."

The pain from so long ago shimmered fresh and new in his voice. Angry as she was with him, Aurora ached to comfort him.

"She swore she loved me," Cole said, "and I, young fool that I was, believed her."

"How old were you?" she said softly.

"Eighteen," he said. "Two years a Ranger

and tough as whit-leather. But she flat broke my heart."

Aurora's heart broke, too, right then, for the boy he had been.

And she fell in love with that boy. He might be a hard man now, he might be just like all the other men she'd ever known, her father included, who were selfish and unsentimental and considered themselves the boss of all women, but long ago, when he had been a boy of eighteen, Cole McCord had truly loved a woman.

But that was then and this was now. And what did she care, anyhow?

He straightened in the saddle and put his heels down, speeding up a little.

"Turns out the old man was doing her a favor, though," he said harshly, "and she was smart to listen to him. I would've been nothing but bad for her."

"That's not true!" Aurora cried, even though she would've agreed with him only a few minutes earlier. "She made a terrible mistake."

Cole threw her a startled, sideways glance, smooched to his horse, and moved on out. Her horse kept pace.

"Seems to me that's a pretty strong statement for you to make about a man you hardly know," he said.

"I know you . . . some," she said, seeing the mysterious shadows in his eyes again.

"You think you do."

"You really loved her," she said, "I know

that much. And that could never have been bad for her."

"Aurora," he said solemnly, "you don't have the slightest notion of what you're talking about."

"Yes, I do. You're a good man, Cole, and you loved her, so what more could she want?"

"I'm a good man with a *gun*. That's why you hired me, so let it go at that."

They found a fine place for the nooning, better than any they'd had since the drive began. It was a large, open meadow, bounded on two sides by tree-covered hills, with a narrow, rushing river running through it. Aurora's heart lifted as soon as they came around the bend in the trail and saw it—it was a homey little nook set beside the endless trail.

"*I* know! Let's have a picnic!" she said as soon as they rode to the edge of it. "In fact, let's stay the night and not travel this afternoon. Oh, Cole, wouldn't that be fun? Everybody's tired."

She turned to see Cole grinning at her.

"Speak for yourself," he said. "I'm good for forty more miles at least."

"We can rest our horses," she said, frowning at him because of the way he was looking at her. "You and I can ride our favorites again tomorrow."

"*My* horse doesn't need to rest," he said.

"*What?* Why are you smiling at me as if you're humoring me or something?"

"I am. You're like a little kid sometimes."

"Because I want to have a picnic? You'd do better to be a little more fun-loving yourself."

He cocked his head as if to concede that point, still smiling at her as if she were a precocious ten-year-old.

"And you don't need to be bragging on that rangy nag you're so fond of riding," she said. "My Shy Boy can leave him to eat dust any old day of the week."

He gave her a narrow-eyed stare.

"Be careful," he said. "Watch that busy tongue of yours or it'll get you in trouble."

"I'm not worried. I challenge you to a horse race."

He shook his head.

"See what I mean? Can't even wait for the others to get here for the picnic to start, just *like* a little kid. Or . . ."

He fixed the most infuriating grin on his face.

". . . or are you afraid for the whole crew to see Shy Boy get beat?"

"All right. Now you've done it. We'll go back and guide the others in and as soon as the herd's here, I will run that broomtail of yours right into the ground. Shy Boy can beat him by no less than two lengths."

"You're gonna get calluses from patting your own back," he said. "Border and I'll help you out by leaving you so far behind you'll have time to think about it."

They exchanged playful insults all the way back to Cookie's and Nate's wagons. Then, after giving them directions to the pretty valley, they headed back to it again with Cole scouting both sides of the trail in long semicircles. He never got out of sight of Aurora, though, and she liked that.

Until she thought about it and realized how much she was relying on him. *That* was why she got those feelings of connection to him sometimes. *That* was why she needed to learn to shoot for herself and become more independent, so by the time they reached her new home she'd be feeling *dis*connected from him. Thank goodness, he wasn't riding right beside her and talking to her all the time.

Cookie and Nate weren't far behind when they rode for the second time into the expanse of green grass cut in two by the silver river. The place soon looked like the coziest, most beautiful camp in the world, with the wagons placed on opposite ends of the flat and the coffee making over the fire. Newt came in with the remuda, and the herd followed.

With so much grass and water close at hand, the cattle settled in swiftly, even though they weren't particularly tired and had been driven only slightly more than half their usual distance for a day. As soon as they'd eaten the meal Cookie hastily prepared, the men immediately fell into the spirit of the holiday.

"We're celebrating that we'll cross into New Mexico Territory tomorrow," Aurora told them, as the first ones finished eating.

"And we'll put our hearts into it, too," Monte called back, as he threw his dishes into the wreck pan. "No telling when we'll have any more time off."

"First event of the day!" Cole shouted, throwing his in, too. "Our trail boss has challenged me to a horse race."

Cheers greeted that information, and everyone started gathering around, looking from Cole to Aurora and back again with big grins.

"Which horses?" Frank shouted.

"My bay roan and her sorrel."

"Shy Boy will win," Aurora said. "You boys all know how fast he is."

"What you don't know is that my horse is a running fool with no quit in him," Cole said. "Put your money on me if you don't want to lose it."

"Don't listen to him, men," Aurora shouted. "I'd hate to see half of you broke before you even draw your pay."

"Border Crossing got his name because he carried me across the Rio Grande ahead of a whole passel of Federales," Cole said. "He's saved my bacon more times than I can count. Think about it, boys."

Aurora started for her horse, Cole strode toward his. At Shy Boy's head, she turned, and they looked at each other while the crew stopped wagering to watch and listen.

"From that tree over there until a hoof splashes in the water?" she called loudly. "Loser gets dunked in the river?"

Loud cheers from the crew approved the plan.

Cole cocked his head and looked her over, and her mount, as if he'd never seen them before. His dark eyes took on a wicked glint.

"You're on!"

"On the count of three!" Cookie yelled, and hurried to station himself at the starting line.

Once there, with Cole and Aurora mounted and trotting to him, he shouted again.

"Monte. You and Frank. Stand at the finish line in case there's any question."

"Better get out of your boots," Cole yelled, loud enough for everyone to hear, while he grinned at Aurora.

He lifted one foot and then the other to pull his off and drop them, spurs clinking, to the ground.

"Take a deep breath, too, Aurora, 'cause I'm fixing to hold every inch of you under the water. I'm glad you thought about that dunking business—makes the race even more interestin'."

"How come you've still got that gold watch in your pocket, then?" Aurora shouted back. "Better leave it with Cookie so it won't be ruined."

"Don't you be worrying about my watch," Cole said. "I don't aim to get wet above the knees."

"You're in for a big surprise, then," Aurora taunted him. "Leave your hat here, too—I'd hate to ruin it."

Cole laughed.

"Run that broomtail for the sake of your honor," he said.

The men lined up between them and the river, still making wagers.

"One," Cookie shouted, "two, three."

He brought his bandana sweeping down. Both horses leapt forward and stretched out into a flat-out gallop.

# Chapter 9

Aurora's heart beat hard enough to take her breath away, her hair blew wild, stinging her cheeks, her hat bounced on its strings against her back. Shy Boy moved beneath her, strong, sure, and fast, confidently stretching out farther and farther, reaching for the river shining in front of them as if he'd never had a shy day in his life.

But Cole's Border Crossing was pounding alongside them, nose to flank, she could hear his hooves separately, somehow, in the thunder both horses were laying down. Half a dozen yards from the water, the bay roan passed them in a blur of color and motion, a bloodcurdling cry of victory coming from Cole's throat. Passed them easily, with her Shy Boy giving everything he had in his big heart.

Seconds later, Border Crossing plunged into the river, and Cole brought him wheeling around, throwing glimmering drops of water high into the air and onto his own laughing face.

"Sorry," he called, "we just couldn't help ourselves."

The next instant, as Shy Boy hit the water, Cole was bounding out of his stirrup to lift her from the saddle.

"It's too cold," she yelled, laughing, too, through her disappointment. "Bet's off. I admit you beat me."

She tried to push him away, tried to cling to her saddle horn, but her strength was nothing against his. Even with her struggling and bucking in his arms, he was striding toward a deeper spot in the river without missing a step, while the crew—her own, *loyal*, Slash A hands!—were all shouting encouragement to him. Along with teasing remarks to her. She'd never hear the end of this, never!

Before she could draw a deep breath, Cole dropped her into the water. The water! Oh, the water was so much colder than she'd expected that it slammed all the air out of her lungs in one fell swoop. Still, she managed to throw her arms around his neck and cling with all her might. She fought, unsuccessfully, to put her legs around his waist. If only she could pull him down with her!

Slim chance. He bent lower and dunked her, screaming, hair, hat, and all, with a swift, strong motion that wet her to the bone and left him dry above the knees, just as he'd planned. Except for his arms, of course, which plastered themselves against her when she came up into the stiff breeze again.

"Turn me loose!" she cried, gasping between every word.

Instead, he dunked her again, just as thoroughly, and she came up fighting, screaming as she could get breath back from the shock of the freezing water. A great burst of laughter rolled toward them, along with indistinguishable shouts. Abruptly, she quit struggling. Nothing would be funnier right now to *everyone* than the trail boss flailing her fists uselessly against Cole's chest with him laughing at her.

She glared at him through narrowed eyes.

"You didn't have to do it *twice!*"

He grinned his devil's grin.

"When you chose the wager, you didn't say how *many* dunkings."

"You are a sneakin' coyote!"

He gathered her closer against him.

"No, no, you've got my name wrong. My Chickasaw name is Rides-Like-Running-Lightning."

For half a second she stared into his so-sincere brown eyes and almost believed him.

"It is *not*," she said. "Now carry me to the bank."

He didn't move.

"Why do you say that's not my name?"

"Because an Indian never tells his real medicine name. Only the person who gave it to him knows what it is. I've heard that my whole life."

He laughed.

"Thanks for that bit of lore," he said. "Is it true of all tribes?"

"Yes."

He laughed again.

"What you need to learn from this is not ever to challenge a man named Rides-Like-Running-Lightning and a horse named Border Crossing to a horse race."

"Never challenge a man who won't go by the rules is more like it," she said hotly.

"Your exact words were, 'Loser gets dunked in the river,'" he said, "not 'Loser gets dunked in the river one time only.'"

"You are so mean," she said. "You just couldn't resist doing it again because you made me scream."

He gave her that same, heavy-lidded look he'd used on the street in Pueblo City.

"I always like to make the ladies scream," he drawled in his low, reckless voice.

A thrill ran through her in spite of her anger, a thrill that had nothing to do with the cold water and the breeze. She shivered.

Thank goodness she had the presence of mind to pretend, however.

"Take me to the bank right now so I can change my clothes."

"I'll keep you warm," he said, holding her closer.

"I'll walk."

She was feeling his hard, solid heat right through her chill. Mad as she was, she was liking being in his arms. Liking it a lot. Too much. *Far* too much.

Kicking, she struggled to get down.

"I'll walk, I said."

He turned and started toward the bank, toward the men who were hooting and calling to them.

"Learned your lesson?" he said.

"Oh, sure," she said sarcastically, "but Rides-Like-Running-Lightning is not your Chickasaw name. And it *ought* to be Sneaky Coyote because that's what you are."

He grinned down at her.

"I'm only trying to surprise you now and then, help you learn to keep your guard up at all times."

His calm, superior, authoritative tone enraged her. She started beating at his chest in spite of all her good intentions.

He grabbed both her wrists.

"Uh-uh," he said, in that same infuriating way, "careful, careful. You don't want to let the men see you're a sore loser. That's a bad rep to get."

She glanced over her shoulder and saw that they were coming closer to the whole laughing crew.

"Especially when you're the challenger," he said, low, into her ear. "This horse *and* the dunking was your idea."

Aurora smoothed her face into blankness and let her hands fall.

"I know," she said, using a chastened tone.

His grip loosened a little.

She grabbed him around the neck, threw herself suddenly to one side, and as he staggered in surprise, twisted in his arms to slam her leg across the back of his knee just as he took another step.

"Whoa!"

The crew laughed and cheered as he sat down in the water, hard. But he didn't even come close to losing his grip on her, and when she struggled to push him over backwards, he let her do it, taking her with him full-length into the shallow water, rolling over instantly to wet her again from head to toe. But this time both of them were laughing.

"That's our *other* lesson for the day," she said, gasping from the cold between every word. "We *both* have to learn to be good losers."

"We *could* both be winners."

Staring into each other's eyes, they stopped laughing. Aurora realized that her arms were still wound tightly around his neck, but she couldn't move. His were around her body, feeling like iron ropes under his skin, pressing her breasts against his hard chest until the heat from his flesh poured into hers in spite of the freezing water.

*We can't keep from touching each other, no matter how hard we try. We couldn't even keep from talking to each other this morning, even when we were so angry we were all rattles and horns.*

He knew it, too. She could see the knowledge in his eyes.

It scared her senseless.

"Turn me loose," she said, through lips nearly paralyzed from wanting his kiss.

He knew that, too.

"No chance," he said, and took her mouth with his.

Desire, pure, crushing desire for his body, for all of him, ate her alive in an instant. She reached deep inside for her fear, for her anger, for *some* other feeling to save her.

Making herself struggle against him took nearly all her strength, but she did it, while her treacherous mouth kissed him back. Then, his mouth was gone and he was scooping her up out of the water, carrying her to the bank.

And all the hands were gathering closer to try to see exactly what was going on.

That made her fear full and real, made it roll in waves over her. The attraction between them actually was real, too, enough for other people to see it.

"You only kissed me because everyone was watching," she said tightly. "Don't you dare ever do that again. And don't you dare kiss me in private, either."

He gave her a look that set the desire to pounding harder in her blood.

"Don't challenge me, Aurora. Haven't you learned that yet?"

She narrowed her eyes and looked daggers at him while he laughed.

He set her down onto her own feet the minute he stepped up the bank and onto the grass, but he did it so slowly, so deliberately that she had to restrain herself from slapping his lingering hands before she turned to face the others. She fought not to show it, so she wouldn't seem a sore loser.

"Pick another finish line, boys, if you're going to race," she said, wringing water from her riding skirt. "This one's got a deep hole you might fall into."

That made them all laugh, except for Cookie.

"Well, it's about time you got outta that river," he called. "When you two come down with the pneumony in both lungs don't expect me to haul you down the trail in my wagon."

Cole stepped back into the water to bring the horses out. Trained to ground-tie wherever their reins were dropped, they stood where they'd been left.

"And don't expect me to be loanin' you my extry pair o' boots!" Cookie yelled at him angrily. "Nobody held a gun on you and forced you into that river."

Cole ignored him.

Cookie was worried about the attraction between them, too, that was why he was suddenly so cranky. Aurora turned and smiled at him, straight into his blistering glare. If he only knew, he wasn't half as worried as she was. She had to get a grip on herself and *stay away from Cole*.

The men were busily collecting their bets and paying their debts, but as she walked to her wagon for dry clothes, they called to her.

"You did give him a run for his money, Boss."

"His hoss stands a full hand taller with a lot longer stride. Yours ain't no slouch."

"Fine ride, Miss Aurora. You was burnin' the breeze."

"Thanks, men," she called, and climbed up into the hoodlum wagon, as thankful for the privacy it offered as for the dry clothes it held.

The holiday afternoon became more and more of a success, with several horse races, a few wrestling matches, lots of mumblety-peg, and some much-needed baths in the bend of the river. Skeeter came back with a deer across his saddle as the sun was sliding down toward the top of the mountain.

Cookie sliced steaks to fry while the other men teased Skeeter about needing nearly a year to get one little deer.

All afternoon Aurora had avoided, as much as possible, talking to Cole, but as she was helping Cookie roll out the dough for the fried pies he made out of dried fruit on special occasions, Cole strolled over and sat on an upturned bucket by the chuck wagon's tailboard to sip a cup of coffee.

After he'd changed into dry clothes, he had taken a fresh horse from his mount and scouted around the valley for a little while, then he had spent a long time cleaning and oiling both his guns. He had seemingly been as determined to stay away from her as she was from him.

But now he spoke to her and settled down to be cozy.

"You'll have to move in a minute," she said testily. "When I start frying these and bringing them back to the platter you'll be in the way."

"Sure wouldn't want that," he said in his most infuriating drawl.

He wasn't trying to stay away from her at all. He would be no help to her in that pursuit.

" 'Course, as your bodyguard, I'll have to stay pretty close whether I'm in the way or not."

She gave an unladylike snort of derision.

"That is so like you—always using some feeble excuse to help you get your way, no matter if you do know you're in the wrong."

He laughed.

"Now, now, no need to cast aspersions on my honor," he drawled. "First you try your best to drown me and when that doesn't work you assassinate my character. I think *I'm* the one needs a bodyguard."

"*Who* tried to drown *whom?* You're not guarding me, you're aggravating me, and you know it. Go away."

"Aurora, I just have a feeling . . ."

That brought her around to glance at him sharply. He met the look with a knowing grin that brought heat to her cheeks.

"No, that's not what I'm talking about—we can discuss that later if you want."

She tossed her head and went back to her work.

"What *are* you talking about, Cole?"

"Just be extra careful and let me escort you whenever you go to the bushes."

She felt her blush deepen.

"Can't we just have one nice day, one afternoon of fun, without worrying about an attack? This is a secluded little valley. We're a ways off the trail."

"As if a rank greenhorn couldn't track two thousand head of cattle," he said sarcastically.

He tossed out the rest of his coffee, got up, and walked away.

She and Cookie finished preparing the meal, and the men ate mostly in silence, as always, then two of them rode out for first guard and the others began a card game. Aurora sat in the shadow of the chuck wagon, idly watching and listening to them.

And wondering where Cole had gone.

They finished one hand. While Frank was shuffling and dealing, Skeeter looked around for Aurora.

"Miss Aurora," he called, "if I was to let down that tailgate to the hoodlum wagon and offer you a hand up, would you be inclined to give us a tune or two? I reckon if I'd dance with ol' Frank I might save him from losin' all his money."

Frank looked up from the saddle blanket, where he was dealing out the cards.

"I'd not dance with you if you was the last partner on earth," he said in his rough tenor voice. "But I would admire to hear some music, Boss. It's been a right nice day."

"That it has, Frank," Aurora said. "I think I'd like some music, too."

She stood up and started to walk toward the wagon where the piano waited, but when she'd gone as far as the fire, the whole world seemed to explode into a dozen things happening at once. The ominous cracks of several shots rang out, the shocked men ripped out oaths, and something hit her in the back, sending her reeling out of the circle of firelight and into the shadows.

For the barest instant, she thought she'd been shot, but miraculously she felt no pain, and she kept her feet under her. Then, a man was bumping into her, a gun blasted from an arm's length away, and she was falling, shoved from behind.

"Get *down*," Cole said, in a stranger's voice, a voice so dangerous it sent cool goose bumps springing to life all up and down her arms, "and stay in the dark, no matter what happens."

He fired three rounds so rapidly that it seemed almost like one. Those were from his handgun; she recognized the sound, but she didn't think of that until his rifle spoke. All of it happened so fast that it was a blur of noise in her ears. She couldn't see a thing.

Out in the dark, somebody let out a high, sickening scream that made her stomach turn.

Then she could see. Shots split the night with

flame, coming fast, one after the other, and either Cole was everywhere at once or the other Slash As were shooting, too. But they couldn't be because none of them had been wearing their guns and they hadn't had time to get to them.

Or had they? Already, this madness had lasted a lifetime.

Another yell of pain echoed against the mountain, an awful, impotent, lonesome sound, and then a hate-filled call.

"Damn you, McCord, I'm hit."

Even though the voice was shaking from pain, she knew it. Gates. Lloyd Gates himself, not just his flunkies, was following her now.

What an honor. Usually he hired people to do his dirty work, but he had come in person to try to kill her.

Gates hated her that much. She had damaged his pride *that much* by hanging onto the cattle and the horses. He was determined to have his revenge, and Gates was an implacable man. What he had done to her father had proved that.

Fear numbed her whole body, but she dragged herself deeper into the shadows and crunched up at the foot of a juniper tree. Its sweet, tart scent floated past her, but her senses were too full of fear to take it in.

"Don't you know you're working for a cattle thief?" he yelled, his voice shrill and trembly. "Whaddya think *that's* gonna do for your precious rep, McCord? What'll all the Texans think about *that?"*

Cole didn't answer. She could barely see him now, he was in shadow so deep, but he fired again, and the next instant he was two yards away from where he had just stood, lifting his rifle, firing toward the sound of Gates's voice.

Another agonized yell, but the voice didn't belong to Gates. At least she didn't think so.

"Now you've hit my best shooter, so we'll ride," came Gates's shout, as much anger as pain in the words this time. "But we'll be back, and we'll bring the law next time. *You* Slash A outfit, you! Every man jack of you will hang for a cattle thief!"

Cole took one more shot, but hoofbeats were already pounding away.

"Forget them, boys, and get to the herd," he called in his new, cool voice of implacable authority. "They may try a stampede."

Only then did she become aware that some of the Slash A crew were running for the night horses, already saddled and tied to the wheels of the chuck wagon. She should've noticed that before and given the order herself.

Yet she couldn't imagine getting even one sound past her lips.

One of Gates's men fired again, and Cole answered with his rifle. A muffled yell floated through the dark; he cocked his head and listened to the retreating horses.

"Five of 'em," he said briskly. "But there may be more surrounding us. Don't go anywhere near the fire, and don't leave my side."

He turned and walked straight to her, although she would've sworn he hadn't seen where she had gone to ground.

"I hate it when I miss like that," he said nonchalantly, reaching to help her to her feet.

Aurora could barely move. The numbness had left her, but she was shaking with fear from finally realizing how close she had come to being killed. She had made the perfect target in front of the fire.

She felt fear instead of relief, fear largely fueled by the horrible noises still ringing in her ears. The pain-filled cries of the men who'd been shot still turned her stomach and made her skin crawl, even if they *had* come from her enemies.

"You *didn't* miss," she said, and was appalled at the thin, weak sound that was supposed to be her voice.

"I should've killed 'em all," he said flatly.

He *would* have killed them, too, without the faintest glimmer of remorse. That certain truth showed in every line of his stance, every nuance of his voice.

She hadn't known this about him. She had known he'd been a Texas Ranger with a rare talent for using a gun, she had known he'd been given many a perilous job during the few months he'd grown famous in Colorado for giving bad men no quarter, but, in spite of all that, she hadn't known he could wish he had killed someone with no more emotion than he might wish it would rain.

She shivered uncontrollably as he lifted her to her feet.

What kind of man was this who held her life in his hands?

"Cole," she said, when he had led her to the shadows in front of the chuck wagon and seated her on the bucket. "Stay here for a while."

She had to know, had to find out as much as she could about him tonight, had to see whether she could still see into his heart from time to time. Hadn't he himself told her he was bad? No good for Mary, the girl he had once loved. Maybe if she tried, she could see a badness in him that would make her stop thinking about him and remembering his kiss.

But was it bad to defend himself . . . and her?

"I'm not going anywhere," he said, taking a cup from the tailgate of the wagon. "Gates may have more men around here someplace. I'd bet no on it, though."

That brought her up short, reminding her of her job, and she stood up.

"If there *are* some more, they *may* be waiting to stampede the herd," she said, starting for the remuda, since the men had taken all the saddled horses. "Come on, we need to help."

When he didn't answer, she stopped and turned. He was calmly pouring coffee—he wasn't even looking at her. And he wasn't even shaken by the battle they'd just been through.

She watched him, as if looking at him long enough could actually let her see into his mind. He had told her, that night in the saloon, that she didn't know whether he had honor or not. Did he?

"The crew can handle the herd," he said. "You don't hear any ruckus, now, do you?"

She listened. Somebody was starting to sing a slow, sad song. Bits jingled, and hoofbeats, moving at a walk, made a steady rhythm against the earth as their sound floated to her through the night. There were a few men's voices, too, low and calm, so as not to spook the herd, but with an edge of excitement, still.

"No," she said.

"They'd already be yelling and popping slickers at your cattle if Gates had left anybody for that. They wouldn't want to get left too far behind their buddies, in case we mounted a pursuit."

Slowly, she walked toward him, her nerves relaxing a little as she realized they probably wouldn't be dealing with another attack. But tension still strummed along her spine.

She blurted out a question before she even knew she was going to speak.

"Why were the Federales chasing you? I thought you used to be a lawman, not an outlaw."

He turned and walked toward her, handed her the cup.

"Sometimes along the border, there's not a dime's worth of difference."

The careless way he said it brought the danger in him to all her senses again. She saw the shifting of shadows in his eyes. What all had he done? What *would* he do?

The cool breeze freshened. She shivered. Hard.

He reached for her hands, wrapped them around the hot cup. His rough palms felt hotter.

"Drink it," he said.

She didn't care if he *was* a cold-blooded killer. All she wanted was for him never to take his hands away.

"I . . . I don't know what's the matter with me."

"You're shaken up because you've just been shot at."

"And you're calm because you're used to it."

He shrugged.

"You might say that."

He dropped his hands, turned away, and went to get another cup.

"Cole," she said, "I can't *be* like this—all upset in a crisis. I have to be able to protect myself and my new ranch."

"You will be." He poured his coffee, then walked toward her with that panther's stride of his.

"You, on the other hand," she continued, "were as cool then as you are right now."

He kicked the short log into the shadows and sat down astraddle of it, facing her.

"Think of it as having to grow up fast one more time," he said. "You did what you had to do then, you can do what you have to do now."

She stared at him.

"Yeah. But then I wasn't making anybody scream with pain or killing anyone."

"Get over that," he said. "If it wasn't them screaming and dying, it'd be us."

"I guess so."

"I *know* so."

She took another drink of the bracing coffee and didn't answer.

He looked at her for a long time with a hard, keen stare.

"Aurora," he said, "you need me until we can take care of Gates and you can learn to shoot. After that, you'll make up your mind whether you want to keep your cattle and your ranch or give them away to the first sidewinder that might scream or die if you shoot him."

For the first time since the attack, she laughed a little.

He smiled, too, but his eyes didn't.

"If you think you can or you think you can't, either way you'll be right," he said. "It's up to you to choose."

*I choose that you stay with me. I choose you don't leave when we find my ranch, no matter what kind of man you are.*

And that thought held the most terror of all.

# Chapter 10

~~~✦~~~

The next afternoon when they headed north to find Cookie and send the chuck wagon on to make camp, the wind rose in a sudden, whistling gale. It made the horses dance sideways and Aurora grab her hat to tighten its strings beneath her chin before it finally, gradually lowered to the boisterous force it had been all day, blowing steadily against every step they made. Scattered drops of rain slapped their faces.

"That's all we need—a downpour for camp tonight," Aurora said wearily.

"Ah, now, what's a little rain? I'd think you'd like that better than a gunfight."

"I would. I'd get more sleep, even in a flood, than I did last night," she said.

"Nobody's fault but your own," he said. "I was on guard right outside your wagon."

"It wasn't that," she said. "I wasn't scared. I was just . . ."

*Thinking about you. Remembering your kiss. Wishing for the feel of your hands . . .*

"Just what?"

"Thinking about the advice you gave me. Remembering I can do anything I think I can."

But he wasn't listening to her, wasn't even looking at her anymore.

"That storm's coming on fast," he said, raising his voice as the wind picked up again.

She followed his gaze to the west, to the tops of the mountains forming that side of the Raton Pass.

"Welcome to New Mexico Territory," she said wryly.

The scudding clouds were mixing and gathering, their gray and dark blue mixing with the purple and red rays of the lowering sun. Lightning flashed low, not far above the green pines.

"This could be a wild one," he said thoughtfully.

"Maybe we should hold the herd north of the pass," she said, although he was already lifting his horse into a lope, and she knew he'd had the same thought.

"Yeah. Out here they've got too much room to run."

The wind rose again in a shrieking rush and howled a warning into her ear. A small, cold knot she'd discovered newly formed in her stomach grew larger.

They pushed the horses faster.

"Thank God we changed horses this afternoon," she called to him, and Cole nodded, pulling his hat down harder on his head.

So he felt it, too. Tired as the cattle were, this

storm was going to be bad enough to make them run.

They picked up the pace, but they were too late. Border Crossing pointed his nose at the sky and whinnied long and loud to the remuda, coming out of the pass at that very moment right behind Cookie's wagon, then Nate's.

Aurora and Cole moved as one person, going into a long lope at the same moment, looking constantly west at the rising storm. But there was no time.

The whole southwestern sky went black while they looked at it, the lightning cracked faster and faster, breaking like gunshots through the noise of the wind. They were closer now, within a half mile, maybe, coming closer to the end of the pass, but then Brindle and Lead Steer burst into view at a quick, hard trot, leading the whole herd south as if their very lives depended on getting out into the wide-open spaces.

Lightning flashed again, blindingly bright, trying to grab them out of the valley and singeing its way along the mountaintops all at once. Almost instantly, thunder broke the ground in two and echoed endlessly against the rocks.

The point rider on this side of the herd was Frank; she recognized the stocky gray gelding that was the best in his mount. He saw the space spreading out before him, started to wave his hat and try to turn the herd, then realized, as Aurora just had, that if too many of them were trapped in the pass they'd trample each

other to death. They had to let the herd through
and try to hold them out here.

Cole slowed his horse and started turning
south again. He had figured it out, too.

Lightning flashed again, and the wind went
crazy. The last clear look that Aurora had at the
herd before the driving rain began was a sight
to strike terror into the toughest trail boss's
heart. Long, wicked fingers of lightning reached
for the cattle, found a place to play along their
horns, hit them sizzling, quick licks and then
ran and danced in eerie blue balls of fire that
jumped from the Lead Steer to Old Brindle, to
the cow behind her and then the next, sending
the poor beasts into a state of pure terror.

She saw all that, somehow, in one thin, mi-
raculous sliver of time, and she saw the leaders
turn at the slightest angle toward the southwest
and commence to run. But more than seeing it,
she sensed it, that great mass of living,
breathing animals armed with horns and
hooves, gathering in greater and greater num-
bers to run straight at her and Cole.

Then, in the space of one heartbeat, the sheet
of rain became a wall she couldn't see through.

She couldn't hear, except for a raw, raging
roar. She made one mighty effort, but she
couldn't think, either. Only one word: Cole. He
had to stay safe.

Her instincts did work, though, flooding her
arms and legs with the strength to hold on, her
body with enough calm to settle deep into the
saddle and Shy Boy's rhythm. She was strong

and vigorous, there was hardly a glimmer of memory that she might be tired. This was a stampede, this was life and death, and there was no such word as tired.

This was survival for her horse and herself and her cattle, and, by the God who had brought them alive out of Colorado, they were all going to survive. With a primal knowledge that streamed into her body on the breath she snatched from the wind, she knew that Cole rode behind her. The two of them were the only riders who had a chance to turn the herd. Frank could help, but the leaders had got past him.

She only hoped the speeding Border Crossing would sense her and Shy Boy before he ran over them—there was no way Cole could see them before they would collide. There was no way she could see him and know if his horse was still on his feet.

The wind sucked her breath. She bent over Shy Boy's neck until the saddle horn bruised her stomach and she rode with no air in her, with all of it outside her and her horse swirling away, stolen away into the ruthless arms of the storm. The sky lashed her with rain like a madman with a buggy whip in his hands. But the herd would turn.

They would, by God, turn. She and Cole would *make* them turn.

Somehow, by some miracle, she loosened the ties behind her cantle and pulled her slicker free. At first, she had no power to lift it against the wind, but she managed to wrestle it for-

ward to rest against her leg. Then she lifted it—
she couldn't flap it, but she did drag it across
some hairy, wild-eyed face. Then she slapped it
against a shoulder, caught it on a horn that
could impale Shy Boy—or her—like a sword.

The horn cut a long slit and tore her weapon
into two parts with one long, dark stroke. The
wind died for a second, and she heard shots.
Cole or one of the men trying to frighten the
cattle into a turn.

They would, by all the strength in her body,
*turn*, damn their rotten hides! She had not de-
fied Lloyd Gates and risked dying by Virgil
Whoever's shotgun blast to let these creatures
scatter from here to kingdom come.

"You're going to *Texas*, damn you!"

She shrieked it into the whipping wind and
it was lost in that instant, way before it ever
reached a cow's ears, but it made her feel more
powerful somehow. At least she had snatched
back enough breath to speak.

That meant she would live through this. That
meant that she would win.

*Oh, please God, keep Cole safe, too.*

She found enough leeway against the wind
to lift the shreds of the slicker, to move them at
the one cow . . . she slitted her eyes against the
rain, for her hat was long since off her head and
streaming out behind her with the stampede
strings cutting into her neck until they choked
her . . . Old Brindle!

There had been a miracle, and she had
reached Old Brindle. She flapped the slicker as

best she could into the mottled face, over the wild and rolling bloodshot eyes and prayed to keep her seat in the saddle and her feet in the stirrups.

And for Shy Boy to keep his feet under him and his speed up until it was safe to slow down.

She did. He did. And finally, after what seemed another whole lifetime, Old Brindle began to turn. Shots sounded from several directions, the cow turned more, shaking her horns angrily back and forth, but doing what Aurora wanted. The lead steers followed, yielding to pressure that had to be from Cole, although she couldn't see him yet.

Aurora stayed with them, giving no quarter, feeling Cole behind her, somewhere near in the lessening storm. But when she threw a quick look back over her shoulder, she couldn't see him. He was there. Surely he was.

A subterranean panic welled up in her, surging toward her heart. Border Crossing, good as he was, was a mortal horse. Any stumble, any fall, and Cole would've been trampled.

She twisted in the saddle and searched again. The rain still stabbed at her face, but it was thinner now; she could see a little. The wind whipped her hair around her face instead of trying to rip it from her scalp. She faced front again, looking at the cattle, looking for other riders.

And she resorted to patience and faith. If she waited to look again while she counted to twenty, Cole would be there when she turned around.

Tears mingled with the raindrops running down her face. Cole had to be all right. Everyone had to be all right. The whole Slash A outfit, on whatever side of the herd they'd been riding when it started to run, had to be all right or she'd never forgive herself. Those men risked their lives for her sake every day, and they had to be in their saddles and unhurt when the storm passed.

It was moving away already, thunder crashing, but less loud, lightning out of sight. The cold rain lessened even more, although it still drummed down on her bare head.

The cattle were slowing for sure, starting to mill. Shy Boy was slowing with them. He was blowing some, but he was all right, she could tell by the feel of him beneath her.

"Aurora!"

She took in a great lungful of air, as if she hadn't drawn breath for an age, and wheeled the startled Shy Boy around, rushing toward the sound of Cole's voice. He was headed to her at a long, fast trot, bareheaded, his smile flashing white, sitting his horse as easily as if they'd been on a pleasure ride through a flower-strewn meadow. He was soaking wet, however, and scraps of yellow slicker hung from his saddle.

Without a word, without breaking the look, they rode to meet, standing in their stirrups too soon to reach for each other, unable to truly believe what they saw until they touched. He caught her up with a need so fierce it took her breath away, pulled her into his saddle with him, into his arms, into the hot haven of his mouth.

His kiss struck flame in the center of her being, banished the cold from her body from the inside out. It lifted her high above the earth, where she would never again have a need for solid ground.

His mouth was her sun, her heat, her light. Her world. She clung to him with hands that trembled, he caressed her throat, her breasts, gathered her up so close against him again that their wet clothes glued them together against even the air.

Every place that his body touched hers its heat consumed the chill in her skin, it flamed in her blood and penetrated her flesh all the way to the bone. He drew back, broke the kiss so he could look at her.

"I never was so scared in all my life," he said, his eyes blazing with the same passion as his kiss. "I'm not tough enough to see you hurt, Aurora."

His gaze devoured her as if trying to burn her image into his memory.

"I wasn't worried for a minute about you," she lied. "I figured that after the Federales a few thousand head of longhorns wouldn't even put you and your running horse into a high lope."

He started untangling her stampede strings

with one hand, but he kept the other nestled firmly at the small of her back.

"Can't keep from reminding me of my old sins, can you?" he drawled. "Reckon I'm gonna have to commit some new ones just to give you a change of subject."

His fingertips touching her throat here and there, hot and tantalizing as they were, couldn't break the unguarded look shimmering between them.

"Any ideas to suggest?"

*Yes. Right now. Except it would be so right it wouldn't be a sin.*

"I . . . I . . ." she whispered, her lips aching so with the desire to kiss him again that she could barely speak, let alone think.

"Hey!" someone shouted, off in what seemed to be another world. Then again, closer, "Hey, Monte!"

She reached to help Cole with the strings to her hat.

"The . . . the men," she managed to say, although her tongue was already demanding to taste his again, "the men and the herd. Cole . . ."

They both looked around them, at the milling, bawling herd and the rain-slashed land, as if they'd never seen any of it before.

"I need my horse," she said, but made no move to get down from his.

Her gaze went right back to Cole's mouth, which she needed even more.

"He's right there," Cole said, but he didn't even glance in Shy Boy's direction.

"We make a pair, don't we darlin'?" he drawled. "You and me, we turned a stampede."

Her whole body thrilled at the endearment. At the tone of his low voice. At the look in his dark, dark eyes.

*We make a pair. Yes, we do.*

"We only did it because you're so stubborn," he said, his dark eyes twinkling with mischief. "I was gonna let 'em scatter from Santa Fe to El Paso, but I was ashamed to quit if you wouldn't."

She laughed.

"That's the reason I kept hanging on," she said. "I hated for you to disgrace yourself in front of the whole Slash A outfit."

The circling herd was growing as more cattle poured in from the pass; it was shifting closer now, bawling and clacking horns. The cowboys rode tighter circles around the edges, pushed the cattle in on themselves even more.

"Miss Aurora, you all right?" Monte called.

Aurora began to pull herself back together, quickly finished untangling her hat and put it back onto her head.

"I'm fine," she called back, realizing how she must look up on Cole's horse with him. "My hat strings were about to strangle me, is all."

She thought Monte gave her a questioning glance, but he would never say anything, nor would any of the other men. They would think and talk to each other about it, plenty, though, and she had her authority to think about.

Dear Lord, she had her whole crew, the whole outfit to think about!

"Is everybody accounted for?" she called to Monte across the short distance and the heads of the cattle.

A wave of frightening guilt swept through her. How could she forget about everyone and everything except Cole?

"Don't know yet . . ." Monte said, the last of his words lost in the noises of the herd.

Aurora thought he said something about the chuck wagon. She turned to Cole.

"Oh, dear God, Cookie! Were he and Nate able to get the wagons out of the way when the herd began to run?"

She began scrambling to get down, but Cole, as if he couldn't bring himself to let her go, tightened his arms around her, stood in the stirrup and dismounted.

"Cookie's been through more than one stampede," he said comfortingly. "He's probably built a fire and is stirring up some supper about now."

That helped her a lot. The more she thought about it, the more she remembered the wagons and the remuda being far enough ahead to be out of the stampede.

Cole held his hands out for her to step into and boosted her up onto Shy Boy.

"That helps," she said. "My legs seem to be just a tad bit shaky, for some reason."

"Mine, too," he said, looking up at her with his irresistible grin.

With his knowing, tempting brown eyes that wouldn't let her look away.

"Oh, sure," she said sarcastically. "You seem about done in to me."

"Let's lay over all day tomorrow and take a nap," he said. "I need it."

"You've got a job to do, cowboy. No naps."

He shook his head in mock dismay.

"Stubbornest woman I ever did see," he said to Shy Boy. "She's liable to work us both to death, boy, if we don't dig our heels in."

She smiled wickedly.

"I'm going to change horses and let him go as soon as I find the remuda," she said. "You'll have to rebel all by yourself."

He laughed up at her, and she wanted nothing so much as to reach down and touch his face, trace the shape of his cheekbone, smooth his wet hair into shape behind his ear.

"You needn't run this stubborn business into the ground just because I told you it was your best feature," he said. "Can I at least have a minute to change clothes?"

She frowned while she looked him over, head to toe. That was a real mistake, because the sight of his magnificently muscled body showing through his clothes, soaked to the skin, sped up her pulse until she thought her heart would beat out of her chest.

"You'll dry," she said, grinning at him. "Cowboy up."

He pretended not to hear that.

"I was thinking maybe you could *help* me change," he said, dropping his voice to a sultry tone that sent a new, more urgent heat through her blood, "and then, maybe, I could help you?"

The images that suggestion created in her mind took what little strength was left in her limbs.

"Turn about's fair play," he drawled coaxingly.

"Will you mount up and ride?" she said briskly. "If you want to go down the trail in the summertime, McCord, you'll have to learn to do your playing in the winter."

He grinned as if he'd won a great victory.

"Well, then, Miss Aurora, you've got a date for the winter . . ." he said, reaching to tip his hat that wasn't there.

Monte rode up to them. Cole paid him no attention.

". . . but right now I've got to go find my hat, which I lost trying to save your cattle, which, I might remind you, is not part of my job."

He turned and threw a careless smile at her segundo.

"Monte," he said.

Monte was too busy looking from one of them to the other and back again to answer.

"Twenty head of those cattle, I might remind you, are yours," Aurora said. "Those are, no doubt, the ones you were trying to save."

Laughing, Cole sauntered back to his horse

and stepped up onto Border Crossing. Aurora had to force herself not to watch every move he made, had to wrench her mind away from the memory of his touch. She practically had to take her head in her hands and turn her face to Monte.

"We was a mite worried you coulda been trampled," Monte said, still looking at her, then at Cole.

"No," she managed to say in a fairly steady voice, "but right now I feel as if the whole herd had run over me."

"Shoot, Miss Aurora, better cowboy up," Cole drawled, as he pulled his horse around and trotted away, "you ain't seen nothin' yet."

Aurora stared at Cole's back in spite of all she could do. She could feel Monte's eyes on her profile, but she was powerless to pay him any attention. Cole wasn't looking for his hat, she knew that and he knew she knew it—if that hat wasn't trampled to shreds in the mud, it had blown all the way to Texas. He was riding away from her because when Monte rode up, they were on the verge of ending up kissing each other senseless or going off to crawl into her wagon and make love.

Her hands were shaking, and not from the stampede. Her heart was pounding, and she felt so hot she could strip off her wet clothes right there in the cold wind that had blown away the storm. Cole's taste on her tongue and the shape of his hands on her body had her blood racing with . . . desire. Never, ever had she known the meaning of that word before now.

She thought she had known, yes, when he had kissed her before, but this was different. This was so primal she didn't have a choice.

"Um, Miss . . . Aurora?"

Slowly, with the greatest of difficulty, she tore her gaze from Cole and looked at her segundo.

"Yes?"

"Reckon we oughtta plan to hold 'em here for the night? Where we've at least got the mountains at our back?"

She stared at him for a moment, as if he'd spoken in some language only vaguely familiar, which she could neither comprehend nor speak. With a great effort, she figured out what he had said.

Standing in her stirrups to look at her surroundings with *her mind on her herd*, she considered the place as a bedground.

"Why . . . yes," she finally said. "This spot will do. I'll go find Cookie and tell him."

She rode off in the direction she'd seen the wagons and remuda take when they came through the pass, but she couldn't keep from glancing behind her from time to time, looking for Cole. At first she told herself it was the herd she was looking at, but it wasn't. She could barely even remember where she was headed and why.

What *was* this connection she'd always felt between her and Cole McCord? Was it all physical desire? Would she ever be free of it again? She let herself look over her shoulder one more time after she found the wagons headed back toward the herd, but he was nowhere in sight.

She rode to meet Cookie, and when she told Shy Boy "Whoa," she sank down in her saddle and just sat there for a moment, exhausted. Not by the horrendous run they'd all been through but by the effort it took to think of something else besides Cole.

If she didn't feel his arms around her again, and soon, if she didn't have his hands on her skin, she would not survive this wanting.

"Well," she managed to say to Cookie, "I see you came through in fine shape."

"Dern tootin'," he said, and gestured for Nate to keep on driving the hoodlum wagon toward the herd. "Takes more'n thousands of crazy cows t' run ol' Cookie into the ground."

She smiled, really seeing him at last. "You still look a little pale around the gills, however."

"Somethin' wrong with your eyes," he retorted. "You gonna keep me jawin' here all night or you want hot grub and coffee for your men?"

She laughed and turned Shy Boy back toward the herd, too. He slapped down his lines, and they all moved on at a trot.

"Monte said you'd probably already have a fire built by the time I found you."

"Monte's a right smart man," he said, chortling. "I got dry wood in the *cuna* and sourdough in the pot."

When they had reached the bedgrounds and decided on the best place for both wagons, Aurora got off Shy Boy, unsaddled him, and rubbed him down. He was eager to roll, though, and to start chomping grass, so she turned him into the remuda and went to change her clothes. She was making progress. During all that, she'd only looked for Cole three times. Or maybe four.

She climbed up into her wagon and began stripping out of her wet shirt and riding skirt, peeling away the thin underthings plastered to her skin. Even the cool air seeping in around the canvas door to brush her bare body here and there reminded her of Cole's hot touch. Where had he gone? Why was it taking him so long to look for a hat he knew he'd never find?

Reaching into one of her wooden boxes, she pulled out a towel and began drying herself, but every friction against her flesh heightened her longing. She wanted him so much. Oh, dear God, she had to feel his arms around her, his hands on her skin.

This torment was too much to bear. Never, ever would she get close enough to him to let him hold her or kiss her.

She knew better, though, deep down in her woman's heart, and that scared her all over again. Was she going to feel this feverish for the rest of the drive if . . . she couldn't let herself finish the thought.

Yes, she could. If . . . she went to his bed to-night . . .

An overwhelming urge to open her trunk, to take out a real dress, to slip into something soft and flowing, something that made her feel like a woman came over her. Instead, she reached for another set of work clothes.

She couldn't deal with the comments around the campfire that her sudden change to a dress would create or the sly looks from the men, who would all be talking about her and Cole by tomorrow if Monte shared his wonderings with any of them. There was precious little entertainment on the trail—besides stampedes and other disasters—and the least nugget of gossip occasioned jokes and teasing no end.

So she slipped into a dry shirt and riding skirt, fixed her hair as best she could, and went to eat her supper. She already felt like a woman every time Cole looked at her.

Oh, Lord, what was she going to do? Her legs shook as she climbed down out of the wagon. She couldn't wait until she saw him again, she *had* to see him, right this minute.

And there he was, standing talking with some of the men between the chuck wagon and the fire, looking truly wonderful in his clean shirt and Levi pants, both miraculously crisp and starched, although his shirt was wrinkled from being packed into his bag. He was also wearing the pale-colored Stetson he always wore, which looked totally undamaged by the storm.

But seeing him turned out not to be enough. Now she needed, with a pervading desperation spreading through her, to touch him again. To kiss him again.

He turned his head slightly and looked at her the instant she stepped onto the ground, as if he'd heard her, when she'd hardly made a sound. His steadfast gaze melted her.

She would never have managed to stiffen her legs enough to walk to the fire had he not turned back to the conversation again. She went straight to one of the logs they used for a chair and sat down. By the time Cookie had the food completely cooked and the coffee made, maybe she could trust herself to eat.

He must've felt her watching him, for a moment later, Cole turned and strolled toward her. Right then she decided that she'd never be able to stand up or walk again. His hat looked exactly the way it always did: silverbelly colored, Texas brimmed, worn enough to have personality. But *definitely* not battered enough to have come through a storm.

"You're looking mighty fine and fresh, Miss Aurora," he said, studying her ostentatiously. "A man would never know you'd just been through a stampede."

"You're too bold for your own good, Mr. McCord," she said, pretending to take offense at his manner.

"That's true," he said and nonchalantly sat down beside her. "I try my best, but I can't seem to get over it."

He smelled of something spicy he'd used after shaving—he had *shaved* when he'd changed his clothes. He looked and smelled wonderful.

"You're a bit on the fine and fresh side, yourself," she said. "How in the world do you have ironed clothes way out here?"

"Ingenuity, ma'am," he said solemnly. "Have 'em ironed before leaving town, then roll 'em just right into the bag and wedge it between the sideboard and the pile of cowboys' gear in the wagon."

She tilted her head to one side and examined him as thoroughly as he had done her. He gave her a long, deep look. Her pulse quickened, her blood heated in an instant. She wasn't sure she could talk, but she did.

"I had no idea when I drove into Pueblo City to hire you that you were the most *dapper* bodyguard in the West, as well as the most dangerous."

He shrugged.

"There are those who call it dapper and others who call it a disguise," he drawled.

"Disguise?"

"For the bad character underneath," he said, showing that devilish grin.

"Who said that?"

He shrugged, feigning a sudden sheepishness.

"Mostly angry ladies, I must admit. And maybe a few enemies here and there."

He paused, taking time to charm her with his mischievous glance.

"Perhaps, also, a few opponents losing at cards."

She laughed, in spite of the small twinge caused by the thought of ladies who knew him well enough to be angry with him.

"Well, they're all wrong," she said. "Your character is the last thing that worries me about you right now."

He raised one black eyebrow.

"Oh? And what's the first?"

*The power you have to ruin my mind because I can't think about anything but you.*

"Your carelessness with your health," she said. "Since you're wearing your hat and it looks unscathed, I can only assume that you took it off on purpose—at the risk of pneumonia or worse—and carried it in your saddlebags through the storm."

He smiled at her, holding her gaze, never letting her see anything but him.

"Wrong. Cookie brought it to me," he said. "Wind blew it right into his wagon."

She looked him straight in the eye, trying not to laugh. Trying to keep from reaching out to touch his face.

"We usually save the tall tales until after supper," she said, "and tell them while we're sitting around the fire."

"I can think of better things to do by the fire."

His steady, deep, dark eyes told her what those better things were. The look made her legs turn to jelly.

"Co-o-me and git it, a'fore I throw it out!" Cookie yelled.

Cole stood up.

"Let me serve you, ma'am," he said, with an exaggerated tip of the hat in question. "You just keep your seat right there."

So Aurora sat, helpless not to watch him, while he got two plates and filled them, brought them to her, and then two cups of coffee.

They soon realized they were starving, so they ate in silence in true cowboy fashion, as the others did. Aurora hardly could swallow, however, because she was so close to Cole. It was torture, being so near him and unable to touch.

As soon as she'd finished her meal, she stood up and took her dishes to the wreck pan.

It was unbearable, being near Cole. He was looking at her now, following her with his eyes, and she ached to turn and run back to him. Another three seconds, and she'd be throwing herself into his arms in front of her entire crew.

"Good night," she called to him, and then looked around to include all the others. "You all better turn in pretty soon. It'll be an early start tomorrow to look for strays."

"Don't you worry, Missy," Cookie said. "I'll run 'em into their bedrolls. I'll cut their coffee off."

Cole gave her a small gesture of salute, then turned to say something to Frank as she left the campfire. She went straight to her wagon and climbed inside, closing the flap behind her, driven by a desperate need for refuge.

But it was refuge from wanting Cole that she needed, and that she didn't find. The wanting came right on into the wagon with her.

# Chapter 11

The first guard had come in to bed, the second had been wakened and gone out. The exhausted cattle stayed where they'd dropped, mostly silent, mostly sleeping. The camp lay quiet except for the shifting, slow stirring of the wind. The only storm remaining was the one inside Aurora.

She got up, wrapped a blanket around her, held aside the canvas flap to her wagon, and stepped out into the night, washed silver by the moon. Cole was out there, somewhere, waiting for her either to come to him or to learn to live with this wild restlessness that refused to be tamed.

From the minute she'd seen him after the run, she had known which it would be. Now was the time.

She jumped to the ground and walked swiftly toward the trees that grew all the way down to the foot of the hill. They formed a crescent-shaped nook that opened its arms to the camp toward her wagon and caught the moonlight. She could see her way plain as day.

An instant before Cole spoke, she saw him, too. A dark shadow inside a darker one, he was a graceful shape, with his shoulders leaning back against a tall pine, one long leg bent at the knee, his heel propped on the tree trunk, too. He was hipshot and loose and very, very sure of himself.

And of her. It made her smile.

"Once you finally came out of your lair you came straight to me," he murmured, his voice like a song on the night breeze. "You never hesitated. How'd you know where I was?"

"I can feel you," she said. "I always know where you are."

That surprised him for a moment, then he chuckled.

"Miss Aurora."

His voice was low and sweet, it warmed her more than the blanket did in the cool wind.

And then he reached for her and she was *riding* on that wind.

"You're supposed to be my bodyguard," she said, teasing him, "and here you are way out here. It would've taken you a long time to get to me if I'd called."

"You just call me and see how long it takes."

The hard significance in his voice sent a thrill all through her.

"I didn't even have to call, you were watching for me."

"Ready to guard your beautiful body," he

said, laughing low. "Come here to me."

He set his feet wide apart and took her into his arms, folded her close and, securing her breasts against his hard chest, tucking her head beneath his chin, held her to him for a long, trembling moment. She felt his face in her hair.

"I thought you'd never come," he murmured. "Lord, Aurora, I was about to come blasting into that wagon after you."

"And scandalize the whole crew?" she said, dropping a kiss into the open neck of his shirt. "Your skin smells like rain."

His hand slipped inside the blanket, stroked her back, hot and hard through the thin fabric of her gown. It slid downward to caress her hip. Her blood began to blaze.

"You smell like heaven," he said.

His one hand pressed her closer to him, brought her belly against his hardening manhood.

"What does heaven smell like?"

"You."

She laughed and went on tiptoe, lifted her face to his.

"Were you really about to come after me?"

"Damn straight. I just didn't want Cookie coming after *me* with a shotgun, that's all."

He gave a low moan, he held her closer yet, but still he wouldn't kiss her. She brushed her lips back and forth on his skin, she touched the tip of her tongue to the sweet hollow at the base of his throat.

"Stop that, now. I have to give you your present first."

She pulled back to look up at him.

"My *present?* I have a present from you?"

He chuckled low in her ear.

"Greedy. You'd rather have a present than a kiss from me."

"I would *not. You're* the one who won't kiss *me!*"

Laughing, he swept her up into his arms, and she wrapped her arms around his neck and clung to him, her heart roaring in her chest. How had she lived this long without him?

He carried her only a few steps back into the trees, into a tiny cove of a clearing on the side of the hill that had a floor strewn with pine needles painted silver by the moon.

"I don't know," he muttered, "you made me wait so long and waitin's so hard for me to do, maybe I ought to keep this present. Might teach you a lesson."

"You don't dare," she said dangerously. "No one has given me a present since . . . I can't remember when."

But they both had trouble breathing as they talked. He pressed a quick, hard kiss to her temple, she tasted his cheek with the tip of her tongue and wrapped herself more tightly around him. The gift really wasn't important at all.

She couldn't even tear her gaze away from his face long enough to see what it was.

The shadows flickered across his eyes, the

moon laid a ribbon of shining silver across his mouth. Her very heart turned over inside her. His gorgeous, sensual lips, full and slightly parted, curved at the corners in the ghost of a smile. A smile on that fiercely handsome face could make any woman weak with desire.

He knelt, and she felt a soft bed beneath her, but she couldn't loose her arms from around his neck.

"No use trying to distract me now . . . ," he said, dropping hot, sweet kisses onto her cheeks and hair, her forehead, the last one deliberately, tantalizingly close to the edge of her lips.

She turned her face to try to catch his lips with hers, but his mouth danced away.

". . . I'm a stronger man than that."

"*You're* the one distracting . . ."

He turned her around, settled her back against his chest, surrounded her with the iron safety of his arms.

"There," he said. "For you, Miss Aurora."

A huge bouquet of flowers shone at the head of the bedroll he had spread there, some lighter, some darker, but all silver in the moonlight. All silver and all wonderfully beautiful and all for her.

Sudden tears blurred her eyes. To think that he would do such a thing!

"Gorgeous," she whispered. "Oh, Cole."

"I saw 'em when I was hunting my hat," he said, "and stole a bucket from Cookie to put 'em in."

"Oh, Cole."

" 'Course they were already soaking wet from the storm, but I didn't know how long before they'd wilt."

"Oh, Cole."

"In the morning you can see they're the color of the sky—and your eyes."

*"Oh, Cole!"*

"You've gone to repeating yourself somethin' terrible," he said, and began rubbing his cheek against hers, his lips seeking hers, demanding her kiss. "We're gonna have to put a stop to that."

His mouth, hot and hungry, took hers, and she turned in his arms like a starving person.

"Ah, Aurora, *darlin'*," he moaned into her mouth as he drove her down beneath him on his bed.

He broke the kiss only for the most fleeting instant, though, and she fell into it with a passionate abandon that wiped away the world. Nothing else existed, nothing, except Cole, hard and strong and wanting her, bringing her flowers, melting her against him until she needed nothing more.

Except more of him.

His tongue twined with hers, talked to her without words, tempted her and tantalized all of her body, set her blood to rolling high, filled her with fire. His hands opened the blanket, slipped beneath her gown, stroked her ardent skin.

She reached for the buckle of his belt, ran her palm over the bulging buttons of his Levis. The touch made him moan with pleasure.

The buckle came undone.

"*Boots*," he muttered against her lips.

Finally, with an incoherent sound of protest that came from deep in his throat, he tore his mouth from hers and sat up to pull off his boots, but with one hand still touching her almost all the time, with his mouth coming back to hers again and again. Aurora found the fly of his jeans with both hands, began work on the buttons.

One by one they popped open, the huge hardness of his manhood beneath them swelling beneath her fingers, torturing her trembling hands. He gave a desperate groan and ground his mouth into hers, cupped her breast in his hand, kneading it, rubbing the standing nipple with his thumb through the thin fabric of her gown. With the other, he began to help her, and somehow the two of them managed to divest him of his pants without breaking the kiss or removing his hand.

She ran her hands up under his shirt and rubbed the muscles rippling under the smooth skin of his back with her palms. Until she could no longer stand any barrier between them.

"Quick," she said, gasping for air but wanting nothing but his mouth again, "get this off me."

He did, while she ripped open the buttons of his shirt and pushed it off his huge shoulders. He shook it off his arms and away, and they fell back into each other's arms. She arched her back enough to rub the hard tips of her breasts against his chest, and he gave a rough, primal cry of wanting, *needing*, needing *her*, that melded her to him.

*"Darlin',"* he whispered.

The endearment was only the lightest feather drifting on that one long breath of his, but it floated all the way into her heart. How could she ever have lived for twenty-four years without this? She hadn't. She had only existed.

She'd never have the power of speech anymore, those had been her last words, ever, because for the rest of her time on earth all she was going to do was give her mouth to Cole, take his mouth with hers, kiss him brazenly and mutely for the rest of her natural life. That's all she would need, that and his hard, hot length on top of her. And his hands caressing her skin.

And . . . yet, something more.

Cole knew that. He broke the kiss and slipped his hand beneath her back to arch her up again and hold her gently, like a treasure newly found. He lowered his head to her breast and took her hard nipple into his mouth, surrounded it with his tongue and suckled it with his lips. All power of thought left her, too.

Moving on pure instinct, she thrust her fingers into his hair to cradle his head in her hands, to hold it carefully there so he could never stop what he was doing, never, ever. He was creating heat in her blood that rose all the way through her skin, he was sending thrills

along her skin that sank all the way into her
bones.

He was making her tremble all over, making
her womanhood weep for him.

He was destroying her, for she would never
be the same. And she did not care, all she
wanted was more.

She let him move to her other breast, but she
kept running her fingers through his hair, kept
holding his mouth where she wanted it, willing
this delight never to end, until he began stroking his calloused palm over her hip, over her
thigh, along the inside of her thigh. Then his
fingers moved higher and into her and her
hands fell away from him, she collapsed with
her arms at her sides, lost in the sensations Cole
created, lost in the magic he made that filled
every one of her senses.

To make her beg in helpless silence for more.

He knew that, too. He heard her begin to
whimper deep in her throat, he felt her arching
to him, pleading with her breasts, her wordless
tongue.

But it was not until she was able to lift her
hands and to find his hard shoulders, to rake
her nails over them and cry out in incoherent,
frantic supplication that he lifted himself over
her and she brought him in. A sting of pain ran
through her at that first moment, but then she
melted around him and moved with him in the
ageless, seductive rhythm of a woman and a
man.

And then the lightning struck again, into the

midst of this new, mighty storm, struck *inside* them both as one, and they were burning, together, like the flame of a tall pine in the wind. Dancing through the sultry air together, flashing like one glittering star in the dark of the night.

When their blaze became a conflagration, it consumed her, heart and soul, for Cole tore his mouth from hers, threw back his head, and called out her name.

He woke at first light. For one long, delicious moment, no thoughts came to him, only the feel of Aurora, nestled in his arms, and the scent of her. The warm satin of her skin against his. The cloud of her hair tickling his chin, shining like the spun gold of a fairy tale, even in the last feeble light from the moon. The soft, gentle sound of her slow breathing, deep as a sleeping child's.

She was a woman, for sure, though. He'd never known one with such passion.

So how could he have known that he was the first man for her?

He couldn't have, so he shouldn't feel guilty about that. After all, hadn't she talked about suitors from here to Philadelphia? Hadn't she come to his bed in her nightgown?

A tenderness took him, anyway, and he held her even closer, although already they were fastened together everywhere they touched like the bark on a tree. And he was gratified by every inch of it. He could barely remember what it was like to wake up with her *not* in his arms.

That was a damned dangerous position to be in, for an old renegade like him. He never stayed the night with any woman, ever.

He hardly ever even cared to be with any woman twice.

Right now, he wanted to be with Aurora forever.

He ought to tell her, as soon as she opened those big blue eyes of hers, that this would never happen again. That was it. He was her bodyguard. That was all.

Just waking up holding her was heaven, though. He waited a minute more.

Finally he kissed her shoulder, then gathered her to him and squeezed her tightly for one heartbeat, then two.

"Aurora," he whispered. "You don't want to miss your namesake, do you?"

She opened her eyes and shifted in the curve of his arm to turn to look at him.

"Your skin's soft as a foal's nose," he said, stroking her arm.

Her slow smile made his heart turn over.

"Well, well, that certainly is an improvement," she said, her words slurry with sleep, "better than 'Aurora, you're stubborn as a mule' by a long shot."

He laughed.

"What was it you said when I woke up?"

He looked into her eyes and forgot what the question was, much less the answer.

"Something about my namesake?"

"Oh. Yeah. The dawn. Doesn't Aurora mean dawn?"

Her face brightened. She was coming awake now.

"Yes, and it's very romantic of you to mention that, Mr. McCord. Almost as romantic as bringing me flowers."

*Romantic.* For sure nobody had ever called him that before.

"Hey, thanks," he drawled, "but you don't know that."

"Yes, I do."

She flipped onto her stomach in a heartbeat, tight as he was holding her, and reached for the bouquet.

"These are so, so gorgeous," she said, and brought them closer to bury her face in them. "Thank you, Cole. You are so thoughtful."

Dear God. She was making too much of him.

"Hey, watch it there, missy," he said, wiping at the drops of water coming off the stems of the flowers, "you're getting our bed all wet."

*Our bed.* He should tell her right now. This was a one and only one-time happening, for they mustn't get attached to each other. Sleep with her once more and no telling what'd be coming out of his fool mouth.

But she was looking into his face, blue eyes twinkling.

"That's a laugh, coming from the champion of dunking people in the river. Decided you're made of sugar? Afraid you'll melt?"

He only grinned at her. That was all he could think to do, since he couldn't remember what he'd started to say.

Her mischief faded into a misty look.

"I dreamed about you," she said, brushing her cheek against the petals of the flowers.

His heart contracted. When had *anyone, ever,* dreamed of him?

"No, darlin'," he drawled, "you were awake. You only thought it was a dream."

She laughed.

"You always think I don't know my own mind, but I do."

Then, with a smile that melted him, she reached over and stroked his cheek with her soft fingers. Velvet fingers.

"Keep on wearing your gloves for riding," he said. "It's paying off."

She grinned.

"So you approve of *one* thing I do."

He let his gaze wander down the length of her, over the one shoulder that was bare and the leg twined with his on top of the blanket.

"I approve of *many* things you do."

She laughed and blushed, a little bit embarrassed, which made him smile.

And made him think about the fact that he was the first man who'd ever lain with her.

The sound of pots clanging together and then Cookie's voice floated up to them from camp.

"No!" she whispered, and snuggled closer to run one tantalizing fingertip down the middle of his chest.

"Don't do that," he whispered back, "I'm leaving you now."

*Coward. Yellow-bellied, craven coward.*

He opened his mouth.

He looked into her eyes and closed it again.

Lowering his head, he took a quick, hard kiss from her lips, then let himself have another light one from the tip of her nose.

"We don't want to set the boys' chins to wagging, now, do we?"

"Fine with me," she said, her blue eyes wide and fixed on his. "What the boss and the bodyguard do is none of anybody else's business, I've decided."

He already was hard, longing to feel her around him again, and that sent a sharp shaft of desire straight through him.

"I've got to get away from you, Vixen. I'm scared you're gonna corrupt me."

She laughed, and she looked so beautiful, lying there in his arms with her hair curling all around her face in a soft, blonde cloud, that he came within an inch of losing his control. He forced himself to put her down gently, disentangle them, and reach for his pants.

"Better get your blanket on, ma'am," he said. "Folks is stirrin'."

She sat up and looked around while he was pulling on his boots.

"Why, you can see my wagon from here, plain as can be! It's not far, either, as the crow flies."

"Bodyguard position," he said. "I wasn't

sure whether you'd come out here or not."

"Liar, liar, pants on fire," she said, and leaned forward to hug him from behind, the mass of flowers still in one arm. "You even had a bouquet for me. Next time I'll bring a bottle of wine."

Her bare breasts against his bare back were exquisite torture.

Her words were torture, too. *Next time.* What had they started here?

He said good-bye with one more quick kiss and got out of there and into the trees, carrying the rest of his clothes. In the nick of time. Looking for the cold creek to jump into before breakfast and a wagonload of courage.

Aurora slipped down the hillside to her wagon, keeping to the shadows, which were vanishing fast in the rays of the rising sun. She ran along the offside of the hoodlum wagon and climbed up onto the tailgate on the side away from the fire. It was true what she'd said to Cole, though, she really didn't care what anybody thought about her coming in from the woods wrapped in a blanket with her arms full of flowers. She just didn't want to listen to Cookie's ranting about her and Cole, that was all.

She smiled to herself as she climbed up onto the tailgate and slid in behind the canvas flap. Her and Cole. Cole and Aurora. Aurora and Cole.

Quickly, she looked through her clean clothes

and chose the new blue and fawn jacket and riding skirt she had bought in Pueblo City. She might not even need it to ride into a town before they got to Texas, they might not even go near any town. Besides, she wanted to wear new clothes to celebrate. They had all survived a stampede with most of the cattle, hadn't they?

She put on her wrapper, gathered her towel and wash pitcher, and, smiling, stepped out of her wagon into the pink and yellow dawn of a great new day. All during breakfast, all during the saddling of the horses and her telling off the riders—giving assignments for the search for the strays—she couldn't stop smiling. She tried, because she didn't want old eagle-eye Cookie quizzing her, but she couldn't, because this was just the most wonderful day since they'd started the drive. Since she could remember, actually. The attraction between her and Cole *was* physical, but not *just* that.

The two of them took the southeasterly quadrant for their share of the search so that they'd also be able to scout the way they were headed with the herd. He was disinclined to talk much, but most of the time they separated anyway to look for strays. They stayed within sight of each other, though, at all times, and she could fairly feel the bond between them in the air.

Aurora found a half-dozen strays and rounded them up, started them to meet Cole, who had come across about as many and was heading them in her general direction. One of the steers Aurora had in her gather was a big, rangy black with one horn tip broken, whom the men had nicknamed Snarly. He was a truly mean-spirited creature who already had caused much grief on the trail by alternately attacking his companions and trying to break away from the herd, and as she and Cole threw their finds together, he was up to his old tricks.

"Hi-*ya*!" Aurora yelled, riding around the others to try to slap at him with a coiled rope. "You hateful thing, you, get away from her."

She looked across the jostling cattle to Cole.

"I don't know why I'm waiting until we get to the new ranch to make barbeque out of him," she said.

Cole was circling the little herd of strays to tighten them up before they started them back to the main herd.

"Yep," he said. "You'd save all of us a lot of trouble if he was supper tonight."

"I know," she said, as he rode up beside her. "But we have plenty of supplies now, and we might need him worse next winter."

She smiled at Cole.

"When we're catching up on our playing, like we said, after all this summer's work."

He gave her an odd look she couldn't read. His shoulders flinched as if she'd dealt him a blow. He looked straight at her, but he didn't smile back.

"Do you like barbeque in the wintertime?" she said. "Or would you rather have an enormous pot of stew with onions and potatoes and lots of jarred tomatoes?"

Still, he was strangely silent for a moment. Only an instant too long.

And then, only a shade too carefully, he said, "No telling what I'll be eating this winter. No telling where I'll be."

A swift shard of hurt rolled through her, sharp points hitting, then missing.

"Hey," she said, trying to force a light tone, "that's your business. I'm only going by a remark you yourself made about next winter's activities."

He smiled, but it wasn't quite the same.

"I reckon I oughtta curb my tongue," he said. "I'm old enough to know when to stop flirting, knowin' what a beautiful woman you are."

She stared at him, an intolerable cold spreading all through her.

"Now, if you'd said, 'knowing what an *ugly* woman you are,' or hateful or grouchy or irritating or whatever, then I might be able to make some sense out of what you just said."

He grinned at her, his old devilish grin. Almost.

Then he sobered.

"I should've left you alone. I should've known I couldn't resist you."

Anger was beginning to fight hurt for her main reaction to this shock. And anger was winning. By a long haul.

"Let me see if I can puzzle this out," she said tightly. "Now that you've learned that you 'can't resist me,' you're hot to leave me at the end of the trail? *Before* that you were thinking of maybe wintering with us?"

"Aurora," he said.

Now he was his old self again, his old, arrogant self who had told her to get lost the moment she'd asked him to come with her, his old, obnoxious self who didn't hesitate, didn't equivocate. He cocked his head and gave her a look that she already ought to know whatever he was about to say.

"Aurora, if we wintered together you know damn good and well that we'd be nothing but crazy for more when spring rolled around. You have got to know that, after last night."

She blinked.

"Well, yes, I suppose I do. However, if this is your usual morning-after attitude, that could slow things down some."

The corners of his mouth twitched as if he might smile.

She, however, didn't feel the least bit inclined to smile.

"What's the matter, Cole, are you thinking that because we . . . spent one night together that I'm expecting you to stay all winter and marry me in the spring? Is that what's galling you?"

All of a sudden, a sense of aloneness came down on her worse than she'd ever felt it before. It weighed a ton. Two tons. She sat up very straight in the saddle beneath it and called up her pride.

"Because if that's it, you can give up your

worries and rest easy—I'll *never* marry anyone. I'm finally in control of my life, and I will never give up that freedom to any man."

Her throat hurt hideously from the huge lump of pain that had formed there, but there was no trace of it in her voice, for which she was thankful.

"Good Lord, Cole," she said. "Last night was one of my adventures. One experience. That's all."

What a lie. God help her. Cole had walked right into her heart.

"I know that's what you think now," he said, in his smoothest, deepest, *surest* voice. "Aurora, I know you aren't expecting marriage, but it would come to that. It always does. Women think along those lines, and you're an emotional woman."

"And a stubborn one, as you're so fond of pointing out," she said coldly. "What's the matter, afraid I'll have you hog-tied and branded before you know what hit you?"

He did smile then, but only for an instant. A sadness passed over his face, a lonesomeness that reached out and touched her through all the other feelings exploding inside her.

"You're a good woman," he said, "and I'm a bad man for you in every way except what you hired me to do. We'd best stay away from each other."

"Not an easy thing considering what I hired you to do."

"You know what I mean. Except for the job."

Her fury rose like a storm. He was saying that last night had meant nothing to him, nothing at all, and had meant the world to her, the emotional woman.

*"Oh?* Well, if *you* were a more emotional *man* you might get a little more out of life! What do you think, that I'll sit around mooning over you for years and years, remembering what happened between us last night?"

She probably would. God help her, she would never forget it.

"I'm trying to tell you I'm bad for you, Aurora. It's only fair that you know."

"Bad in what way?" she cried. "What are you *talking* about?"

"I'm a renegade, always have been. I don't play by any rules but my own. Until I got to be captain myself, I nearly got thrown out of the *Rangers,* for God's sake."

"So that makes you a big, bad one," she said sarcastically. "Let me tell you, I am so impressed. Maybe you haven't noticed, but I make *my* own rules, too."

"Aurora," he said, in the coldest tone she could imagine, "I'm responsible for the death of a man."

"You're responsible for the deaths of many men. That's why I hired you. That's life on the frontier. It doesn't mean you're bad," she said stubbornly.

Why, dear God, was she defending him, when what she wanted was to drag him off his horse and pummel him thoroughly?

He turned away and stared into the distance, and she opened her mouth to say something else. But he spoke.

"Riders coming."

It took a moment, but then she saw them: three horses and riders, coming toward them from due east through the tall grass. Her stomach knotted even tighter than it already was.

"Who could they be?"

Cole shrugged.

"We'll see. Stay back, keep me between you and them."

"I can take care of myself."

She reached back for the gun she carried in her saddlebag.

"Leave it," he said, without even turning around. "I can take care of three. Look around and see if there're any coming from another direction."

She did as he said.

"No sign."

"Good."

It seemed forever, but the men finally reached them.

"Hello, the Slash A," one of them called.

"Hello," Cole answered.

Aurora noticed that he dropped his hand to the handle of his six-shooter and left it there. They looked pretty respectable, though, as they rode up and stopped their horses facing her and Cole. They all had an honest air about them.

"Milo Thomas of the Circle T," said the oldest man, the one in the middle.

"Cole McCord."

Milo Thomas introduced his men by name as two of his top hands and then fixed his direct, gray gaze on Aurora.

Cole deliberately did not introduce her.

"You know who we are," he said. "What can we do for you?"

"I'm interested in buying your herd," Milo said. "My information has it that the lady's the owner."

Aurora rode forward so her horse was even with Cole's.

"I'm Aurora Benton. I *am* the owner. But I'm not interested in selling."

"Sorry to hear that, ma'am," Milo Thomas said, with a tip of his hat. "I'm looking for some stockers, and it'd sure be handy to find 'em right here. I'd give top dollar."

"I'm sorry I can't accommodate you, Mr. Thomas, but it's completely impossible."

Her tone rang so strong and final that Thomas didn't argue. He and his men stayed visiting just long enough to be polite, then turned and rode back the way they had come.

As soon as she saw their backs, Aurora started pushing the ten or so head that they'd gathered toward the big herd. She could see it in the distance, and the sooner they reached it, the sooner she could get away from this stupid conversation with Cole.

Then, to her complete shock, it became even more insane.

"You should've at least thought it over," he

said. "That was a good chance to save yourself a whole lot of miles chasing Old Snarly."

She ignored him, wouldn't even look at him. Damn him for patronizing her.

"I'll be glad to ride after Milo Thomas and say that you'll think it over until tomorrow."

And damn him for knowing her so little that he took her silence for consent.

She turned on him viciously.

"Why don't you mind your own business? And why don't you come right out and say to my face that you don't think I can get these cattle through to Texas? Why don't you just admit that you are exactly like all the other men who think women can't do anything on their own?"

His face flushed with anger.

"That isn't true! You're such a stubborn-hearted she-wolf I know you can do *whatever* the hell you set out to do. I'm trying to save you a world of grief, that's all."

"Well, don't bother yourself! And don't lie. What you're doing is trying to get this drive over with fast so you won't have to deal with an *emotional* woman jumping into your bed every night because she can't resist you and then begging you to marry her every morning after!"

The expression on his face would have made her laugh if she hadn't been so completely furious.

"Well, dream on," she said, "because it ain't

gonna happen. I wouldn't touch you again with a ten-foot pole, Cole McCord!"

She held his gaze with a hot, sharp stare.

"You better not be laughing at me inside," she said dangerously. "You could not have stopped that stampede without my help, you know that, don't you? I did a man's job and just as well, maybe better."

"I know that. You may recall that I said as much."

There was no laughter in his voice, so she finally, disdainfully, swept her gaze away from his and got back to her work.

"You're my *employee,* for goodness sake," she said, "and that's all. You have no more loyalty to me than any other hired gun would have, and that's fine. The only thing that matters in my life is that I'm going to have a ranch of my own or die trying."

And she would hold last night as a precious memory for her old age, because it'd be that long before she could bear to think about it. She could never live with Cole McCord, and he was right about one thing: making love with him again would only make her want more, so from this moment on she'd be sticking tight to her promise never to go near him anymore.

Yep. From now on, Aurora Benton, owner of the Slash A Ranch, wherever in the Panhandle that ranch might be, would be all business.

All the time.

# Chapter 12

Cole filled his lungs with the new, storm-washed morning air and set his gaze firmly on the plains stretching out ahead. During the endless time since they had made love—and war—he had made great progress. He could ride beside Aurora now without being so constantly aware of her that he couldn't think about something else at the same time. Today he was going to prove that to himself beyond question: he was going to fix all his instincts on discovering the whereabouts of the disappearing cows. He wasn't going to think of Aurora as a woman, not once.

Maybe that would ease the pain in his gut.

Hadn't part of it gone away when he'd learned to bear the cross of her constant physical allure? That was now a given in his life, since she lived and breathed right beside him or within a stone's throw of him night and day. No, the misery inside him wasn't desire for her any more.

Now the powerful pain in his gut was himself.

That and the fact that some two-bit lowlifes were stealing cows out from under his nose. How embarrassing was that for the most dangerous man in Colorado?

With a wry shake of his head, he scanned the plains in every direction, searching for a glimpse of long horns shining in the sun or a white-spotted hide almost hidden in the tall, lush graze. Or a spiral of smoke rising from a branding fire. Or the crowns of the hats of men on horseback out to the side of the herd somewhere, riding the coulees so as not to throw their silhouettes on the horizon.

"Do you think I've gotten good enough with a gun to go up against them?"

The sound of her low, husky voice after a long silence affected him like her warm hand on his skin. But the words struck him with cold fear.

He whipped around in the saddle to look at her, fighting the quick, blunt answer that sprang to his lips. Three. Count to three and then speak. Don't destroy her confidence, because she might need it bad.

"You're a lot better," he said, unable to resist a glance at her trim waist and rounded hips, both emphasized by the heavy gunbelt she'd insisted on wearing since the first loss of cows.

"But . . . ? I can hear the 'but' in your voice."

"But you shooting at empty airtights and

men shooting back at you are two entirely different things."

"I know that."

"Not until you've been there."

"I have been shot at!"

"But you haven't shot back. And you felt sorry for the mewling, whining sidewinders when *I* shot them."

"*Anything* is pathetic when it's screaming in pain."

"In a gunfight, forget pathetic. Think, 'Him or me, who would I rather see dead?'"

She nodded, her eyes solemn and fixed on his.

"I can do that. Every time I remember waking up to another dozen head missing."

He laughed.

"That gets your dander up more than remembering Gates trying to kill you when you walked in front of the fire in your own camp?"

She laughed, too. "Makes me sound as money-hungry as he is, doesn't it?"

"Yep. And crazy enough to risk your life for the sake of greed. If you're dead, it doesn't matter who has your cows, Aurora. Let me take the lead if we scare 'em up today."

"Oh," she said, "so you *don't* think I can shoot well enough to . . ."

"Now, I didn't say that," he interrupted irritably. "What I'm saying is that we might get the drop on them and not have to do any shooting at all."

"So first you worry that I won't shoot because I feel sorry for them and now you worry that I'd shoot them in the back."

He turned on her.

"*Aurora!* Hush! You're gonna have my spurs so tangled up I can't even talk at all."

She was grinning her most mischievous grin.

They both laughed, then, and things felt easier between them than they had at any time since the blowup.

"One small detail," he said. "We have to find them before we can shoot or not shoot them."

"I think it's Gates," she said, for the thousandth time.

"You never know," he said, also for the thousandth time. "Thomas may have got his back up when you refused to sell and decided to take your cattle any old way he could get 'em. Or it could be brand blotters from parts unknown."

"It's been a week exactly since the stampede," she said thoughtfully.

"Seems like a year," he muttered. "Matter of fact, seems like a lifetime."

And that was the God's truth. He had never lived through such a stretch of misery in all his life, and he had been through some hell in his time. What was she *doing* to him? All the damned soul-searching he'd been falling into was because of her somehow, and he didn't even understand why.

He dragged his scattered thoughts together and forced them back to the problem at hand.

"*Whoever* it is, they didn't cause the stampede, though," he said.

She turned in the saddle to face him so suddenly that it nearly made him jump. "We've said all this so many times we're getting as predictable as Cookie," she cried, pounding her fist on her thigh. "We have to *do* something, and fast, or we'll have no cattle at all by the time we cross the Texas line. *What* can we do to stop them?"

For a minute he didn't even take in what she'd said. Her mouth was so sweet that all he wanted was to taste it again, reach across the narrow space between their horses and pull her into his arms.

But that was what had got him into this predicament in the first place, wasn't it? This weird state of mind where his sins haunted him and he longed to bury them all forever? Where he wanted, dear Lord, to make things right somehow so he'd be good enough for her?

A protesting shiver ran down his spine. So that was it. For the first time in all these wild, wolf-howling years, he was regretting the truth of his old line that always saved him from a woman's clutches and kept him moving on: "I'm bad for you, darlin', someday you'll know that. I'm not good enough for a woman like you."

He gave a great sigh. Well, at least now he knew what it was that had been keeping him awake at night—besides the rustlers. Besides his body longing for Aurora in his bed, if he was going to tell the whole truth.

"*Cole*," she said. "What are you thinking about?"

Her husky voice that never failed to surprise him somehow broke a little on the last word. He tried to steel himself against its magic.

"You," he said.

He had not meant to say that out loud.

She straightened her back and leaned a little away from him. She was stronger than she looked, actually stronger than he was, because her startled gaze immediately got lost in his, and her blue eyes plainly said that she wanted him to reach for her as much as he did, but she made no move.

Every fiber of his body gathered to reach for her. He wanted her so much, she wanted him, too. They could forget all about shootings and cattle and rustlers and danger. They could spend all day in a wonderful world of their own, a world of sweet-smelling grasses and huge, blue skies and bright sunlight and hot kisses and dizzying caresses on their skins.

No, they couldn't. Because her honest face had filled with yearning. With caring. For him.

He couldn't let that happen to her. Or to him. She touched him in too many places—like his heart and his loins and his head.

She saw the exact moment that he recovered control, and she put her guard up right then.

"Don't be thinking about *me*," she said. "I need you to do the job I hired you for, Cole."

"I'm guarding your body at this exact instant," he said, but lightly, not seductively.

He was never going to seduce her again. He was bad enough for going ahead with making love to her, even if she *was* the one who had come to him, because she was far more inexperienced in every way—except managing cowhands and cattle—than he had thought that day in Pueblo City.

She laughed a little.

"My mind's part of my body and you have to guard it, too, because it's going crazy over this rustling."

Her tone was as light as his, her wonderful voice only a little bit strained. It was best for both of them to keep the distance between them. It wouldn't be *too* hard to do.

"We'll find 'em," he said. "I've decided that I won't sleep until we do."

A sudden mischievous grin lit her face. That was one thing that made it so hard for him—she fascinated him, for he never knew what she'd do or say next.

"Great! I won't, either! We'll lie in wait!"

"N-o-o," he said firmly, unable to resist grinning back at her. "This isn't one of your famous adventures. And why lie in wait all night when there's never any tracks in the morning? That's not what I meant."

"Well, whatever you meant, I'm going with you."

He lifted Border Crossing into a short lope for a change of pace.

"Nope."

Then he bit his lip. The one thing he *could*

predict about her was that telling her she couldn't do something was sure to make her do it.

"Look," he said quickly, "this is nothing but an augurin' match. What we're gonna do is whatever we *have* to do when we figure out who's thinning our herd and how."

"Oh, yeah," she said. "I forgot to tell you that it's your twenty head that they took so far."

He looked at her and laughed.

"Last I heard from ol' Monte's count, we've lost around sixty head, all told. Some of 'em's bound to be yours."

"You're right! So that means I ride beside you to get them back."

He shook his head.

"Tricky," he said. "Tricky woman. I have to watch you like a hawk."

"As if *you* can be trusted," she said. "Nearly drowning me in the cold river when the bet was that I'd get dunked only once."

"I'm not getting into *that* argument again," he said, chuckling, giving her a teasing glance. "What's done is done. You've already been dunked twice."

She made a face at him.

"You look about six years old," he said, as she stuck out her tongue.

He tried to imagine her as a child. Had she been a little tomboy? Or a pretty little lady?

"Aurora, what did you mean that time you said you had to grow up fast?"

She stared at him.

"When did I say that?"

"When Nate was getting attached to your dog. I said he had to get tough."

"I'm amazed you even remember that."

*I remember everything about you. Probably every word we ever said to each other. Every look we ever exchanged.*

"I remember. That's always been a big help in Rangering."

She nodded.

"I meant that I've had to take care of myself almost since I could walk and talk. Mama died when I was ten, but she was sick in bed a lot before that and Papa was always caught up in ranching. Cookie tried to look after me and I rode with Papa some, but mostly I did as I pleased."

Loneliness from the past echoed in her voice.

"I reckon that explains it, then," he drawled.

"Explains what?"

"You still think you ought to do as you please. No questions asked."

Her laughter rewarded him.

"*You* should talk, Cole McCord."

After a moment's comfortable silence moving across the fresh, new country, she turned to him again.

"What about you? Did your mother take good care of you?"

"She tried, in between working in the fields and cooking and trying to make do. When the work was done every fall, she took me to see her Chickasaw people. But she died when I was sixteen, and, since I never got along with my pa, that's when I joined the Rangers."

"Any brothers and sisters?"

The question shot a lump into his throat.

"One brother who died young," he said gruffly. "And a partner who was more than a brother to me."

All the old pain slammed into him like a wall of water roaring down a dry gulch. Helpless. God Almighty, he had never been so helpless as he'd been that hellish day. His limbs felt paralyzed just thinking about it.

It was sure too late now. There was nothing he could do to redeem himself.

"Tell me about him," she said, so softly he almost didn't hear.

"Travis," he said. "Trav Henderson. He was one to ride the river with."

"Was?"

"Shot to pieces," he said, and nearly choked on the words. "Last year. On the Nueces."

"I'm so sorry, Cole."

He couldn't look at her for a while. When he finally did, her blue gaze caught his and comforted him, told him she understood. She didn't ask any more, she didn't say everything would be all right.

Because it wouldn't, and she could see that. Because she was hurting because he was hurting.

He wanted to be in her arms. He wanted his head on her breast.

"I was goin' back to Texas anyhow," he said,

tearing his eyes away and staring straight ahead, "to see a woman."

He told it as a lie to throw up a barrier between them. But as soon as the words were out of his mouth, he knew he couldn't let it stand.

It made him feel hollowed out so much he could blow right off his horse and away in the wind. He couldn't do it. Aurora needed to know he was bad, all right, but he couldn't do that to himself—let her think that he'd made love with her while he was riding hundreds of miles to see another woman.

Besides, suddenly he knew that it was the truth. This *was* one reason he was going back to Texas.

"Travis's widow. I want to see if she needs anything."

"That's good of you," Aurora said quietly.

She waited, sensing something more. From the very minute they met, she could read his mind. She knew him, or she was beginning to. Nobody else but Travis ever had.

He couldn't say any more, though, he *wouldn't* say more. And that was all right with her, too.

They rode on in silence, watching the horizon, while he tried to calm the turmoil in his heart. It wasn't all guilt and regret over Travis, either.

Layered over all those old feelings was one that was brand new. Was he really going to see Ellie to keep Aurora at a distance, to have a reason to leave her at the end of the trail, to keep her from thinking she was important enough or persuasive enough to him to have brought him on this upside-down and backwards, north-to-south trail drive?

Or was it to confess everything and ask for Ellie's forgiveness? To try to make himself a better man, one more deserving of Aurora?

God help him if that's what it was.


After the nooning, Aurora remounted and waited for Cole to catch his fresh horse. The men were throwing the cattle back onto the trail, Cookie and Nate were breaking camp, and, after a hot meal and a rest in the shade, everybody seemed ready for a long afternoon's drive. If they drove far enough, fast enough, could they outrun the rustlers?

The very question made her furious. She had to think of something. She had to *do* something.

Monte came trotting toward her and jarred her out of her reverie.

"I've done a quick, rough count," he said, "and I'd say we've lost another ten head or so."

"You mean since we've been *here?*"

"Since sunup. I counted then."

Monte was known for his ability to ride through a herd and estimate its number to within a cow or two. Some men could do that, just as some men could throw a rope onto anything that moved and some men could ride to a standstill every bronc they climbed on. Monte was not mistaken.

A chill ran through her. Her cattle were being

spirited invisibly right out from under her nose.

Cole rode up to them.

"From the looks on your faces I think I know what you're talking about," he said.

"Ten head," Aurora said. "Since sunup."

But Cole was looking at Monte.

"What position did Skeeter ride this morning?"

Monte immediately cocked his head and gave Cole a sharp look. Aurora's breath stopped.

"Cole!" she said. "There's no call for that! I told you, Skeeter's been with us . . ."

Cole held up his hand to hush her, but that wasn't the reason she closed her mouth.

Her mind whirled, trying to think of a way to smooth over the fact that he'd asked one of the men such a leading question before. It was one thing to voice his suspicions of Skeeter privately, and entirely another to say something to Monte when the very question was an insult to one of his crew. Among the Slash A riders, as among the cowboys of any ranch or trail drive worth the name, an insult to one was taken as an insult to all.

But Monte didn't take offense. He didn't bristle with indignation. "Drag," he said, eyeing Cole as if trying to read his mind. "He ain't one of the newest men, but he likes to eat dust, I reckon."

Cole nodded. Skeeter had been volunteering for one of the two drag positions, which most cowboys hated to ride. Monte had told them that without actually informing on Skeeter.

So. Monte must have his own suspicions.

A sick feeling spread through her.

"Right drag?" Cole asked.

"Right."

Cole nodded, and the two men exchanged a look she couldn't quite read before Monte wheeled his horse and rode away.

"Let's lope on out to our own usual position," Cole said, "and once we're over that ridge yonder we'll double back."

"To the breaks over there to the south."

He gave her a long, straight look that held a warning. And sympathy.

"Let's ride," he said.

She worried in silence while they followed his plan, passing the front half of the herd, riding off to the southeast as if on their usual scout, then doubling back under cover of the roll in the land so that when the Slash A riders came on, she and Cole would be out of sight. Then she started worrying out loud.

"We have to be very careful what we say to Skeeter or about him until we know for sure," she said. "I still can't believe it."

He didn't answer for a minute.

"I'm sorry," he finally said. "But if you can drive a herd to Texas, you can face life. It's a hard fact that sometimes people you trust will betray you."

"If we accuse Skeeter without proof, though, the whole crew might quit."

"We'll be careful about that."

His tone held so much empathy for her that

she felt foolish. Cole could handle this.

But she didn't know whether she could, no matter how much noise she had made about being the trail boss. She forced her mind into the present moment.

"You guessed right drag because of the broken country over there," she said.

"Yes. The trees are thick in spots and, in the low places, somebody could hide quite a little herd."

"So you think Skeeter is cutting them out or letting them stray . . ."

"Or even driving them into cover when it's handy," Cole said encouragingly.

"Then Gates's men are gathering them and changing the brands."

"That's about the way I picture it."

"That would explain no tracks to or from the herd in the morning dew," she said.

"And Skeeter calling you to walk in front of the fire the night they shot up our camp."

She turned in the saddle to stare at him. She felt sick, sick enough to throw up.

"We can't prove that," she said. "And how can we prove he's in on this, even when we find the cows? He's long gone with the herd."

"Somebody'll talk," he said. "A noose in a rope does wonders for loosening tongues."

They had to be quiet, then, because voices carried on the wind and bounced back and forth against the rocky land. They kept to dirt footing so as to save the noise of hooves scraping on stone, and they kept their eyes on the sky, looking for smoke.

Along about the middle of the afternoon, they saw it, both of them at almost the same instant.

"By their reckoning, we're too far gone to see the smoke," he whispered. "I'll bet they brand this time every day."

Then, as the smoke grew clearer and closer, he said, "No more talking from here on in."

Thirty yards later they dismounted and tied the horses, crept on in closer to the fire. Aurora found them the best cover, while Cole led her to the most secure spot to see out of it.

Two men, which made sense because Gates was notoriously cheap, were working over a branding fire. Grazing in a small, creek-fed valley were the missing Slash A cattle. Aurora recognized several head of them. Silently, they watched for what seemed to be hours.

Finally, Cole nodded.

"Looks like there're only the two," he whispered. "We'll creep down close and round them up. Yours is the one in the blue shirt. All you have to do is be ready to shoot if he goes for his gun."

She swallowed hard.

"I can do it."

"Play it as it goes. Stay close to me until I signal."

And so, with Aurora's blood roaring in her ears and her heart pounding out of her chest, they made their way closer to the unsuspecting thieves. Finally, Cole waved her away and pointed to a small tangle of bushes. She crept to it, into it, and began to watch and wait some more. Sweat trickled between her breasts and down her spine although the afternoon was a cool one.

She took her gun from her holster and held it in both hands, muzzle trained on the middle of the blue shirt shining in the sun. Trying not to breathe so as not to shake, she prayed that whatever Cole was about to do, he would do it fast.

The rustlers' voices muttered low, the branding iron clinked against a rock when the blue-shirted one turned it in the fire. The other started toward his horse, building a loop to catch another calf.

"Hands up and turn around!"

Cole's voice rang like iron on an anvil.

The roper dropped his rope and whirled, she heard a shot fired, but she didn't let herself look toward the sound even though it jangled everything inside her. The *other* one was her man, and she could only help Cole by taking him out of the fight.

Blue Shirt threw down the branding iron and went for his gun, whirling around to face Cole as he started to stand up. She sighted down the barrel of her gun and jerked the trigger. It seemed to take forever to do that, much less squeeze the trigger slowly, as Cole had taught her.

Blue Shirt fell.

The next thing she knew, she was running, she was out of the bushes and running toward Cole, who was already standing over the man he had shot, bending to pick up his gun. He was taking Blue Shirt's gun when she got to him.

"Are you hurt?" she cried.

"No," he said, looking down at her target.

"I killed him," she cried, following his gaze. "Oh, Cole, I've killed a man."

"Not quite," he drawled, "it's more like you've stunned him."

The fall had knocked the man's hat off, the bullet had left a barely bleeding crease across the back of his neck. But Cole had hit his target more seriously—blood was spreading fast over the man's chest, running down his sleeve.

For a long moment Aurora couldn't speak, couldn't breathe, couldn't think what to do. Cole stuffed both rustlers' guns into the waist of his pants.

"Can you go get their horses?" he asked. "Aurora?"

She looked directly at him. His coolly satisfied expression jolted her back to herself.

"Y-yes."

And she forced her trembling legs to carry her toward the horse saddled and tied to a tree a dozen yards away. The other one saddled for the roper to ride was the other she was supposed to take to Cole. That's all she had to do before she could sit down: get two horses and take them to Cole.

By the time she had done it, though, her heartbeat had slowed, her legs had stopped shaking, and she had realized completely that these cattle with the ugly, messed-up new brand that she couldn't even read were her cattle, part of the only thing she owned and the only livelihood she had. She welcomed the anger that swept through her.

The man she had shot was stirring slightly while Cole tied his hands behind him. The bleeding man was already tied.

"You best git me some help," he said, " 'fore I bleed plumb to death."

"And send the doctor bill to Lloyd Gates?" Cole said. "Reckon he'll take it out of your pay?"

The way he sounded so friendly, so conversational, was a wonder to Aurora, considering the hard set of his jaw. He jerked the last knot tight and dragged Blue Shirt to his horse, threw him over the saddle, and tied him on.

"I may be dyin'," the bleeding man said.

"You ain't that lucky," Cole said in that same nonchalant way. "You'll have to decorate a cottonwood tree before you turn up your toes."

He ripped the man's shirttail from his pants and tore strips of it off. Very quickly, so fast her eyes could hardly follow, he competently packed some of the cloth against the wound and tied the bandage on.

"Too tight," the man gasped.

"Shut up," Cole said.

He dragged the man to the horse Aurora held

and practically threw him into the saddle.

"Let's go," he said.

Each of them leading a horse, they started toward the spot where they'd left their own.

"I kin tell you one thing," the conscious rustler said, "I don't aim t' hang fer Lloyd Gates, the tightfisted son of a bitch. I'll never work fer him agin."

"You're as good as hanged already, son," Cole said. "Save your breath."

They reached their horses and untied them.

"Turn us loose, little lady," the thief said, "and we'll take that snake in the grass Skeeter with us. I'll git rid of him fer you. I never could abide a man that signed on and then wouldn't ride for a brand."

Aurora's eyes met Cole's. Her heart sank like a stone through the soles of her feet. Cole had been right.

But he didn't say so. He only looked at her to see how she was taking the proof she'd demanded.

Never, in all her life, had she wanted to touch him so much as in that instant. She wanted him to kiss her hair and press her head to his chest, cradle her cheek in his big, calloused hand. She wanted it desperately. She wanted him to hold out his open arms and take her in to safety, because her childhood and the world she knew had just been cut out from under her.

She knew by his eyes that he saw that need in her face. But he turned away from it.

"Nice shooting, pardner," was all he said.

# Chapter 13

$\sim\!\!\circ\!\!\mathcal{O}\!\!\mathcal{O}\!\!\circ\!\!\sim$

**"L**ucky* shooting, you mean."
He chuckled.

"After you've shot a thousand rounds you'll know just *how* lucky."

"*You're* the salty shooter."

But she still couldn't think enough to actually have a conversation. As if the whole experience with the rustlers and the disappointment about Skeeter wasn't enough to overwhelm her, the devastating longing for Cole was hollowing her out inside. It was all she could do to turn her back and walk away. She made it to her horse and, after two tries, swung up into the saddle.

"Speaking of rounds," Cole called to her, "always reload as soon as you can."

Her hands were shaking, but she fumbled in her saddlebags for the box of bullets and broke open her gun.

"I hope I never have to shoot at anybody again."

"So do I," Cole said, sympathy in his voice, "but that's not too likely."

It was true and she knew it, but she couldn't worry about it now. And she couldn't bear to think about Cole. Or to look at him. If she saw the same understanding in his eyes that had been in his voice, she'd fall out of her saddle into his arms.

Painful as it was, the best she could do was concentrate on Skeeter to keep her mind off everything else. That thought brought back the sick feeling full force.

Skeeter was Slash A, he was one of her crew, and he had ridden for her father's Flying B ever since she could remember.

She balanced the box of ammunition in front of her and forced her trembling hands to finish loading her rounds. This was life. This was the way things were, sometimes, for no credible reason, like her father killing himself over losing his money. She was a grown-up woman, and she had to accept some facts that made no sense to her.

But her heart and her memory weren't that easily convinced.

"How could he steal from me, day after day? How could he put his buddies to so much trouble riding all those extra miles looking for the missing cows?"

Cole met her anguished look as he stepped up into his saddle.

"Some men ride for a brand with everything in them," he said. "Some don't. Some men tell the truth and some lie. Now you know which kind Skeeter is."

"After twenty-some *years?* Cole, I would've sworn I knew him."

"I'm telling you, one person never truly knows another."

*But I know you. You're still trying to scare me away but I know you. You're good, even if you think you're bad. Even if you can kill your enemies without compunction. You're a good man.*

She replaced the gun in her holster and made sure it was seated safely, slipping the belt around so that the six-shooter was under her hand.

"Skeeter chopped wood for me all last winter. He made me a beautiful headstall and reins to match. He always saddled Shy Boy for me when he was around headquarters."

"And he tried to get you killed," Cole said as he turned his horse and headed back toward the herd, leading one outlaw's horse as Aurora led the other.

"I want to talk to him," she said. "I want to ask him why."

"I want to be there when you do," he said, "but even a woman of your persuasive powers will be wasting breath. I doubt he'll say a word."

She never had a chance to reply. A shot cracked, the bullet whizzed angrily past her ear, close enough to make a breeze against her cheek, near enough to make her scream, and she threw herself prone along Shy Boy's neck. He began to run, the outlaw's horse bumping against them because she'd jerked it up by instinct.

From the corner of her eye she glimpsed Cole pulling his rifle from the saddle scabbard and working the lever in one long, smooth motion. He fired so fast it didn't seem possible. He fired again.

There were more of them! That was the only thought she could hold for more than an instant while she tried to bring her horse around. Gates hadn't been as cheap on hiring help as she'd thought. There were more of them.

She wrapped the reins of the horse she was leading around her horn and reached for the gun in her holster. No telling how many of them Cole was fighting all by himself.

But when she got Shy Boy turning, she saw that Cole would have to fend for himself. There were even more of them.

Two men came on at a high lope, headed straight for her out of some trees, directly to her right, directly behind Cole. She couldn't resist one more glance in his direction. Two. He was fighting two men, two more were coming, so Gates had paid six long riders to come after her cattle.

*Gates.* Rich as a new mother lode and still determined to take everything she had. She lifted her chin as she lifted her gun. She'd show him the meaning of "determined."

Way too soon, she fired one shot, but then she got control. No time to reload, so she had to make the rest of her rounds count.

The one in the lead half-turned in the saddle and yelled, "Hold your fire. Take her alive, remember!"

So. What did dear Lloyd have in mind next? Torturing her until she signed a false bill of sale?

She saw the surprise on the grizzled face of the first outlaw when he realized she was keeping on coming, that she was riding toward instead of away from them. Then she leveled the gun, holding it against her thigh for balance, veered sideways, and fired, wishing she could stop still and use both hands the way Cole had taught her.

The shot missed. A shiver of fear ran through her, then the cry of pain shocked her. The *second* outlaw fell forward, reaching out with both hands as blood spread over the shoulder of his tan shirt. She had fired at one man and hit the other!

Immediately she cocked the gun and levelled it at the first rider again, because he was coming closer, faster. But before she could fire, in the very next instant, he was jerking his horse around, bumping into his partner's horse, and the partner was coming headlong out of the saddle.

When she got there, holding the gun on them with both hands, they seemed to have forgotten her. The man she'd shot had dived off his mount and grabbed onto the tail of his friend's horse, maybe to keep him from riding off and leaving him, and the horse was turning in a frantic circle to get rid of him, his rider trying to help.

"Hands up!" Aurora shouted. "Get your hands *up!*"

The uninjured man complied. The horse kicked the other man, who let go and dropped, unmoving, into a heap at his partner's feet. The horse ran away a short distance to join the other one, taking their long guns out of reach.

Aurora sat her horse, stunned, trying to take it all in while holding her six-shooter as steady as she could. Guns fired and men shouted behind her, but she didn't dare take her eyes from her captives.

"Take off your gunbelt and toss it away," she said, "or I'll shoot."

The unshaven man did as he was told, and not a moment too soon, because in the next instant she had to risk a glance away from him. A horse was pounding toward her, fast.

"Aurora!"

*Cole.* A great terror she had barely recognized gave way to pure relief.

"Still lucky, I see," he said dryly, but that same intense relief was in his voice, underlying the cool nonchalance.

That unfathomable connection between them grew stronger in one leap.

"I shot at this one," she whispered, as he rode up beside her, still leading the horse carrying the first trussed-up rustler, "and hit the other."

He chuckled as he tied the reins he was holding to the saddle horn of the horse Aurora was leading.

"Keep that between us," he said, "at least until I get him tied up."

She held the new rustler in her sights while he went through the process of tying the man's hands behind him.

"Pretty soon you'll be trying to borrow my Chickasaw name," Cole said, and from his tone she realized that he was intending to calm her, to soothe the wild beating of her heart.

"Which is?"

"Shoots-Like-Striking-Lightning."

"It is *not!* You tell me a different story every time."

"But not about the scalping," he said loudly, and threw a fierce look at his captive before he turned him toward his horse. "That story's always the same, right?"

"Right," she said, perversely enjoying the terrified look that flashed across the thief's face. "I think I know how to do it now that you've explained it all."

"Hey!" the man shouted. "You can't do that! This here's not Indian country!"

"It is if I say it is," Cole said, dragging him to his horse. "Do exactly what I tell you if you want to hang with your hair on."

"*Hang!* What're you talking about? All my partner and I are doing is riding through."

"We'll see about that. We've got one of your buddies, who's just itching to tell the sheriff all about it."

"I don't know why you'd believe him instead of me! Ol' Carlile's so windy he'll blow you away."

"You know his name, you know what he'll say, sounds to me like you all are in cahoots."

"Who? Know whose name?"

Cole and Aurora laughed.

"Must shore have been a funny fight," someone shouted. "Sorry we missed it."

Monte and Frank came riding up and swung down to help Cole with the captives. Again, Cole was bandaging the wound with the speed and dispatch of long practice.

"It was a mite serious fight right there at the beginning," Cole said, "seeing as how my partner ran off and left me."

"I did *not!* Shy Boy got spooked having another horse slapping his side at every step, that's all."

Cole turned and grinned at her as he helped tie the man onto his horse, since the rustler obviously couldn't ride, although he was coming around.

"Best to get your horse good broke, then, before you go out gunning for trouble, ma'am."

Monte and Frank laughed with them, everyone needing the relief.

"You can put that hogshooter up now," Cole said to Aurora. "Reckon it'd be safer for us if you'd holster it."

He told Monte and Frank about her missing her target, and they immediately started the inevitable teasing.

She had shot a man and she had meant to do it, although she'd hit the wrong one. It was a strange feeling. But they would've shot her if they hadn't been ordered to take her alive. They had been stealing her cattle with no compunction at all.

Yet the groans of the man she had wounded made her feel terrible.

Gathering the rustlers and their horses, they all started back toward the scene of Cole's battle. Abruptly, he changed directions.

"Let's head for the herd," he said. "Those two aren't going anywhere, and we need to let the trail boss here give out the orders about getting her stolen cows back."

Aurora shot him a grateful look. He was reading her mind again.

"I wanta see that low-down Skeeter with his hands tied, too," one of the rustlers said. "That skunk is guiltier than we are, since we don't even know you, ma'am."

Monte jerked around in the saddle and sent a questioning look at Cole, who answered with a quick nod.

"They mentioned him first thing," he said. "Reckon he's in on it."

Monte and Frank both looked quickly away, embarrassed to hear such a thing about a member of their crew.

"Surely not," Frank drawled in protest.

"Looks bad for him," Cole said.

"I never done such a thing as hanging a compadre of mine," Frank said.

Aurora's heart stopped and then sank. She couldn't imagine hanging anyone, especially not Skeeter.

"We won't hang them," she blurted. "I . . . I want them to stand trial."

Cole looked at her with disbelief.

"You can't spare men from the herd to take them to the nearest law, wherever that is . . ."

"I have to," she said, shocked to think that the fate of these outlaws, their very lives, in fact, rested completely in her hands.

She tried to think.

"Gates isn't here. Are you going to let him off scot-free?"

"No. I'll kill him the next time he crosses my path."

"But what if he doesn't? I can't hold the herd here while you ride back to Pueblo City to find him, and I can't go on without you."

She couldn't break down, not now, not here, but her voice trembled with emotion. Cole heard it, too.

"Sure you can," he said, teasing her with his irresistible grin.

The message in his dark eyes was plain: Buck up. You're doing fine so far. You can get through this.

It made her feel stronger, strong enough to steady her voice and explain herself.

"If there's a trial, the truth will come out about Gates, and maybe he'll be arrested, too."

"Nobody'll believe these waddies against upstanding citizen Gates," Cole said with a gesture of disgust.

"I'm thinkin' they will," said one of the rustlers, the one whose horse Cole was now leading. "I know plenty on Gates, and I aim to tell it all t' try t' save my own skin."

"I'm with you, Petey," said the other fully conscious one. "I've worked for the son of a buck for a lot of years."

"Always as a brand artist?" Cole said.

"No. Everything from salting gold mines to stolen horses sold under a false bill of sale."

"There might be some proof on paper of some of that," Cole said, "but Gates is smart, and he's had a lot of practice at rubbing out his backtrail."

They fell into their own thoughts as they picked up the pace. Aurora's heart grew heavier still with dread as soon as the wagons came in sight. She hated so much to confront Skeeter, yet she had to know why he would betray her after all their years of friendship. The very thought made her want to cry.

Cookie had built a fire and had coffee ready.

"Sounded like a war out there," he said, looking Aurora over with sharp concern in his eyes. "You ain't hurt?"

"Only my feelings," she said. "Where's Skeeter?"

The same embarrassment as Frank's and Monte's passed over the old man's face. He turned away.

"I reckoned we'd need stout coffee and boilin' water, both," he said.

"You were right," she said. "Where's Skeeter?"

"Skeeter's gone. Skedaddled."

"Did he say where he was headed?"

"Said the owl hoot trail."

He turned to face her again.

"He said t' tell you he'd give his right arm to change things if it would. Said Gates had him plumb trapped into followin' his orders or gettin' hanged fer somethin' Skeeter done a long time ago. He heerd them shots you all was throwin' around and he lit outta here like a scalded hound."

"For all Skeeter knew, these men could've died in the fight and he could've gone on like before with none of us the wiser."

"Nope. Said he'd druther ride the coulees than live another day all wire-edged and walkin' the fence."

The hollow feeling inside her grew larger and larger. Skeeter was gone. Skeeter was guilty. There was nothing she could do about him.

"Want us to carry this bunch back to the trees and have a little necktie party, Miss Aurora?" Monte said. "Now that Skeeter ain't amongst 'em?"

"No!" she said, more fiercely than she'd intended. "We'll take them to the law."

She turned and rode away from them all, around behind her wagon, and stopped in its shade. After a moment, she stepped down and then just stood there, leaning her forehead against Shy Boy's sweaty shoulder.

"So Skeeter's gone," Cole said.

She whirled to look at him, tears welling up at the sympathy in his voice.

"At least he had a *reason*," she said. "At least he was trying to save himself and not stealing from me out of greed."

"I reckon that's right," he said softly and looked at her closely before he swung down off his horse.

Oh, dear God, if only he would hold her! She needed the comfort of his iron arms around her and his hard chest beneath her cheek like she had never needed anything else in all her life. He walked straight toward her.

"But you have to see it plain, what he did to you, and not cut him too much slack," he said. "Remember how tough you have to be if you're going to carve a ranch out of nothing."

She managed a shaky smile.

"I know. It's just that Skeeter always . . ."

He opened his arms and she went into them, into the hard circle of comfort that his body closed around her. She laid her cheek on his chest and wanted, with all her being, to melt against him, into him.

But he wasn't holding her that way.

"You can't be sentimental," he said. "In the future you'll have to hire men you don't know, so you must judge them with clear eyes."

The trembling she'd felt earlier came back

through her, and she nearly froze. How could she *do* it alone?

Suddenly it sounded entirely overwhelming, the thought of hiring strange men, riding herd on the cattle, building some kind of shelter for her and her men, and shooting outlaws and rustlers on top of it all. She didn't even know a decent *location* for her new ranch—what if it had to be in a place that was hard to defend?

"Oh, Cole," she said, "I don't know if I can handle it all."

"Yes, you can. You've come too far to back out now if you wanted to. And you don't want to. Building a ranch of your own is entirely possible."

"But how can you say that? You had to do most of the shooting today, although I did do a little. The crew is taking care of the cattle— I'm scouting, yes, but I'm not herding or branding or cooking . . ."

She was on the verge of bursting into sobs, but he wouldn't let her. He took her chin in his hand, turned her face up to his, and fixed her with a straight, stern look.

". . . what if I had to try to do it all myself?"

"You couldn't. Neither could a man rancher. Don't let this one traitor make you think your whole crew'll leave you. They're decent men. They'll stick until you can replace them if they want to go—and don't think that's special treatment because you're a woman. It'd be the same with a man."

Already, the helpless feeling was leaving her.

"Sometimes I just think what in the world have I done, dragging these cattle and this crew—and you—way out here to go even farther down the trail, risking everybody's lives without even knowing what we'll find when we get to the Panhandle."

"We know we'll find grass and plenty of room," he said, still holding her with that sharp look. "Listen to me. You've made the right decisions, time after time. You've proved you can defend yourself—and without letting go of your first rustler to boot!"

She swallowed hard around the lump in her throat.

"That's what spooked my mount. I should've turned the other horse loose but I couldn't uncurl my fingers from around those reins."

"Now you're talking, Rory. Never give up a prisoner."

The nickname sent a thrill running through her. No one else had ever called her Rory.

"Cole," she said, "thanks for encouraging me. And thanks for not saying 'I told you so' about Skeeter."

"Never," he said. "You lost a friend."

That made her tears well up and spill over. She fought them back and resolved not to think about Skeeter any more.

"So you really think I can do it?"

"I know you can. You're fractious today because of the gunplay and the blood and your own cowboy betraying you. But that's why I'm trying to toughen you up, because this is real, it's the way life is. Don't worry, you can ride it to a standstill."

"Not so long ago you were telling me to sell the herd."

"Because of days like this. You could've been killed. My God, Rory," he said, and he tightened his arms around her, opened his stance just a fraction to pull her closer in, "you could've been captured and . . . mishandled."

She shivered. She hadn't even thought of that.

"I'd hate so bad to see you hurt," he said in that low, slow drawl that poured pure heat all the way to her bones.

Without thinking, she clung to his slender waist, came up onto tiptoe to bring her mouth nearer his.

But he didn't bend to kiss her. He wanted to, though. She could feel it.

"But if any woman can build a ranch in the Panhandle of Texas, you're the one," he said, looking deep into her eyes. "You're a strong woman. Now it's time to get stronger."

She shook her head.

"This is the biggest irony. Remember the first conversation we ever had? You have completely switched sides, Cole McCord."

He gave her his mischievous grin.

"That's because it's too late for me to back out now."

She stayed where she was, but still he made no move.

"You're too far from home down the trail with your fate in my hands, is that it?"

"Right," he said, flashing that grin again as if he'd never wanted to kiss her in his entire life. "That's why I want you strong and savvy."

"And sassy, too?"

She tilted her head and smiled up at him in her most flirtatious way, letting her gaze wander from his eyes to his lips, waiting for him to kiss her. They had never felt so close. At least he surely would *kiss* her!

But when he took her shoulders in both his big hands he set her a step away from him instead of pulling her up to take her mouth with his.

"Remember what you said today about me being a salty shooter?"

"Yes, Lightning, I remember."

He smiled but quickly went solemn again.

"That's what I am," he said fiercely. "That's *all* I am. Don't be thinking I'm more."

A cold wind blew through her.

"So that proves you're bad, is that what you're trying to tell me?"

He gave that quick, abrupt nod of authority that always made his silences more commanding than other men's words.

She looked at his strong, brown hands on her shoulders, at the right one, then at the left.

"And holding me away from you when I want to kiss you and hug your neck as I would any other friend is . . . what? A noble gesture? If you're really bad, Shoots-Like-Striking-

Lightning, you'd throw me to the ground and ravish me right here like you're wanting to do."

The fleeting glint of shock in his eyes made her raise her eyebrows in triumph, but he wouldn't acknowledge it.

"You and I are as far from being like any other friends," he growled, "as a badger is from a bear. You know that."

"I know you're not bad," she said, looking steadily into his eyes. "And I can prove it."

"How?"

"Because you're traveling to see your partner's widow. Because a man who was bad wouldn't bother."

This time she let the triumph into her voice as well as her eyes.

Again he ignored it.

"You don't know enough to even talk about that."

"And you're encouraging me to take heart. You're telling me I can do this incredible thing and you've got me believing again that I can. You care, for *my* sake, whether I can do it."

He frowned at her, but he didn't let her go.

"Bad men don't do things like that," she said.

"You are, without a shadow of a doubt, the stubbornest woman I have ever met in all my life."

"And you are the stubbornest man in mine."

Her calm, judgmental tone made them both laugh. He turned her loose, and they stood looking at each other for a long time.

But still he wouldn't kiss her.

"I've gotta see about our visitors," he said, when she thought she couldn't bear it any more not to reach for him.

He turned away, but then he stopped.

"Your shooting'll improve with practice," he said lightly. "You did fine today. Another week or two of shooting airtights every night and you won't even need me anymore."

*I will! I will need you forever!*

That was the truth. She reached for Shy Boy's solid bulk, felt behind her with both hands for it, clung to her stirrup leather and leaned back against him.

She would need Cole forever.

Without his hard hands on her, without the glint in his chocolate eyes, without the wry drawl of his voice, she would float up into the sky and drift away from the very earth. She felt as if that could happen any minute.

Oh, dear God, what could she do? Surely her need for him was only physical. That must be it. He was the only man she'd ever lain with, and that was why she thought she couldn't do without him.

That and the thought that she needed him to protect her. Soon she'd be able to do that for herself, to rely only on herself, as she'd done all her life.

Yes, by the end of the trail she'd be able to let him go because they weren't going to make love any more. And that was good—she might fall in love with him if they did. That would *never* do. She would be powerless to keep him with her always, for the restlessness in him was infinite.

They weren't going to make love any more. Cole wouldn't even kiss her.

Something changed between them after that day. He learned that he was a stronger man than he had ever thought he could be. He had refrained from doing more than taking her into his arms when she was wanting him to kiss her. Right then they'd grown close as two pine saplings, yet as far apart as the moon and the stars.

But thinking about it did no good whatsoever. Maybe he ought to admit the truth, that instead of being strong he'd only been scared.

His heart had been open right then, open like an abyss, because he'd realized she could've been shot or raped, and that had shaken him to the core. God knew, he had to get a grip on himself, for he cared way too much about her. He'd told her the truth when he'd said he'd be bad for her. For her sake, if for no other reason, he could never stay with her.

Cole stepped up into the saddle and looked ahead, out over the land that should be the last of the two days of dry drive. Dawn was still just a shadow on the horizon, the moon was still high, but they were moving out anyway, after traveling until midnight as they had done for the past two nights. He stood in the stirrups and stretched his arms into the air, moved them in circles trying to get waked up.

Damn! He must be getting old. A hot breakfast in his belly only made him sleepy now, when normally it and the four hours' sleep he'd had would've made him good to ride all the way to the Rio Grande and fight the whole Mexican Army when he got there.

What was he doing thinking about staying with Rory, anyhow? His mind normally didn't run like that, never, for he was nothing but a renegade drifter, and that was the God's truth. He cared too much about her, but it wasn't the usual attraction a woman had for him, he wasn't falling for her or anything like that. He admired her, that was all.

He sat his saddle, rubbing old Border's neck and murmuring to him, trying not to think about it. But his thoughts went right back to her like a stud to a mare.

She was the most courageous woman he'd ever known, and it wasn't blind courage, either. She knew what she was facing, yet there had been not a doubting peep out of her since that day they'd got the rustlers.

The only reason she had faltered then was because one thing Rory was was loyal beyond measure. Loyal to a fault. She could not hurt Skeeter, even though he'd betrayed her.

He grinned and glanced toward her wagon, which was already hitched to its mules, where she was doing God knew what, getting ready to ride. Rory.

He always called her Rory now, and she called him only Lightning, and they tended to read each other's thoughts without words. That was the damndest thing. She had read him like a book ever since they met, but now he could read her, too.

She pulled back the canvas door and stepped down from the wagon, flashing a wide smile at the twin who was on his way through the darkness to drive it.

"Good morning, Nate," she called to him. "Gonna find water today."

"Yes, ma'am! Reckon we'll get us a bath?"

"Could be. I'm sure hoping so, aren't you?"

Her voice was as cheerful as a chirping bird's on the morning air. He shook his head in wonder. That was what he admired about her the most, it must be—her determined cheerfulness ever since that day Skeeter had ridden for the sunset.

A sullenness, a tension, had fallen over the crew as they sat around the fire that night, learning Skeeter's sins from the talkative thief, and the mood wasn't quite gone yet. An anecdote would come up, and before the storyteller could stop it, he'd realize that Skeeter figured in it. Or just in the course of the work someone would mention his name. But it didn't help for everyone to be on guard not to speak it, either. There was a bitterness of betrayal in the air, made worse somehow by the fact that it had gone unpunished, yet when that was stated out loud, others pointed out how bad it would've been to have to turn over one of their own to the law, maybe to be hanged.

And the fact that they'd known the dry drive was coming hadn't helped any, either. They all dreaded that, Rory especially, but she had teased the crew and jollied them around and kept that smile on her face day after day, quicksand or no, cactus or no. Gallant, he'd call it.

Then she was running lightly toward him and her horse, and he stepped off Border Crossing to give her a leg up. Even the feel of her small foot in his palm would stay with him all day.

"You don't have to do that, Lightning," she said softly. "If I'm going to be a rancher I certainly should be able to mount by myself."

"You can," he said. "When you *are* a rancher."

She gave him a playful swat.

"I am now, and you better know it."

"No, you're not. You've gotta have land to put these critters out to graze."

"Boy, are you particular," she said. "I thought I could just keep 'em moving forever."

"Delightful as this trip is," he said as he remounted, "I think we'd finally want to end it. Especially when the blue northers blow."

"Aw, come on, Cole, cowboy up," she said. "Driving in a blizzard is just when it gets interesting."

Then she rode out a little way so she could see most of the crew.

"We should reach water about midday," she

called to them, "and they won't graze well this early, so push them on. Cole and I'll carry the lantern until good daylight but if you men on drag can't see it, don't worry. Let 'em hold a good pace."

"Another good decision," he said as she rode back to him with the lighted lantern Cookie handed to her.

"Thank you so much," she said with light sarcasm. "An old trail hand like you ought to know."

"I've may have gone up the trail all the way to Montana for all you know," he said, as she raised the lantern and led off. "I've had a lot of experiences you know nothing about."

"I don't doubt that for a minute," she said, her eyes straight ahead on the trail, "and I'd be willing to bet that most of them I don't *want* to know."

Then they set a good pace and quit talking.

They were never very far apart, though, even after the sun came up. They never were, not for long, but they both were careful not to touch. He couldn't get away from her because his job was to protect her, yet he couldn't truly be with her because they would become too attached.

It was torture, pure and simple, Cole decided, an ordeal that a god with a sense of humor had concocted to punish him for his sins.

# Chapter 14

Another week of hard driving, but this one with sufficient watering places, and they struck the endless grasslands of the Llano Estacado. Aurora and Cole rode far ahead of the herd onto the lush, waiting range, as awestruck as if they were entering the promised land. The only sound for half a mile was that of their stirrups swishing through the tall buffalo grass. At last, Cole spoke.

"We're here. You did it, Rory."

She turned to smile at him.

"But where's here?"

They laughed. Out here, a person could look for miles in every direction beneath an even more infinite sky.

"You expect to find a ranch house, outbuildings and corrals with a sign reading Slash A hanging over the yard gate?"

"Why not? We deserve that, after all we've been through."

He shook his head.

"Greedy, greedy," he said ruefully. "All I've heard for two months now is 'get this herd to Texas' and now that they're here you're angling for your work to be done already so you can settle down and wait for winter."

A little stab of panic shot through her. Winter. Cole would be gone.

But that wasn't what was making her feel suddenly so forlorn. Not at all, because she was prepared for that. She had always known it.

No, it was the land itself. Somehow, this land felt bigger and more lonesome than any they'd passed through. Maybe the Comanches weren't the only reason the Llano had been left unsettled.

"Building a house and corrals isn't even half of it," she said. "We've got to ride herd on these cattle every day. They could drift from here to Fort Worth with nothing to stop them, straight into the clutches of every outlaw and settler and traveler or trader that comes along."

Cole took a long look around.

"Doubt we'll have that worry today."

She laughed, then sobered.

"I wonder how far we'd have to ride to find another person," she said, some of her desolate feeling creeping into her voice.

"Like a merchant with a store full of supplies or a dressmaker or a milliner or a . . ."

"Isn't that just like a man!"

She put her fists on her hips in mock anger and entered into the game for the distraction he was offering. She had worked too hard to get here to let the awful, let-down feeling take her over.

"You think just because I'm a woman I'll be pining away for new clothes and hats with feathers on them. What do you expect? That I'll be branding calves and sawing logs in my Sunday best?"

He grinned.

"I don't see any trees."

She glared at him.

"Mixing adobe, then!"

"That's my stubborn Rory," he said. "Don't let anything stop you."

That last word rang like a bell in the air between them.

He would be gone. By the time her hands started helping her build a house, *whatever* materials they had to use, Cole would be gone.

*You.* That sounded so strange after weeks and weeks of *we* and *us.*

Soon he'd be gone, and she would never see him again. The thought hollowed her heart right out of her body.

*Don't go. Stay, Cole. Don't go.*

The whishing of their stirrups through the grass echoed the desperate whispering in her heart.

*Stay. Touch me, Cole. I'm dying of this blazing pain.*

How could she have known that going to his bed for one adventure, one new experience, would set her on fire for him? That it would call for more and more, forever?

How could she have known that his arms would be so strong, his hands so skilled, his lips so hot?

How could she hold that memory in her heart for all her life without it burning her to ashes?

For the next few days, while they held the herd on the banks of the Canadian River and made forays to the south and east looking for ranch sites, she fought the mysterious bond that had pulled her and Cole together since the moment they'd met. It had been created from her need for protection from Gates, that was all, and now that need was gone.

Whatever had come out in the trials of Gates's henchmen, whatever had been proved against him, his name had been dragged through the mud sufficiently to stop him for now. Plus now she had taken the herd so far from Pueblo City and into such a vast, untracked country that she would be devilishly hard to find.

She didn't need Cole any more, she told herself constantly. She didn't need him. What she needed was to pay attention to her business of ranching.

Several days in one place and on the lush graze rested the remuda and the cattle and put flesh back onto them at a heartening rate. The last hard weeks of the drive were no longer evident in the animals or the men, who rested while she and Cole rode mile after mile. They found no sign of other people and no good source of water for a ranch site unless they stayed on the river.

One morning, as they were saddling their horses, Aurora began to decide that that was what they'd have to do and said as much to Cole.

"Not good," he said. "Any bandido riding across the Llano—and there are plenty even though we haven't seen them—will be following the river. There are *comanchero* camps on it. We need to get you situated in a more private place because you'll have enough to contend with without every bunch of long riders in the country dropping in for breakfast."

"I'm more worried about them running off my cattle."

"Or worse," he said, pulling his latigo tight and securing it.

"Riders coming," Cookie called from his post at the coffeepot hanging over the fire. "Half a dozen of 'em. Lookin' fer breakfast, no doubt."

In spite of his grumbling, his voice held excitement. It had been so long a time since they had had news of any world but their own or talked to anyone not in their outfit that all the men except the two who were assigned to the herd wandered back toward the fire for another cup of coffee.

"What'd I tell you?" Cole muttered.

Then he turned and called to the crew.

"Could be comancheros. Stay close to your guns, men, and keep your eyes open."

He had already put his rifle in its saddle scabbard, but now he drew it out.

The leader of the newcomers rode out a little ahead of the others.

"Hello, the camp," he called in Spanish-accented English. "Rudy Gomez, *mesteñero*, at your service."

"Wild horse hunters," Cole said. "Watch yourself, Rory, maybe kind of stay out of sight until we find out if that's what they really are."

"Stay out of *sight*? This is my camp!"

He grinned.

"I thought that's what you'd say. But if they're a bunch of cutthroats they might try to take us and carry you off as a prize."

She laughed.

"That's what I hired you for, Cole McCord. To prevent that kind of happening."

"I mean it," he said dryly. "The very sight of you could incite them to kill us all to get to you."

"Light-ning! You should be called He Who Is Full of Hot Wind."

He gave her a crooked, teasing grin, held her gaze with his in that knowing look that bonded them beyond belief. She thought for a minute that he was about to kiss her.

Heat rose in her blood. Never. She could never let him do that again.

She knew it all the way through her bones and her sinews, now that she was living in torment. Cole McCord was a wise man. The kiss she had begged for at her wagon that day would only have made the torture a thousand times worse.

"Have you forgotten our potentially dangerous guests?" she whispered.

He shook his head.

"You *are* beautiful this morning, Rory," he blurted in an uncharacteristically unguarded moment. "You're a definite danger to us all."

She had to reach for more air.

He was still wanting her as much as she wanted him. Oh, dear Lord, what would happen if he made her be the strong one?

Finally she found a few words and a light tone.

"Are you getting sick? Going soft in the head? That doesn't sound like you, Lightning, throwing compliments in all directions at the crack of dawn."

He laughed, but the serious hunger for her flashed in his eyes for an instant. It roused an answering desire in her, one so sharp it took her breath away completely.

"I know you won't hide," he said at last, "but keep your hand near your gun and stay close to me."

*That's all I want to do. Stay close to you.*

Somehow, she made her feet move and her legs hold her up. Somehow, she walked beside him, wishing he would touch her, aching to touch him, and they went out to meet their rough-looking visitors.

Gomez didn't bother with the names of any of his men, three of whom appeared to be grizzled, hard-looking Anglos. But they all sat their horses until asked to get down, and they didn't mention food until invited to eat. They weren't too clean, and their clothes and gear were well-worn, but they seemed to be friendly, at least, and intending no harm. With a hot meal in their stomachs, they rolled smokes and accepted a second cup of coffee.

"Had any luck with the mustangs?" Monte asked.

Gomez nodded.

"We have spotted several small bands of them," he said. "We find them. We look to see if there are bigger bands, then we catch some."

The conversation immediately turned to methods of catching wild horses.

"We used to drive 'em into a lake," Frank said, "tire 'em out fightin' the mud and the water."

"You have a hard time to find a lake around here," a small, older mesteñero said, and everyone laughed. "And this river is too full of quicksand."

"How about box canyons?" Monte said. "It's easy to make a trap to drive them into a box canyon."

"*Si*, we do that sometime," Gomez said, and he and Frank began exchanging advice on that method.

Aurora liked the old mesteñero with the twinkly eyes who had said there was no lake, and she felt bad the others had cut him out of the conversation before he'd gotten into it.

"*Are* there any box canyons near here big enough to hold a band of wild horses?" she asked him.

He widened his snapping black eyes and laughed.

"Big enough," he said wonderingly, and shook his head as he took a sip of his coffee. "Big enough. Is *uno* canyon big enough to hold the earth."

He spoke so reverently, with such awe in his voice, that it piqued her interest.

"Near here?"

He shrugged.

"Mucho, mucho far."

He busied himself with his coffee again, then leaned forward to take the last biscuit from the Dutch oven near the fire. He ate it in two big bites and stared into the distance, seeming to forget the conversation.

"Have you seen it?" Aurora persisted. "This big canyon."

"Oh, *si*," he said.

He held up a gnarled forefinger.

"*Uno dias.*"

One day. He'd been to the canyon one time.

"*Es grande*," he said. "*Muy grande.*"

He set down his tin cup and opened his arms to show how huge it was.

"*Una ciudad*," he said, "can be on its floor."

He stretched his arms even wider.

"*Agua*," he said, "creeks *y uno* big creek. *Los arboles*, the trees, and *muchas* . . . grasses."

He patted the grass where he sat.

An indescribable thrill ran through Aurora's bones. This sounded like the tallest of tall tales, but it wasn't. She could hear the truth in his voice, see the surety in his eyes.

Water and trees. A canyon would be a protected place on these endlessly exposed high plains. It might be perfect for her ranch.

She looked into the bright, twinkling eyes until she saw that the old man knew she believed him.

"Can you take me there, *señor?*"

He stared back at her with a look as serious as her own.

"*Si.*

"I will pay you to be my guide."

He waved away the suggestion.

"No, you must take pay," she said. "Scouts work hard, and they earn their pay."

Cole had been listening to them the whole time, even while he'd been joining in the wild horse talk—she realized that when he leaned across her and spoke to the old man in fluent, rapid Spanish that was much better than her awkward efforts. *Why* had she studied French in Philadelphia? Spanish was what she needed now.

"He'll take you to the canyon for ten head of horses," he said. "He claims money is of no use to him."

"Ask if five head can be delivered when we find the canyon," she said, "and five this time next year. We'll need lots of fresh horses while we're building shelters and getting settled."

When Cole translated that, the old man laughed.

"*La señorita*," he said, nodding sagely. "She will be here next year. She is a tough one, this *señorita*."

He wasn't making fun of her, though. The teasing glint in his eye held an edge of respect, and so did his voice.

He reached up and tipped his sombrero to her.

"Gabriel Martinez," he said.

"Aurora Benton," she replied.

They didn't shake hands, they didn't touch, but they sealed a bargain with their eyes. They trusted each other. They would be friends.

An hour or so later, the mesteñeros got to their feet and said their good-byes. All except Señor Martinez.

"I work for La Señorita," he told them.

And then, in a long spate of Spanish, he bid them good-bye.

"He's staying with you until this time next year," Cole told her, after listening to Gabriel and his friends.

His eyes were twinkling as much as Gabriel's had been.

Then he burst out laughing.

"You've been shorthanded since we threw the cattle on the trail," he said. "Now you have a new Slash A man."

She stared at him, surprised.

"He's staying with us until he gets all his horses?"

"Yes, but it's not because he doesn't trust you to pay. He told his friends he wants to eat some good cooking for a change."

"Oh, no, don't tell Cookie that," she cried, "or his head will be too big for his hat. We'll never hear the end of his bragging."

Cole was still laughing.

"*Or* the end of his grumbling," she said. "He'll whine about another mouth to feed until this time next year."

"Gotta be careful what kind of deals you make, Miss Rory. Maybe you should've paid all the horses up front."

"Laugh if you want," she said. "But I'll gladly feed and shelter Señor Martinez for the rest of his *life* if that canyon is everything he says it is."

Cole rode with Rory and Gabriel south from the herd for several days, finally ending up wandering across the plains with the old man almost in despair because he was so confused by the many other canyons they came across. Cole marvelled that he didn't feel the least impatience with the wild-goose chase, that he found himself perfectly content to ride alongside his pair of unlikely companions over mile after mile of the huge, wild country.

Maybe it was because he and Rory were no longer alone, and, even though that didn't lessen his desire for her, it did set a boundary that made him feel freer to watch her for hours, to drink in the sound of her husky voice and think about everything she said. He was becoming as weak and pathetic as any drunkard or inveterate gambler who ever drew breath, he thought, as he saddled their horses on the morning of their seventh day out from camp. He had to have the crutch of a third person there to bolster his self-control where Rory was concerned, so he must be sliding downhill fast.

"Thanks, Cole," Rory said, as she came to take Shy Boy's reins. "I was just telling Gabe that we have supplies enough for two more days and then we'll have to turn back."

The strangest combination of relief and regret ran through him.

"You think the old man dreamed the whole thing?"

"Oh no," she said as she swung up into the saddle, "it's real and he can find it. We'll just have to go back and re-outfit ourselves."

The flat surety in her tone made Cole laugh.

"Sorry to have asked such a stupid question."

"It surprised me, that's all," she said with a grin, "since you're always pointing out how stubborn I am."

They turned their horses and rode to where Gabriel was waiting with his mount.

"I think ride south," he said, kicked his horse into a trot, and led the way.

Only a couple of hours later, when the morning sun was filling the plains with yellow light and the prairie birds were calling, dipping in and out of the deep grasses, the three of them suddenly rode up onto the rim of a color-flaming canyon whose bottom lay so far down it took their breath away. The level land beneath them dropped away so abruptly that the horses snorted and stepped back and Aurora cried out that it made her dizzy. But she couldn't stop looking into it, and neither could Cole.

Gabriel was clapping his hands with joy.

*"Al fin! Al fin!"* he cried.

"Yes," Aurora said absently as she stared into a paradise watered by a wide creek with willows and cedars growing along its banks. "At last. At last."

Then the three of them dismounted in silence, as if the vision before them would vanish if they spoke again, and peered down into the wild chasm, mesmerized. The entire valley was carpeted with buffalo grass.

"Graze and water," Rory said softly, "and it's protected from the weather and from intruders. I don't even see a trail down the sides."

"Ees a trail to the east," Gabriel said. *"Vamanos."*

But not one of them moved. The sight held them captive, filling their eyes with dozens of shades of spring green, with bold bright stripes of reds and vermilions stacked eight hundred feet deep.

Cole's heart twisted in his chest. It looked like heaven, which is what it would be to live in it with Aurora.

"Come," he said brusquely, "let's see what's down there."

Still hardly able to look away from such beauty, they reached for their reins and mounted up. They rode along the top at a trot, keeping an eye on the way the canyon lay, the way it widened and narrowed.

"We can make the headquarters easy to defend," Rory said. "We can barricade one of the narrow places if we have to."

"Right," Cole said.

Then, for the sake of his own discipline, to prove he could face the truth, he made himself say it.

"You could do that for sure."

*She* could. This would be *her* place. It had nothing to do with him.

But she wasn't thinking about that, not now, with her eyes full of her new ranch. The minute she was settled, the minute she felt secure here, she'd forget all about him.

"The trail!" Gabriel cried, as they rode around a small bend in the rim.

Clearly, it was an old Indian trail, one worn into the side of the cliff by thousands of moccasined feet, a narrow path that wound in and out of the natural contours of the land, hugging the shape of the earth's side, looping back into itself and then leading down again. It was probably a thousand feet from the spot where they stood at the top of it to the bottom on the canyon floor.

"This entrance could be guarded too," Rory said, elation filling her voice. "Let's explore and see if it's the only way in, at least for this section of the canyon. It seems to go on for miles and miles."

How could he ever feel alive again without hearing that husky chortle of hers? How could he ever *be* alive without her?

"Let's go," he said, suddenly desperate to get this over with, eager to be done and be gone, anxious to be free of the torment he couldn't escape as long as he was with her.

Gabriel insisted on leading the way, since he'd gone down this trail and a short way into the valley when he and his companions had discovered it. Cole put Rory in the middle and he followed, trying not to watch her natural seat in the saddle, trying to put his mind onto the surroundings. Danger. He had to think about danger. Anyone or anything could be looking at them from the opposite wall or lurking in the trees in the valley.

Not even that thought could occupy him fully, though, for no bad man or wild animal could be more fearsome than this pain in his heart.

As soon as they descended past the rim, Aurora could feel the magic of the place growing more powerful, could feel its beauty reaching out to enfold her. And she could see that it was even more perfect for her purposes than she had thought.

"Oh, look," she called to Cole, looking back at him over her shoulder. "The caprock will keep in any cattle who graze far up the sides of the canyon—although the thick grass at the bottom will keep them off the sides most of the time, anyway. Oh, and can you believe it actually has plenty of water?''

He nodded agreement after a moment, as if he hadn't been listening to her at first. Then he scowled at her.

''Watch where you're going,'' he snapped. ''It's a thousand-foot drop to the bottom.''

''My *horse* is watching,'' she snapped back.

Stung, she turned around. What was the matter with him, anyhow? They'd just wandered all over the face of the earth for days without a complaint and now that they'd found what they'd been searching for, he had to turn into a grouch.

The scents of cedar and sage floated on the air, along with the cry of a red-tailed hawk. Wildflowers bloomed in scattered patches all along the big, swift-running creek. Or maybe it was a river.

''I want the headquarters to be near the creek,'' she said. ''I want to let its splashing put me to sleep at night.''

''You won't need that,'' Cole said wryly. ''You'll be tired enough to sleep.''

*I hope. I do hope so. I hope I'm so tired I don't have any strength left to think about you.*

Once she reached the bottom, the canyon was like a huge wonderland, tempting her to go in every direction at once. She chose to explore the north side of the creek and then the south, with Cole and Gabriel riding near enough to keep her in sight.

"This feels like a haven," she said. "I can't imagine danger here, at least not from people."

"Imagine it," Cole said. "A whole bunch of cutthroat comancheros could have a hideaway in here."

She made a face at him, but he wasn't looking at her.

"I can feel it," she said. "There's nobody but us in this whole canyon."

"Stubborn," he muttered, but he let it drop.

They explored the canyon for several miles each way, disturbing rabbits and birds. They listened to the calling of crows and the whistle of a cardinal, saw the tracks of deer and turkey in the sand near the river, rode until the sun was directly overhead and then past, hardly talking because the high walls hemming them in and the soothing rustle of the cottonwood leaves in the wind made them feel they had entered the very heart of the earth. At least, that's how it felt to Aurora. The changing light played on the greens of the grasses and the junipers and all the other trees, turned some of the reds on the walls to purples and lavenders, whitened the cottonwood leaves.

Spring. The greens were spring greens—all of the canyon was alive, bursting with spring. All of it called to her, filled up her senses, yet set her yearning for more. This place was meant to be her home.

Cole was feeling that same pull to the earth.

"If a man was ever going to settle down, this would surely be the place," he said as they stopped and got down to drink from the main stream of the river, which was running over rocks—clear water, fine as the air.

And then, before Aurora could begin to sort out the feelings those words roused in her, he quickly tried to recall them. Or deny them. Or something.

"I never will settle, though," he said, and drank from the cold water he scooped up in his hand.

A whole gamut of emotions swirled through her, with a stinging anger on top. He *had* to say that—as if she could pounce on one, unguarded remark of his and use it to rope him and tie him down. As if she *would*.

"Some people don't," Aurora said coolly. "And say they can't."

She bit her lip. She had not meant to say that, had not meant to answer.

"How do you know what another person can do?"

Gabriel threw them a curious glance, responding to the undercurrents in their voices.

"A person can do whatever he or she *wants* to do or *has* to do," she said and finished her own drink, stood up, and turned away.

Let him wander the face of the earth for the rest of his life, for all she cared.

Aurora walked away from the men and the horses drinking from the river and looked up at the marvelous walls of the gorge. A great sense of happiness flowed up through all the feelings churning in her, a sense of powerful rightness. This was her new ranch. Next, the best place for the headquarters would have to reveal itself.

She found it an hour later as they rode up the north bank of the creek, back to within eyesight of the winding Indian trail that they'd taken down into the canyon, the only entrance they had found in their hours of exploring.

"Here," she said. "Stop here."

It was a beautiful spot, a perfect cove in the side of the gorge, wrapped securely by the high walls, watched over by junipers and cottonwoods, watered by the creek that within a stone's throw flowed into one coming from the south and began to swell into the river. Home. This would be her home.

The three of them dismounted and walked around under the canopy of trembling leaves, thinking of protection from the snow and cold, from the sun and wind, from intruders. They could find no fault.

Gabriel led the horses away to be watered again before they began the long climb up and out to go bring back the herd and the cowboys.

"We'll put the headquarters buildings like this," Aurora said, pacing back and forth, trying to see the whole setting at once. "The house over there so that one huge cottonwood can be in the front yard, the first barn a hundred yards to the south . . ."

"That'll work," Cole said.

He sounded completely noncommittal, as if he could care less. And he sounded abruptly impatient, as if he wanted to cut her off.

She turned to look at him.

He stood with one leg bent, his boot heel against the trunk of a mulberry tree, his long, powerful body all hipshot and loose in that way he had of looking relaxed and wary at the same time. In that way that never failed to make the center of her womanhood contract deep inside her, that way that made her yearn to beckon him to come to her so she could watch that panther's prowl searching her out as his prey.

Her breath caught in her throat. He stared off into the blue distance of the sky over the south wall of the gorge, one thumb hooked into his belt, his hat pushed to the back of his head. The sunlight slanted in beneath the leaves to limn his high cheekbones and the curve of his lips, showed his face so darkly handsome that it broke her heart.

He wasn't looking at the house site. And he was nowhere near relaxed. He was waiting. Waiting to be gone from her.

"Well, fine," she said. "Let's go."

She would help him get his job done as soon as possible if that was what he wanted.

That would be best for her, too. She *needed* him to be gone.

Without another glance at him, she walked toward the horses. He couldn't settle in one place, no matter what she had told him earlier. It was his nature to drift, as it was for so many other men. He would never change.

He would never stay.

But then *why* did she have that feeling of being connected to him, a feeling even stronger than her feeling for this valley?

# Chapter 15

~~~◇◇◇~~~

"**P**alo Duro," Gabriel said as they topped the rim and sat their horses to let them blow.

He gestured down toward the beautiful, wild valley they had just left. "*Se llamo* Palo Duro."

So it had a name. She didn't know what *palo* meant, and she was in no mood to ask Cole for a translation, but *duro* meant hard. That was good. She needed to be a "hard girl," as Cookie sometimes called her when she wouldn't listen to him and do what he wanted, to match her new home.

She had to be a hard girl to survive and run a ranch on her own. It scared her how much she had come to depend on Cole.

It took them three days back to the herd and then nearly seven returning to the Palo Duro, letting the cattle graze slowly along the way to preserve the gains they had made while resting on the Canadian. The men of the crew were consumed with curiosity, Cole with his thoughts, Gabriel with satisfaction, and Aurora with the search for her old, independent, self-reliant self. She urgently needed to be that woman again.

But, one early morning, when they rode the last couple of miles from where they'd left two men with the herd, rode up onto the rim of the great gorge once more and looked down into the valley, the sight of it captured her as it had done the first time, and she felt strong and suddenly able to do anything. This land gave her strength, somehow, as if it were home to powerful spirits, Indian spirits, spirits of the canyon itself, from the past. She looked at Cole.

"This place is a gift from God," she said. "It's perfect for me."

He raised one black eyebrow.

"Nothing's perfect."

"This is," she said.

"My stubborn Rory."

She turned to face him, full of fury, but she kept her voice low so the men wouldn't hear.

"Don't call me that! I'm not *yours.*"

He gave her such a calm, appraising look that she almost thought he'd been testing her in some way. What did he expect? For her to throw herself into his arms crying that she *was* his and to do with her what he wanted for however long he would deign to stay with her?

Well, that would be a July day when the river froze over in the Palo Duro Canyon. She was staying *away* from him for what little time they had left.

But a chill ran through her. When would that be? It might be less time than she even thought. Would he help them get the cattle down into the valley's grass and then go on his way that evening? At dawn the next day?

Without another word, he turned away and began riding along the canyon's rim. But he was looking over the canyon again, that was all. He didn't have his bedroll or the rest of his gear.

The men of the Slash A crew were riding along the rim, too, awed and excited about their new home. Oh, dear God, if only it would be their home, if only all of *them* would stay! She couldn't build this ranch alone, but with their loyal help she could.

They were all she needed. The crew and Cookie and Gabriel and her own fierce determination. At least she was here, safe, and Gates might even be in jail. Even if he weren't, he'd never find her in this canyon.

In a few minutes, Cole came riding back.

"What's next, Boss?" he said.

"Let's go on in while they go back for the cattle."

"That'll work," he said.

"Monte, when you get back here look for me at the bottom of this trail," she said. "I'll probably be waving you in. We'll bring the remuda in first, then the herd, and then we'll figure out what to do about the wagons."

"Wagons'll have to stay on top," Monte joked.

Aurora grinned back at him.

"Limber up your rope," she said. "And your muscles. Looks like the wagons'll have to go down a piece at a time."

"Aw, this here's the land of milk and honey. We won't need the flour and beans and cookin' pots in there."

"Keep on dreaming," she said. "I'll wake you up when Cookie comes rattling up here onto the rimrock."

Monte laughed and gave her a little salute as he rode back to gather his men for the last, short leg of the long, long drive.

Then, for the second time, she, Cole, and Gabriel rode down the winding, switchback path worn into the earth so long ago by unshod hooves and moccasined feet. They talked very little—somehow all the words had dried up.

They found the place she'd picked for headquarters undisturbed and the canyon, at least in this section, uninhabited, as before. Aurora rode back past the bottom of the trail in the other direction with Cole not far behind her.

"I think head the cattle down this way and keep pushing them on to that grass," she said, pointing out a long meadow past a grove of willow trees. "The wagons we'll set up at headquarters and the remuda, too, until we can string a rope corral or find them a box canyon."

Cole nodded agreement. They went back to the cove she'd picked for her house site and began building a small fire for the coffeepot

Cookie had sent on ahead tied to Aurora's saddlebags.

"He's determined not to let his reputation for constantly hot coffee suffer just because it'll take hours to lower the chuck wagon and get the supplies down here," she said.

"I'm surprised he didn't give us orders to shoot a deer, skin it out, and put it to cooking on a spit," Cole said, "so he could give the crew a hot meal, too."

Aurora grinned at him. That just sounded so good, all of a sudden, that careless camaraderie in his voice. It had not been there for days.

Oh, Lord, she was going to miss him.

"He did ask me if we heard any bobwhites in the canyon," she said, "but I rode out of there before he could lend me his shotgun."

Cole laughed, and the warmth of the sound spread through her. Their eyes met and held.

"You'll have to watch it, or Cookie will have you hunting meat instead of bossing this ranch," he said.

*You.*

He broke the look, stood up, and paced restlessly around a small willow tree to glance toward the trail.

"They'd better get moving," he said. "This'll take all day and then some."

"How come you're in such a hurry?"

The question popped out against her will, but now it was there, hanging in the air between them.

"I've got places to go," he growled, and strode off toward the river.

He didn't come back and didn't come back and it seemed like an age to Aurora before the wind brought the noises of the herd and Monte's shrill signal from the rim. Cole came back and swung up onto his horse at the first whistle.

Yes, he was desperate to get out of there.

Aurora mounted and followed him to the foot of the trail. And she was desperate for him to go. Much more of this tension, and she'd fly into a million pieces.

*If you're so eager to leave, then go. You've done the job I hired you for. Go, Cole, get away from me.*

But she didn't say it. She just rode behind him, her gaze on his broad shoulders and his easy seat in the saddle, her thoughts and feelings swirling in tangled profusion. Anything could happen today. Anything could happen tomorrow. Cole might decide to stay.

Or he might not.

Monte and Frank came down first, with Newt driving the remuda right behind them to give the cattle something to follow. They all paused at the top, and then the horses started picking their way, single file, down the narrow trail, all of them beautiful in the sunlight, their brown and bay and black and sorrel hides shining against the red-yellow wall of the earth. As the first horse reached the valley floor, Old Brindle started down the path.

One by one, the cattle came, horns bobbing

up and down, trusting that they weren't going into danger, trusting that there'd be grass and water ahead of them somewhere. They were beautiful, too—and they were her whole future, because there wouldn't be any other way to make a living at the bottom of the Palo Duro.

They had gained a lot of weight while resting on the Canadian, and they looked good. They looked healthy. There were plenty of cows and several bulls for growing the herd and quite a few calves, younger ones following their mamas and bigger ones mixed in with the yearling and two-year-old beeves. She would sell those when they got to be great big three- and four-year-old beeves, which they were certain to do on the grass in this valley.

A wave of joy and thankfulness came over her. She was so fortunate that God had sent Gabriel Martinez and that she'd had the sense to believe his tall tale.

The cattle kept coming. It took over three hours—and she and Cole were riding with Monte and Frank, pushing the new arrivals onto the meadow before they were all down—but the chain of cattle taking the trail one by one never broke for an instant. The men on top handled them superbly, never letting one turn back, not making any sudden moves that might spook them. Finally, her heart swelling with pride, Aurora saw the last head come off the trail. Her new ranch was stocked with a fine herd of cattle.

Tears stung her eyes. She'd had a lot of help,

vital help, but she'd been the boss. She had made the decisions. And she'd done it. She'd brought these cattle to Texas. Now she knew she could do anything.

*Even let Cole go?*

She ignored the small voice inside her and tried not to think as Cole rode Border Crossing up to her at a trot.

"Now the wagons," he said briskly.

Her heart turned over. He was in a *tearing* hurry to leave.

"It won't be dark for hours," Aurora snapped, setting her gaze on the cattle so she wouldn't have to see his handsome face. "You don't have to rush around as if your head is on fire!"

She could feel his eyes on her profile, but she wouldn't turn and look at him. Finally she did. He was puzzled, he had no idea what had brought about that outburst from her.

It was gone. For miles and miles and many days they had read each other's minds and feelings, they had been so close. Now that was gone.

At least on his side, it was. *She* could still read *him.* She could tell perfectly well that he wanted nothing more than to be out of this canyon and far, far away.

She kneed Shy Boy around and rode to the bottom of the trail, started him climbing.

"Good idea," Cole said from behind her. "You can supervise the unloading and . . ."

"You have no earthly idea *why* I'm going up

there or what I plan to do when I get there! So just don't be trying to tell me!"

He laughed.

"What's put such a burr under your saddle?"

"If you don't know, then it'd do no good to tell you."

He laughed again, making her frustration soar.

"That makes a lot of sense."

"As much as anything *you* say."

She sat straight as a ramrod as Shy Boy started climbing up the trail. She forced her body to relax enough to fall into rhythm with his. Cole was right behind her—even if she didn't hear Border's hoofbeats, she would feel them there.

"Rory . . ."

"And don't call me that! You have no right!"

What in the name of heaven *was* the matter with her? Her heart was beating like a hammer in her chest, her face felt flushed and hot. She was suddenly *furious* at him with a rage she could not control.

"Turn around," he said. "I'm gonna take you back and dunk you in the creek. You're the one with your head on fire."

She refused to turn and look at him.

"Try it," she said, between teeth clenched so hard her jaw hurt, "just you *try* to dunk me in the creek. You've dunked me for the last time, Cole McCord."

Oh, the sound of his name—the *shape* of his name in her mouth made her wild. This was

purely loco, the way she was feeling. She had
to get hold of herself. It was nothing but sensual
pleasures that attracted her to him, that was all,
and her life would be too full from now on for
such foolishness.

"Aw, remember how much fun we had the
first time we ended up in the river," he
drawled. "We'll do it again. Be ready."

"I *am* ready," she snapped. "Come on, if you
dare. Right now I could whip the entire Llano
full of comancheros with nothing but a quirt
and my bare hands."

He burst out laughing, a true belly laugh this
time.

"If you had a quirt, it wouldn't be with your
bare hands."

She turned in the saddle to fix him with a
withering glare.

"Yes, it would. If they had guns and knives."

His face was so gorgeous when he laughed.
It made him irresistible. It made him so sweet
and so sexy, both at once, that she could not
bear it.

She hated him for going away. She'd like to
take a quirt to *him*.

"Stubborn Aurora," he said, sobering, then
giving her that devilish, crooked grin of his,
"since I'm not allowed to say 'my' or 'Rory.'"

That was so ridiculous it made her smile.
And just that motion of her mouth cooled the
worst heat of her fury, made her want to cry,
made her ache to be in his arms.

His face turned serious, emphatically serious,

as their horses carried them slowly upward.

"What the *hell* has got into you?"

*You're going away. I'll never see you again. You don't care enough about me to stay.*

She came so close to actually saying the words out loud that she had to lock her jaw against them. Lord, all of a sudden she was so full of surging feelings she was liable to say anything. She had better be quiet.

Finally, she succeeded in tearing her gaze from his and faced front, looking only straight ahead until they reached the top of the trail. Cookie and Nate were there with both wagons, staring with disbelieving eyes over the edge of the caprock. Bubba was happily running back and forth along the rim.

"What in this world were you thinking, Missy?" Cookie said. "Why didn't you pick a place for yore ranch on top of the Rockies?"

Aurora had to laugh at the expression on his face.

"Think of this as the Rockies upside down," she said. "Really, Cookie, you'll love it when you see how perfect it is at the bottom."

"This here trail don't look too perfect to me."

"It's not bad," she said. "And just think, once you get down it you don't have to come back up it for a long time."

" 'Less'n' I wanna go to town. 'Less'n' I might be needin' supplies."

"You can take pack horses for supplies and not have to hoist the wagon up and down."

For an instant he was quiet, and she tried to

think when he'd ever complained so much about anything. Cowboys didn't complain and didn't put up with those who did.

"Better start unloading your wagon," she said finally, annoyed that she'd have to tell him something so simple.

"We was thinking maybe we'd ought to let your wagon down first," he said.

Then, at her puzzled frown, he added, "Seein' as how you've done got the coffee made, and all."

That was when she noticed that they were already unloading her wagon with the household items. The wooden chest that held her clothes, the larger one with her bedding, and a great assortment of boxes and bundles sat scattered around on the grass.

She shrugged.

"Fine with me. I don't care which comes first."

"And seein' as how it's a long ways down this here canyon," he said, "we was wonderin', Miss Aurora, honey, if you might be ready to jettison this here pi-anny."

She gasped. The very idea made her feel empty.

"The piano! Why, no! What would I do?"

Then she clamped her mouth shut. She wouldn't be the one lifting all that weight, struggling to carry it a thousand feet down the side of a cliff. The piano was terribly heavy. It might cause one of the men to injure himself, or even to fall off the trail.

"Well, I mean . . . I hadn't really thought about getting the piano into the canyon," she said slowly, her heart sinking.

What would she ever do without the comfort of her music? Especially with Cole gone, she would have to have it. She had just come to depend on him too much, that was all, and she'd get used to his absence after awhile, but until she did, she would just die without her music.

But what if it slipped and one of her loyal crew died beneath that piano? A deep chill moved through her blood. She hadn't really considered this at all.

"It'd take the rest of the evenin' jist for that one thing," Cookie said.

"I guess the Palo Duro isn't quite as perfect a place for our new home as I first thought," she said, trying her best to keep her voice from shaking. "You men have risked so much for me on the drive, I can't ask you to do this, too."

They didn't want to, or they never would've mentioned it. They'd appointed Cookie as spokesman because he was closest to her and they were embarrassed to go against all cowboy tradition and admit that there was something they couldn't do.

"Mainly we're scared of busting it all to pieces right in front of yore eyes, Miss Aurora," Lonnie said, his voice heavy with chagrin and a touch of resentment that she would ever suspect them of concern for their own welfare. "One good lick against a rock on that wall is all it'd take. We ain't worried about gettin' hurt ourselves."

"If you all were worried about getting hurt, then you wouldn't be trailing cattle," Aurora said, and was relieved when they all laughed. "I just hadn't thought about this problem one time . . ."

She straightened in the saddle against the disappointment dragging her down and forced a briskness she didn't feel into her voice.

"It is, more than likely, impossible to get the piano to the bottom in one piece," she said, "plus think of the time and energy it'd take to move it when we need to be moving the things we can't live without."

Cole eased Border Crossing over to the side and stood in the stirrup, ready to swing down.

"Aw, that piano's going to the new headquarters if I have to carry it down on my back all by my lonesome," he said, and stepped off his horse. "Let's get some ropes on it, boys."

A little buzz ran through the group of men.

"Mostly we jist didn't know how to go about this movin' piannys down a cliff business," Tom said, taking his rope from his saddle. "We shore would hate to say we cain't do it, though."

"We can do it," Cole said, not a trace of doubt in his voice. "Look at it this way: it has to come out before we start lowering the wagon, anyhow, and once that's done, we're halfway to the bottom with it."

That drew a lot of laughter and joking and

they all fell to the task with a will. She couldn't stop them now, no matter what she said or did. Cole had challenged their manhood, and she'd never known a cowboy to back down from that.

But Cole had done it in such a way that nobody's pride was hurt, nobody was mad.

And she'd get to keep her piano. She had no doubt that he could figure out how to move it safely.

But mostly she felt elation about Cole, which was insane because he'd be leaving tomorrow. It made her so happy, though, to know it *wasn't* gone, after all, that inexplicable closeness they had shared during the drive. He had seen her true feelings while she'd tried her best to hide them. He knew her well enough to know how much she needed her music.

And he was trying to give her what she wanted. So did that mean he cared about her, perhaps just a little?

At least he cared about her piano.

"Let's not leave any rope burns on the wood," he said, and began pulling the tail of his shirt out from under his belt.

Unbuttoning it as he went, he strode swiftly to the men gathered at the back of her wagon waiting for the ones inside to push the piano to them. He stripped off the shirt and threw it onto the tailgate.

The sight of him half-naked in the sunlight took her breath away. It made her ache deep, deep inside.

He took a stance with his legs set apart, ready to take the weight when it came.

"Let us have it," he called.

The others helped, but when the heavy instrument came over the edge, Cole took the brunt of it. His powerful shoulders and arms bulged and rippled in the sunlight beneath his copper-colored skin, the horseman's muscles in his thighs threatened to burst the seams of his tight Levis.

Watching him melted her right into her saddle.

Mesmerized, she kept her gaze glued to him as they lifted the piano to the ground and set it gently down.

"Give me a minute," he said.

He picked up the shirt and tore it into pieces. "Ropes!"

And then, with amazing patience, he fitted a strip of cloth under every lariat where it rubbed tightest on the edges of the instrument. He was directing the men, who obeyed without a murmur, to make a sort of cradle out of the ropes, which, she could see, would keep most of the weight balanced in the center.

He must not be in *too* much hurry to leave or he'd never have started this. Moving the piano was going to take some time.

"Now the mules," he said.

Cookie had already unhitched them, and now he brought the team forward. Cole had him separate the four into two teams, one on each end of the piano.

She smiled to herself. That was one thing she admired most about him: he never seemed to be in doubt about anything. He was acting as if he'd moved pianos down thousand-foot cliffs for half his life and hadn't put a single scratch on any of them.

He asked for more ropes, with the lengths at the bottom of the instrument, ropes to be held by riders on the trail below it. Squatting on his haunches, he helped pull them under; once those were attached, they were finished and ready to lower the piano over the edge.

The muscles in his arms bulged and then relaxed as he drew the final knot tight. He stood up.

And turned to look at her.

Caught staring, her feelings completely unguarded, she looked back at him.

The dark mystery vanished from his eyes. He smiled at her, a smile so sweet it broke her heart.

*I love you, Cole McCord.*

The truth flashed into her soul like a lightning strike.

She loved him.

No. It couldn't be. He made her feel safe, that was all.

No. She wouldn't love him. She would *not*.

But she did.

His look, still tender, held hers for the longest time. Then he turned back to the men.

"Over the rim, now," he called. "Gently, gently. Lonnie, mount up and come with me."

She continued to stare, to drink in the sight of him as if she'd just found water in a desert, and she was powerless to look away.

Her vision blurred, but she watched him anyway, hungrily, desperately. This would have to keep her warm at night when the cold winds blew across the plains and reached down into the canyon. This and the memory of their lovemaking night.

She had already loved him then.

How could she have never known it until now? Adventure or no, new experience or no, if she hadn't loved him she would never have gone out to him where he was waiting beneath the pines.

Cole went to his horse and swung up onto Border Crossing in one long, fluid movement, a powerful sweep of motion that made her want to watch him forever. He rode to the head of the trail, gesturing for the men to move the piano to a spot a few yards away on the rim of the caprock. Then, without so much as another glance at her, he disappeared over the edge of the cliff.

Tears filled her eyes. He *did* care about her, a great deal, or he wouldn't go through all this trouble to save her piano.

That wasn't like him, not like he was in the beginning, because then he had been all practical, all intent on survival and getting to Texas, nothing else. Her mouth curved up in spite of her tears. Did he remember insisting she should sell that wagon and everything in it? He hadn't cared one whit for her feelings back then.

Yes, on the trail he had changed. He truly had.

But not enough to stay.

# Chapter 16

～～ɔ∽ɔ∽～～

**C** ole put his whole mind and muscle into the backbreaking task of lowering the piano over the edge of the canyon wall and launching it on its long descent. After Aurora looked at him with her soul in her eyes, he rejoiced that he'd started the crazy job and willed it to take him over so he couldn't think about anything else.

He watched his horse's footing. Then he watched the piano, swaying gently in its rope sling, and signaled Lonnie how to help steady it. Then he started looking for the best spot to set it down when the rope played out and they had to move the mules it was tied to. But none of that did him one whit of good. Even when he'd made a quarter of the descent and was using a big part of his strength to hold the downward-inching piano away from the side of the gorge, his heart remained on top of the rim, helplessly beating its life away in Aurora's small hands.

That look she had given him with those beautiful eyes—eyes blue as heaven itself! Dear God, no woman had ever looked at him that way.

He still hadn't gotten over the surprise of it. It was as if she thought he was a hero or something for saving her piano. Never before, not even when he'd rescued Mrs. Bowers's little girl from Carlos Fuentes' gang of bandidos, had he experienced such passionate, admiring gratitude.

But there'd been something else in Rory's face, too, something new. Something he couldn't quite name.

Whatever it was, it had made him feel tough enough to carry the whole *world* on his shoulders, never mind one measly piano.

He whoaed Border Crossing softly to a stop on a bend in the path and stood in the stirrups to take hold of the piano with both hands, straining so hard to keep it from swinging against the cliffside that his leather gloves slipped on the polished wood as if they were slick with sweat. How in tarnation had Aurora Benton cast such an influence over him, anyhow?

What the hell was he doing risking his and his good horse's life to move a *piano*, of all the useless objects a ranch didn't need, anyhow?

How had things come to such a pass that he couldn't bear to think of leaving her here without her music?

*He couldn't bear to think of leaving her.*

Instantly, he smothered the thought.

What was the *matter* with him? This might be expected of a green kid or a senile old man, but he was exactly halfway in between the two and had plenty of experience, so he should have full use of his faculties.

He helped set the piano down on the trail, the men on top brought the mules a way down the path, he and Lonnie swung the instrument out into space again, and it resumed its torturous descent. Lord, Lord, this could take the rest of the week at this rate. No, it wouldn't even take until dark. If it did, he might have a feeble excuse to stay another day.

"Hold it at the next turn, please, Cole," Aurora called over the rim. "We're going to hitch the other team of mules to one of the long ropes."

"Sure thing," he yelled. "Nothin' to it. I sit around on my horse and hold pianos in the air over my head every day of the week."

Her laughter rolled over the top of the cliff to make him smile.

"That'll work," she said.

He grinned, not only because she'd turned his own saying back on him but also because she'd sounded so sincere. She really believed he could make this whole thing work, poor girl, and her blind faith pleased him far out of proportion to the compliment.

All the time that he, Nate, and Lonnie held the instrument on the trail balanced against a ledge in the wall, Cole thought about Aurora. She not only considered him a strong man, but she also believed he was a good man.

His mind kept coming back to that as if to a lodestone. That was foolish, though, because she was way too inexperienced to judge the character of a man like him.

So, then, why did he set such store by her notions? And why did he care so much about her feelings?

He had felt something truly akin to fear whenever she'd faltered in her confidence or grown sad, as she had about losing the piano. And that had been nothing compared to the panic that had seized him when he thought she could've been shot.

None of that was like him at all. As a rule, it was everybody for himself—or herself—around Cole McCord, tender feelings included. He must be losing his mind.

Truth to tell, he thought as the piano resumed its downward progress, he *was* becoming more than a little bit loco. He didn't even recognize himself any more, because Aurora was in his thoughts most of the time.

He wanted her more than any woman he'd ever met and that was the truth. *That* was probably the real reason she was always in his thoughts. This was a physical attraction only. He hadn't been with a woman for a long time before coming on this drive, so he'd attached a disproportionate importance to that one night with Aurora. When he got to Fort Worth, he'd do something about wiping out that memory.

Finally, by some miracle, since his mind was

not on the job more than half the time, they got the piano down safely with only a few scrapes and scratches and much sooner than he wanted, since that set his mind free to obsess on Rory. They spent the hours between noon and dusk lowering both the wagons and the food supplies. The other gear could wait on the rim until morning.

While Cookie prepared the first hot meal of the day and the men took their first rest of the day, Aurora gave what she called a "free, open-air concert" to express her gratitude for all their hard work. He had never seen her happier.

Stretched out flat on his back beneath a fragrant juniper tree, Cole propped his head on his saddle so he could watch her. She had had them set the piano up off the ground onto a detached wagon tailgate to protect it from dampness, and had located a tarp to wrap it in later against the night air.

And she had thanked him a dozen times with that heart-stopping smile.

It was a good thing they'd not shared a bed more than once or he would never have been strong enough to leave her. That smile alone could addle a man as bad as an all-day ride with no shade and no water.

She began playing a melody he'd never heard before, maybe one of her own creation, that made him wonder what the tune was about. It could make a man feel sad and glad, both, with a lot of passion either way, the best he could tell. It might be a love song.

Her hands moved over the keys with a smooth, caressing touch that he could practically feel on his skin. He needed to stop watching her. He had to stop. That night they'd had, their one night, was flowing back into him, feelings and all.

*That* was what the song was about. This music was telling the story of that night to the canyon, to the cool air, to the bobwhites calling and the rushing water. And to him.

He would get up and walk away, he couldn't listen or look at Rory any more.

But the lowering sun was playing in her hair, striking fire in it and burnishing its gold. And her hands moved as they had moved on his body that night to set his blood aflame.

He wanted them on him again more than he had ever wanted anything.

"Come and git it!" Cookie yelled. "Or I reckon I'll have t' throw it out!"

Thank God.

Aurora stopped playing, everyone lined up with plate in hand, and the whole crew ate at once, since the canyon was holding the cattle. Cole made sure to sit across from Aurora instead of beside her.

No one talked much, even once the meal was done, and when the first guard went out, the rest of the crew fell exhausted into their bedrolls. Aurora got up and walked toward her wagon with only a soft murmur to him as she passed by.

"Thanks again, Lightning. Good night."

"Good night, Rory."

But he couldn't sit there and let her go. He tried, he truly tried—he didn't move at all until she'd reached her wagon.

"Rory," he said then, and was on his feet striding toward her before she'd done more than turn toward the sound of his voice.

"Yes?"

He waited until he was so close no one could overhear. Or maybe he waited just to hold her where she stood for an instant more, with her hair catching gold sparks from the fire and her body showing its perfect shape in dark clothes against the pale canvas.

"Tomorrow we need to ride several miles down the canyon, farther than we went the other day. I want to take a look-see for signs of an outlaw hideout or maybe even a stray band of Comanches."

He stopped, but then he forced his tongue to say the words.

"Before I go."

She stiffened.

"I have a lot to do here," she said. "And outlaws or Comanches or not, we're in the Palo Duro now. To stay."

Truth hit him like a slap in the face. Their long, private scouts were over. No longer did he have her all to himself for the whole day as a matter of course. His job was done.

Yet he couldn't give it up.

"I know you're here to stay," he said, "and I don't mean you should run if we find some-

thing. What I'm saying is that you're better prepared if you know what you're up against."

She looked into his eyes for the longest time,
her own a blue, smoky gray in the gathering
dusk.

"All right," she said. "I'll give it one day.
We'll ride out after I get the men started on the
house."

She turned, went into the wagon, and
dropped the flap closed behind her.

That was when he knew the real reason he
had to ride alone with her one more time. He
had to try to tell her good-bye.

They rode down the canyon the next morning
mostly in silence, and he wondered how he
could ever have thought he could talk. But yet
he couldn't keep silent. His throat hurt with the
words crowding each other to fill it and spill
out onto his tongue.

Why the hell hadn't he rolled out of his bed
before dawn and gone on his way? He'd never
had any trouble before now leaving a woman
asleep and unaware of his leaving.

"You think your crew knows how to build a
house?"

There. That had come out without breaking
his teeth or his jaw. They could have one more
good ride, and he could help her make plans
and think through what she had to do next and
in the morning she'd wake up and he'd be
gone. *That* was the way to do things.

She chuckled.

"They'll have to learn if they don't. I can't exactly hire some carpenters from town."

"It's good you're having them drag the logs in from further upstream," he said. "I'd hate to see you lose any of the trees around the house."

He felt like an awkward guest in a stranger's parlor. Why didn't he just keep his mouth shut instead of saying something so stupid?

Evidently, from the quick glance she gave him, Aurora thought the same.

All this home-building talk made him sick, anyway.

"If you thought there were outlaws or Comanches in here, why didn't you say so before you moved the piano?"

He looked at her sharply. She sounded slightly amused.

"I didn't say I thought they were in here."

Her mouth turned up at the corners. She had the most gorgeous, full lips, the most sensual mouth in the world.

But he would not, would *not* let himself kiss her again.

"So we're spending today exploring the canyon in the *hope* we'll find some enemies?"

Her husky voice held a definite edge of amusement.

"I didn't say they'd be enemies, did I? They might be the best neighbors you ever had and bring you squash from their gardens and eggs from their chickens."

That made her laugh out loud. Oh, God, how he would miss that sound!

"Outlaws and Comanches with gardens and chickens," she said. "Civilization has come to the Palo Duro."

"Not to mention music," he said. "You could give one of your open-air concerts in return for the gifts of food."

"Thanks to you," she said, and she gave him that look again.

He couldn't get up before dawn and ride away without a word. He would hate himself forever for a coward if he did, for he had to have every memory of her that he could gather.

"Let's sit by the stream awhile," he said, and rode Border Crossing up to an old cedar growing a few yards from the creek.

Loco was too mild a word for the shape he was in. He had no earthly idea what to say to her.

They dismounted and sat cross-legged in the shade of the cedar, on a grassy bank near a rock they could lean against.

"This is a great picnic spot," Rory said lightly, "but it's too early to eat the one meal we brought. Searching out our neighbors all day will make us hungry later on."

*I want to spend all day making love with you. I'm only hungry for you.*

She was close enough to reach for, close enough to kiss if he bent toward her, but she sat Indian-style, as he was, her back very straight, her manner tense as she faced him. Now the way she looked at him was unreadable.

He wanted this look, whatever it was, off her face. He wanted her smiling at him the way she'd done on top of the rim yesterday.

*That* look would never come again, though, not when he was done talking to her. Then she'd really know him, she wouldn't want him any more, and he would want to go.

Yes, the sooner he was gone, the better.

But he needed one more time in her arms, one more unforgettable time.

Proof right there, if any was needed, that he was a no-good, selfish rounder. Another time with her would only break her heart.

His own heart was beating out of his chest with the effort he had to make not to touch her. A curl of her hair was caught on her cheek. His hand itched and prickled, but he didn't reach out and brush it back to fly in the breeze with the others.

He reached for the strength at his core, for the force that had brought him alive through hails of bullets and days and nights of hunger and thirst, through his mother's death and his brother's, and the galling misery since Travis's.

"Aurora," he said, "I have to talk to you."

"I'm listening."

An edge in her voice as fine-honed as the brightness in her blue eyes made him look at her again. She was wound tight, tight as the wanting that was tearing him apart.

Something in her face told him that she knew this was good-bye. She knew him so well—except for thinking that he was a much better man than he was.

He opened his mouth, but he couldn't speak. The big cedar enfolded them in its shadow, in its spicy smell, and waited with them. Aurora didn't move, didn't take her gaze from his face.

"This cedar," he said finally. "There's a legend about the cedar tree that lots of Indian people know."

She watched him through those sky-eyes of hers, her look steady and straight with a hot light burning deep in it like a sun.

"Lightning can strike near the cedar tree, it can run along the ground and in circles around it trying to enter, but it can't. It cannot split the heart of a cedar the way it does other trees."

"So?"

The huskiness was taking over her voice.

"My heart is the heart of a cedar," he said. "My heart doesn't open. I live in the middle of danger, always, because my real name is He-Stands-In-Lightning."

The corners of her luscious mouth lifted a little.

"At last," she said, "I hear your real name."

He couldn't resist their old game.

"You *think*."

"I *know*,'" she said, and the trace of a smile vanished from her lips. "I know when you're telling me the truth."

She went so solemn so suddenly that his gut knotted. What if she burst into tears? What would he do? If he touched her to comfort her, he was lost.

"My name was given to me because of my life," he said, and he fought to loose the tightness in his own voice. "I'm not meant to have a home or any peace. I never have, I never will."

She only looked at him.

"I'm leaving at sunup tomorrow," he said, and his voice sounded harsh as a crow's cry. "My job's done. I got you here safe."

There. He had told her, honorably, and had not left her twisting in the wind the way he'd left so many other women. He could go now. He could get up and walk away and be able to look himself in the eye.

But her face held him there. So beautiful and so stricken, yet strong. So strong. She was no longer the girl who had badgered him into coming with her. This was a woman to be reckoned with.

"And I'm not meant to marry," she said. "You don't have to run away the minute I start making a home, He-Stands-In-Lightning."

"That's nothing to do with me," he said, and the truth of it was like a knife in his heart.

"I know that. But you're always welcome in my home, we'll always be friends."

"You don't know me," he blurted. "I killed my best friend. *I* killed Travis."

Not one thing changed about her. She didn't pull back in revulsion or stare at him in horror.

"You shot him? Why?"

"No, some bandido shot him, but I put him in front of the bullet. We raided a hideout on the Nueces when we should've waited for help—they outnumbered us six to one and we knew it."

"If Travis knew that, too, then why is it all your fault?"

He wiped his hand across his eyes, but it didn't help. All he could see now was Travis's face when his spirit had left him.

"I wouldn't hear to waiting. I badgered him. I hoo-rawed him."

"He didn't have to listen to you."

"He did when I said I was going in alone. We were partners."

He stared at her, horrified that he was actually talking about this, yet somehow relieved, too. All these months he could hardly bear to think the truth about Trav's death, much less speak it.

"I hate to break the news to you," she said wryly, "but you're only human, Cole McCord. Human beings don't know everything. Sometimes they make a bad call."

It helped. Not a whole lot, but it helped.

"I make more than my share of bad calls," he said. "I brought my little brother into the Rangers, and he got killed within a year. I went off to my mother's people and played in the woods the summer she worked herself to death on the farm."

She looked at him a boundless time with that fierce, blue gaze.

*"You're not God,* Cole McCord. I'm trying to tell you that."

"And I'm trying to tell you that you don't want me to love you. The people I love don't live long."

*"You* don't want to love me," she said in her husky voice.

"No, I don't."

He intended to get to his feet, to go to his horse and leave her then, to ride on up the trail and out of the canyon before he had even planned. But that old trap of wanting to know her opinion, of needing to see how she saw him, held him still. He looked for the disgust in her eyes, the disapproval she might be too polite to voice.

It wasn't there. He saw only acceptance and admiration. And love. That had to be love, that look like the one she'd given him on the rimrock.

"You have to go tell this to Travis's widow," she said. "I know that."

"Yes."

"And you may not come back, I know that, too."

"Yes."

She lifted her hand, then, and caressed his cheek, traced his cheekbone with her thumb. He felt so familiar to her now, although they hadn't touched each other for weeks. That was because he was now and would always be a part of her.

This was her fate, her destiny, to love him. Forever. And somewhere inside her she had known that from the first sight of his face.

"I only want one promise from you, He-Stands-In-Lightning."

"What is it?"

She looked deep into his wary eyes. For the longest time they looked at each other in the growing sunlight, trembling a little in the rising wind. She removed his hat, laid it on the ground, and brushed his hair back from his forehead, coming a little closer to him with each movement.

"Remember this," she said.

"Until the day I die."

They came together like fire and fuel, already alight, already burning before their lips could meet. He thrust one big, hard hand into her hair and took her mouth with a passion that stopped her breath, nearly stopped her heart.

She reached for the buttons at the fly of his Levis, brushing the swelling bulge beneath with her knuckles as she ripped at it with trembling fingers, aching to hold him in her hands. He groaned and cupped her breast in his palm, he tried to break the kiss to help her at her task but, once kissing, they couldn't stop except to kiss again.

He blazed a hot trail down her throat with his mouth, she kissed the hollow of his collarbone and tore his shirt open. She unfastened the buckle of his belt, pushed at the waistband of his jeans, he pulled her blouse from her riding skirt without lifting his lips from her skin.

At last, somehow, without ever letting go of

the kiss, they managed to peel off their clothes, and they fell into the delight of touching each other with no barriers at all. His hands slid down her back, burning her skin, cupping her buttocks in a greedy, quick caress before coming back to her yearning breasts again. He found both her nipples. The need to have him inside her made her lose breath, it hit her so hard.

Their eyes met. Her whole body thrilled to his.

This would be the last time. She'd live the rest of her life on this.

"Rory," he whispered.

His eyes blazed. They devoured her face.

Then he brought her hard against his hot maleness, wrapped her body with his and started the kiss all over again.

*I love you, Lightning. Oh, dear God, how I love you!*

She told him that with her greedy lips and long, slow, importunate caresses of her tongue and her hands that could not get enough of him, she told him with tiny, faint moans deep in her throat, she told him in every way possible except with words. For words would be shackles to him, and he had to be free. He wouldn't be Lightning if he couldn't be free to roam in the storm.

He gathered her to him, sheltered her close in the curve of his big body, began to pleasure her with his hand. When she lay melted and helpless, unable to so much as lift her finger, he drew back and smiled at her, his face warmed with the gold of the sunlight falling through the leaves.

Then he took her breast into his big, calloused hand to cradle it there, and she began to stroke his hair, running its silk beneath her palm again and again until he lowered his head and began to lave its tip with his tongue. Her arms, her hands, her whole body went nerveless except for that exquisite sensation, except for the precious sight of his dark head bent so tenderly over her breasts.

"Never stop," she whispered, "never stop."

But soon her whole body contradicted her, her blood began to race for more. Shameless with need, her hands caressed him everywhere she could reach, her voice made wordless little begging sounds she didn't even recognize.

He knew, he knew what she wanted, what she needed, but still he made her wait.

She writhed beneath him, she gathered the breath to whisper "Please," she rubbed her face against his jaw and bit his ear, and finally, at last, after an eternity when she thought she would die, he wrapped his arms around her, stroked her back, and lifted her to meet him as gently as if she were glass. He entered her.

The comfort was glorious.

But then he moved, and she wanted still more. She wrapped her arms around his bare shoulders, her skin moving on his, and the sheen of sweat they both created sealed them together. She arched up to him, brought him more fully into her.

They moved together then as if this ancient rhythm had been theirs to share for years and years, moved together as if their only other time, that one sweet night beneath the pine tree, had taught them to be one. Always. Forever.

The word came, again, into her mind where, only a heartbeat before, no words had been. This had to last her forever.

She thrust her fingers into his hair, brought his mouth to hers, and kissed him avidly, silently begging him not to leave her with her lips and tongue, her heart and soul. He brought her back to that moment, then made her believe that it would never pass, that no other time would ever come.

He kissed her wild and free and thoughtless again, he held her so close that they could never part, and he consumed her with the hot maleness of his body. She moaned and whimpered, deep in her throat, for mercy.

But he gave her none. His hands swept trails of fire onto her back, and his lips dropped burning kisses at random on her face and neck. He took her deeper and deeper into the conflagration that drew them both like the lost to light.

Until their blood sang and the lightning struck and they rode like conquerors on the back of the storm.

Afterward, they lay entwined for the longest time, skin melded to skin, legs and arms entangled so they could never be separated. They couldn't be parted. Not after this. It would go against the laws of nature, the structure of the world, the form of the universe.

Except that after the dark fell tonight and the sun came up tomorrow, Cole would be gone.

Tears began to roll down her cheeks, they forced their way between the bones of their faces, pressed together, ran into the hollows of their throats.

"Here, now," he said gruffly. "What's this?"

He pulled back onto his elbow to wipe them away, the touch of his rough hand so gentle that it made her cry harder.

Desperate to look at him, to drink in the sight of his face, she raised up and wiped her eyes, trying to see him clearly.

"Who told me she believes in living one moment at a time and that moment to the fullest?"

"Some simpleminded girl who had no idea what she was saying."

He smiled, a smile to break any woman's heart.

"That's all there is, Rory," he said softly. "One moment at a time. You were wise beyond your years."

"Oh yeah, yeah, yeah. I don't want to hear it."

Laughing a little, he dropped a kiss on her hair.

"Cole . . ."

He shook his head, laid a long, rough finger across her lips.

"Now," he said. "This day. Live this."

And he kissed her like a wild man as he drove her back down.

# Chapter 17

Aurora bent over the cookfire to fork bacon from the skillet onto the tin plate. Cookie had the biscuits done, too, even though the last guard hadn't come in and most of the men were still asleep. The sun was rising, sending the faintest of pale, purple light into the canyon. A haze drifted up from the creek.

And Cole was saddling up, getting ready to leave.

She carried the bacon and a plate full of biscuits she'd taken from the Dutch oven to the tailgate of the chuck wagon and began to make them into little sandwiches, amazed at the fact that her hands didn't tremble. How could they not, when an earthquake was shaking the inside of her body to bits? How could they not, when her heart was aching with pain enough to kill her?

When the bacon biscuits and a bundle of ground coffee were all packed in the cloth sack she had already put his wages in, she climbed up into the chuck wagon for tomatoes and peaches. She came out, with her hands and pockets full, to find Cole standing waiting, holding the reins. His saddle looked like a stranger's with his bedroll tied on behind the cantle.

"Oh, Rory, that's too much," he said, when he saw all the food she'd gathered.

"Don't tell me that," she said fiercely. "It's a long way to Fort Worth and no Mattie's Diner on the way."

Her lips went suddenly stiff, and she couldn't say any more.

He stood silent while she took another bag, emptied the first one, and put the heavier airtights on the bottom of each. Then she added some of the biscuits and bacon to both and connected the two with leather straps to hang on either side of his saddle. The straps kept slipping from her grasp, but after an age the job was done.

They walked away from the camp, then, toward the foot of the trail that led out of the canyon. It felt so right to her, walking beside him, that his leaving seemed more incredible than ever.

At the foot of the trail, he stopped.

"You'll do fine here," he said, turning to look down into her eyes. "I told you the truth when I said if there was a woman on earth who could do this, you're the one. Don't forget that."

For an instant the lump in her throat wouldn't let her speak. Finally, although she couldn't swallow it, she could talk around it.

"And don't you forget that you're a good man," she said. "The best."

His dark eyes hardened.

"Don't use this trip to see Ellie Henderson as a stick to measure my character," he said. "I never even thought of it until that day I told you I was going, and I don't usually worry much about other people."

She looked at him straight.

"While I was fixing your food I was remembering what you told me about the day Travis was killed. Cole, one thing you need to remember is that he would've done the same to you."

He frowned.

"What are you talking about?"

"You're blaming yourself for hoo-rawing Travis into the attack," she said, "but wouldn't he have dared you into it if it'd been his idea?"

"It *wasn't*," he snapped. "The fault's all mine."

"But he was the same kind of man as you, right? Since he was your partner?"

"*What* kind of man?"

"Sure of himself, maybe to the point of being . . . reckless, sometimes. Fast at the draw and used to winning. Wild enough to go over to Mexico and do something that would get him chased by the Federales all the way to the Rio Grande. A great rider on a great horse he was used to carrying him out of every scrape."

He scowled at her.

"I guess so."

"Well, then, if he'd been the one in the feisty mood that day, he would've wanted to go on in and not wait for any help, and if you'd held back, he would've hoo-rawed you into it or threatened to go in alone. It would've been the very same deal turned around."

A terrible expression passed over his face. He turned away and threw the reins across Border Crossing's withers.

"What's done is done," he said, his voice even harder than before. "No amount of thinking or talking can change that."

"All *right!*"

Stubborn as she might be, she wasn't going to argue this. It was too delicate of a subject with him, it would only drive him away before they'd even said good-bye.

She stared at his broad shoulders, the copper skin of his neck between his hair and his collar. If only she could put her lips to it. If only she could kiss him all over. Forever. If only he would stay.

"At least take a spare horse," she said. "Take your pick."

"No, thanks."

She looked at him, biting back the tears she would not let him see, waiting for him to turn around.

"You wouldn't be obligated to bring it back, if that's what you're worried about," she snapped, her tone cross and cranky, her voice about to break.

The muscles tightened across the top of his shoulders. He went stiff and still.

She shut her mouth. Hadn't she promised herself she'd be brave? That she'd be dignified and self-possessed in his last memory of her?

He whirled on his heel.

"Take care of yourself, Rory," he said, in his low, rich voice that held no anger in return.

Unsmiling, he searched her face, and for one heart-stopping moment she thought he would reach for her.

He didn't. He turned to his horse, stuck the toe of his boot into the stirrup, and swung up into the saddle.

"If I touch you I'll not let you go," he said, in the raw, rough voice of a stranger.

"Then don't."

It came out in a venomously hateful tone.

She brushed back her hair and looked up at him, silhouetted against the rising sun.

"I didn't mean it that way," she blurted. "I love you, Lightning."

He stared down into her eyes, he searched her face.

"I'll never forget you, Rory."

Her heart stopped. Every cell in her body went quiet to listen.

But that was all he said.

She was completely amazed that she could speak, or even think of anything else, but she said, "What'll I do with your twenty head?"

"Brand 'em," he said, "with the Slash A."

"They already *are* that—it was the trail brand.

I'll take a new one for my new place."

"Then mark 'em yours," he said.

He reached down and touched her face, just once, so lightly it could've been the brushing of a feather.

"Don't forget to carry your gun," he said.

Aurora stared up into his unfathomable eyes. "So long, Rory."

And then he tore his gaze from hers, faced the wall of the gorge, smooched to Border, and started upward.

She stayed there, watching breathlessly as he took the narrow, winding trail. Sunlight was building into the canyon now; soon it would burn the haze away. It washed Cole and Border Crossing with a blinding yellow light on the outside bends of the trail, shaped their dark silhouette in the shadows on the inside.

Pain paralyzed her. How could she ever have thought that she'd already faced the worst life could throw at her? How could she ever have guessed that she could hurt so much and still live?

It would be easier, far easier, if Ellie were a woman he loved. Or, better yet, a woman he'd thought he loved until he held Aurora in his arms. Then, competing with another woman, she might have a chance.

She didn't have a prayer against Travis's ghost.

She stood rooted where she was until he had climbed every inch of the narrow, winding trail back up into the wide world, never pausing until he reached the top and rode out onto the caprock. Shading her eyes against the sun, she walked backwards a few steps to try to see him better.

On the rim of the gorge, he sat his horse and looked down at her. He lifted his hand, and she waved back. Then he rode away from her.

Cole traveled like a man possessed. If it hadn't been for the fact that he would've killed his horse, he would never have slept in all those many miles. He rode toward Fort Worth and Ellie Henderson—if she was still there—as fast and furiously as if she could help him somehow.

That thought twisted his lips in a bitter grin as he made camp that last night, close enough to see the lights of town. Nobody could help him. He had left Rory to survive as best she could in the wildest country left on the frontier. He had left Rory. The only woman who had ever truly loved him.

Those words from her brought him a flash of happiness every time he recalled her saying them, a brief joy in the instant the memory came to him, but then it always added to his old storm clouds of black guilt and shame. He didn't deserve her love and, in not returning it, he'd broken her heart.

Staking Border Crossing on a rather thin graze, he patted him in apology.

"Too many travelers been camping here," he told him. "We should've gone on in to the livery tonight so you could have grain."

But only God knew whether he'd be able to face a town full of people tomorrow, even. He didn't care if he never saw another human face to face. Unless it was Rory.

And he could never do that unless he went back to stay.

He spread out his bedroll without eating, without even making a fire, shucked his boots, and crawled in. Going back to stay was nothing but a loco wish, even if it had come to him in a dream, even if he had had the dream every night since he left the Palo Duro.

The dream was another punishment for his sins, along with its twin, the one where Travis was the one pushing *him* into going in after ol' Garza and his gang, laughing like crazy at the answers Cole was giving. He wished he'd never told Rory anything about that day in hell.

And God help him, now here he was, he'd see Ellie tomorrow and he didn't even know why he'd ridden all this way. What could he do for Ellie if she *was* miserable or in trouble, except maybe get her some money from his account at the Bank of Ft. Worth?

What would he say to her? *If you're too lonesome since I got your husband killed, I'll marry you myself?*

That'd be like serving a jail sentence for life. That'd be a punishment, at least, so it might make him feel better.

The wind turned to come from the west and sent a chilly breath down his neck. He turned on his side, pulled the soogans up over his shoulder and his hat down over his face. Blowing sand sifted in under it anyway, into his mouth, onto his tongue. No matter. He *sure* couldn't sleep inside a hotel tonight.

Being under a roof, being inside four walls didn't seem right, not while his need for Aurora was a cold rain in his heart.

He did manage to be around people enough to visit the barber shop for a bath and a shave and a mercantile for clean clothes before he visited Ellie Henderson. Not only was she still in town, he learned upon inquiring about her while he got his haircut, but she was setting up her own business there, making hats. From what little he'd ever seen of her, Ellie had been a shy, retiring woman, not given to dealing with the public. This was his fault, that she'd been forced into a life she didn't want.

That thought drummed through him over and over again as he walked toward her shop, then past its windows filled with fancy women's hats. The fateful decision he'd made that September day reached out in all directions, and its consequences went on and on.

In spades. Because when he stepped into the shop and glimpsed her reaching to take down a hat from a shelf, he saw she was going to have a child. And very soon. God help him, he had orphaned a baby!

"Ellie Henderson?" he said, although he knew her immediately.

He removed his hat. *How* would he ever get through this? *What* the hell could he say?

The bell tinkled its warning as the door closed and she turned to face him.

"I'm Cole McCord," he said, although his mouth seemed filled with cotton.

Her wide brown eyes looked him over.

"I know who you are," she said, and walked slowly toward him, holding the brightly colored hat in both hands.

"I didn't know if you'd remember, since we'd only met once or twice."

"I could never forget you," she said.

His gut tightening, he waited for the rest of it. *Because you're the one who killed my husband.*

But instead, she said, "This brings back such memories, Mr. McCord. Won't you sit down?"

"Call me Cole," he said, "please."

She nodded absently.

"Ellie," she said.

Then she seemed to realize for the first time that she was still holding the hat, and she made a motion toward the counter with it, changed her mind, and walked toward the two chairs sitting at a small table in the corner. He followed, his heart thumping in his chest.

It had been a damn-fool idea to come here in the first place. *Why* had he done this stupid thing? He'd told Aurora the truth when he'd said this wouldn't change anything. He could already tell that it wasn't even going to make him feel any better.

Ellie sat down, though, and indicated the

chair facing her, so he sat in it. His knees felt like they'd bump his chin at any minute—these dainty armless rocking chairs were obviously meant for ladies only.

For a little while they just stared at each other, holding their hats in their hands, waiting for Cole to say something. But his tongue felt frozen.

Finally, Ellie said, "Someone told me you left the Rangers."

That brought his purpose back to mind like a slap in the face, but it didn't put any words in his head. He swallowed hard.

"Yes. I . . . couldn't stay without Trav."

Her eyes misted.

"I know how you feel," she said kindly. "I thought the same way when he was first gone."

"He'd be here now if it wasn't for me," Cole blurted. "I killed him."

Her gentle expression changed to one of shock.

"Captain Haley said when he brought Trav's body home that bandidos killed him."

A dam burst inside Cole.

"Bandidos shot him, yes, but I'm the one who set him in the path of their bullets, sure as if I'd picked him up and dropped him in the line of fire. I insisted that the two of us raid that Garza outfit, Ellie, when I knew they outnumbered us, bad. Haley and Martin and their partners were on the way to meet us. It wouldn't've been more than a half day more for us to hook up with them and come back to take the outlaws, but I wouldn't wait . . ."

She leaned forward and touched his hand.

"You didn't kill him."

"I *did*," he said, clamping his jaw tight. "You don't understand. He hesitated, he said wait until we had more men, he counted seven of them against the two of us and we couldn't see 'em all."

Sweat was popping out all over his face, running down the sides of his cheeks. He pulled out his new handkerchief to wipe it away.

"Trav was a captain, too," she said. "He held the same rank as you. He didn't have to follow your orders."

"I told him I was going in alone," he said, nearly choking on the words. "Like a green, cocky kid too young to know *he* could be the one killed instead of the other guy. Like an *idiot* kid. And me thirty-three years old and veteran of so many campaigns I can't count 'em."

Confessing to that foolishness tangled his tongue into uselessness.

Her face and her eyes had long since lost all shock and surprise. Now she looked at him with such calm and such wisdom that he was reminded of pictures he'd seen of the mother of the Christ child.

"You're a man, Cole. Travis was a man. Men set great store by their courage, and that's as it should be."

"There's a difference between courage and foolhardiness."

"And you were his partner," she said slowly, as if he hadn't spoken. "He wouldn't let you go in alone."

"Right. I'll never know why I wasn't the one who stopped that bullet instead of him. If there was any justice I would've been."

She smiled.

"Surely you're not thirty-*four* years old now, Cole, and still expecting life to be fair."

He made a little sound of ironic agreement.

"I pushed him, I even hoo-rawed him, Ellie. Still he wouldn't budge. Not until he thought I'd try it alone."

She nodded, still calm as glass.

"You would have done the same for him, don't forget. I know what it means to be partners. I know what you meant to him. I know his work was his life. Travis wouldn't have had it any other way."

He stared at her for the longest time. She meant that, and she held no resentment.

"What about . . ."

His gaze darted to her huge abdomen and then, embarrassed, away.

"He loved me," she said, "and he would've loved this baby. But he would never have stayed at home with us very long at a time."

"I feel so small," he blurted, without having the slightest warning that he was about to say that. "I had a petty fear when you-all married that you'd become Trav's best friend instead of me. He'd been my partner for years. He was the only person I'd ever been truly close to."

"*I* was never close to him," she said thoughtfully, "and I know now I never would've been."

"You can't know that. You were only married to him for four months."

"And I only knew him for two weeks before that. But I have a . . . comparison," she said, blushing. "A gentleman caller with whom I'm very close after only a few weeks. He has asked me to marry him, and I said that I would, but only after my confinement is done."

Well. He didn't know beans about anybody else's life, so he could stop thinking he did.

"Are you shocked? That I'm making these plans when Travis has only been gone for eight months?"

"No," he said honestly, "but I'm shocked at your whole situation. I'd never imagined you with your own shop, or a baby, much less a suitor. I thought you were too shy and retiring, that you were helpless without Travis, that . . ."

She laughed.

"I've never been helpless, Mr. McCord. I never will be."

She laid the fluffy hat on the little table between them and folded her hands across her lap, although she barely could reach around it.

"That's why I'm keeping my shop after Mr. Siddons and I are married. He agrees with my reasoning."

Cole searched her sweet face, looked at her quiet hands.

There'd be no punishment here, no life sentence to serve to take away his guilt.

He shook his head wryly. He had assumed too much, and too much importance for himself all around. Aurora had been right when she'd told him he wasn't God.

The bell on the door tinged again, and a woman came in, shopping basket over her arm.

"You have a customer," he said and stood, bending to take her elbow and help her to her feet. "And I must be going."

"I'm glad you came to see me," she said. "Please come back in a year or so and see the baby. I'd love for him to know you so when he's older, you can tell him stories about his daddy. That way, he'll feel he knows Travis a little bit."

"I'll try," he said. "I have no idea where I'll be."

"Wherever it is," she said, "let go of your worries. You would have done the same for Travis if things had been the opposite that day, and you know as well as I do that they easily could have been. Travis was just as . . ."

She paused. He supplied her with words.

". . . foolhardy? Wild and crazy?"

Smiling, she shook her head.

". . . bravely impetuous as you."

She gave him a pat on the arm and went to serve her customer. He put on his hat and went out onto the street.

Ellie was incredible. How'd she get to be so much smarter than he was, although she obviously was a good ten years younger?

But it was Aurora who had first told him that Travis could have been urging him into the attack instead of the other way around. He'd never really heard her until now, had never *wanted* to hear because his guilt was all he knew, all he had left of his old life.

He'd been clinging to his guilt so hard he hadn't let himself hear any hope.

So it had taken two women to make him see that a man is only a man. No matter how strong he is, how fast with a gun or close with a friend, he cannot control his own fate, much less that of his partner.

It was true. Travis would've done the very same damn thing to him if he'd been in a salty mood that morning in the wild, brushy brakes of the Nueces. And Travis did, sometimes, have his salty moods.

His mind was opening up, trying to take that in, and he didn't see anything as he instinctively walked to the livery stable and collected his horse. All he wanted was to be horseback and out of the bustle of town so he could think.

But once he was mounted and riding out beneath the overhead sign of the stable, his brain darted from one thought to another like a scared rabbit. Where should he go? What direction should he take when he rode out into the street? Left or right?

Border Crossing, with no tug on the reins, no touch of Cole's foot, and with no hesitation at all, turned west. Cole let him.

Why hadn't he listened to Aurora? She had

told him he would've done the same for Travis. She had also told him he wasn't God. Yet somehow the truth of it hadn't soaked in until he'd heard the same from Ellie.

Until he had confessed to Ellie.

It all went back to Aurora, though. She'd been the reason he'd even *thought* of coming to see Ellie in the first place—admitting he'd been wrong was so foreign to him. As a matter of fact, he had first admitted it to Aurora.

Panic seized his gut.

Rory. God in heaven. He needed her more than he'd ever needed anyone or anything. She had healed him.

Would she be glad to see him if he went back? He had left her to whatever dangers might befall her, he had broken her heart when he'd climbed the canyon wall.

If he did go back, he'd never be able to leave her again, that much he knew for sure.

He grinned. Not only would he not be strong enough to tear himself away from her but she would kill him if he tried to leave again. She'd take a rifle and pick him off as he climbed the canyon wall.

But what if he did go back, and then, after a while, he wanted to keep on drifting around, looking for danger as always, as Travis had done? What if he didn't want to spend much time at home?

Ellie had been right. Even with a baby, Travis would never have stayed home more than a week or two at a time.

Like Travis, he was a wandering man, used to a wild, hard life filled with danger and challenges.

His grin broadened.

Life with Rory would be wild and hard, full of danger and challenges.

He stopped the horse in the middle of the street.

He loved her. He'd known that for a long time, but he'd never admitted it, even to himself.

Now that he had, he'd have to do something about it.

Slowly, he squeezed Border's sides and moved him down the street at a trot, to keep from getting run down by a buggy or a wagon. That thought, too, brought an image of Aurora, careening toward him in her gig wearing a saucy blue hat that matched her eyes.

Evidently, everything he ever saw or thought of for the rest of his days would remind him of her. He might as well head for the Palo Duro and find out whether she'd accept his love. But what if she sent him packing?

The very thought of it made him want to ride down to one of the saloons by the stockyards and pick a fight, let some no-good, horse-stealing long-rider shoot him and put him out of his misery just as he'd wished he could do ever since Travis had fallen backwards into his arms with the life gone out of him. But even that probably wouldn't cure him. He'd probably just wander around in the Spirit World forever, crying for Aurora.

# Chapter 18

Aurora woke to the raw, sweet smell of newly cut logs and the spice of cedar. Her home. This was home, now.

She lay in her blankets, staring at the roof that wasn't there yet, looking for daylight, seeing the stars but imagining the dark was fading. Day passed much faster than night, that was a law of nature she'd noticed since Cole had left.

The window opening was there, too, cut squarely into the wall, standing empty and uncovered, she knew it, but all she could see was black. The air felt softer now, though, like there would be some dew to greet the sun, or maybe a haze hovering over the creek. Dawn was coming. The birds were beginning to slide from night calls to waking ones. Since Cole had been gone, she'd learned the feels and sounds of every stage of the night, she had become an expert, and she wasn't wrong now.

She threw off her covers and began to dress, trying to get ready, get outside and get busy

371

before she could even think, before she could count. If Cole had had good luck and had reached Fort Worth in fifteen days . . .

Her mind stopped still in the ruts she'd created running through the problem over and over again. She'd promised herself not to think about him any more. She was *not* going to think about him any more.

But if he'd had good luck going and coming back, if he hadn't wasted any time, today would be the first day he could possibly reach her.

Why would he come back? He wouldn't.

He wouldn't come back, though, he wouldn't come back. That became her silent litany for facing reality as she threw on her clothes and went out into the darkest part of the night to walk along the creek. He wouldn't come back. Telling herself that was the only way she could save herself from being consumed by the impossible hope that he would.

Dawn broke over the canyon in a bright spill of pinks and yellows, painting the thin mist that floated on the tall grasses, turning the deep red walls of the gorge into flames of a primal fire. She walked out of the trees by the creek and up the slight slope toward the house, holding her breath until she could see the trail to the rim. This would be the only time she would look at it today. This and right before dark fell.

She had disciplined herself to watching the trail only twice a day, and she wasn't going to lose that progress now, even if it was the first day he could possibly appear. Pretending no interest at all in the trail, she waved to Cookie, who was just stirring up his fire, and to Tom and Monte, who were heading for it with coffee cups in hand, but then, a stone's throw from her start of a new house, she let herself stop and look up at the rimrock.

Nothing. No one. Exactly as any sane person would know.

She swept her gaze down, toward the floor of the canyon. The corner of her eye caught a movement. Something on the trail.

Walking forward without looking at her path, she shaded her eyes from the sun in the east and peered intently. Horse. Rider. Someone was coming.

The sight froze her where she stood. Insane hope battered in wave after wave like the ocean crashing against her wall of reality.

She couldn't give in to it until she knew for sure who was there. Even if it *was* Cole . . .

But who else would have started down that twisting trail—or even found it—in the dark? He was already three-fourths of the way to the foot.

And who else rode a tall, leggy bay roan who moved like a Thoroughbred race horse?

The wall of good sense surrounding her heart tumbled down, and hope spilled into her blood. It was Cole, she'd known it from the instant she'd seen him. She could recognize him as far as she could see him by the way he sat a horse, if nothing else.

Yet he might not have come back to stay.

She tried to remember that, she let the chill of it wash through her, she put it in the front of her mind as she watched him come. Maybe he'd decided he couldn't do without his cattle, that he'd earned them and he might as well take them.

Perhaps he planned to start his own ranch somewhere. Maybe he even planned to lay claim to another part of the canyon. He had loved it the first time they rode through it.

But he was no rancher, he was a renegade, a far-rider. He was wild, and he had to be free. She'd known from the minute they'd met that he was as different from other men as a stallion was from a gelding. Surely he would never let himself be tied down to one place, no matter if he *had* realized that he loved her.

Then she took a long, cleansing breath and blew all the thoughts away so she could live that moment, so she could remember it well if it turned out to be only another memory to add to her priceless remembrances of him. He rode with the horse, as always, with Border's rhythm as he leaned to take the bends in the trail. They disappeared, and then, when she thought she could not bear it any longer not to be looking at him again, Cole filled her sight once more.

She stood without moving to watch him come.

Not until he rode into the edge of the yard did she walk toward him, slowly, through the pearly dawn. They met beneath the big cotton-wood tree.

"Morning, ma'am," he said, pushing his hat onto the back of his head as he sat looking down at her. "Reckon a man could find a hot breakfast at this ranch house here?"

The early sun highlighted his cheekbones, glowed hot in the copper of his skin. He was exhausted, worn to the bone, she could see it in the dust on his clothes, in the way he folded his arms and leaned on the horn the moment Border stopped moving. She could see it in the deepened lines of his face, and she longed to reach out and smooth them with her fingertips.

His eyes showed no tiredness, though. They searched her face with a mission. What could he be asking of her? He knew how *she* felt. He himself was the question.

"Reckon he could," she said, her voice gone husky with tears. "Get down and come to the fire."

She walked to Border Crossing's head and rubbed his soft muzzle. He snuffled at her and nudged her with his nose.

Cole swung his leg over and dismounted.

He moved with the same fluid sureness, he held himself with the same calm power that said he could cover the ground he stood on, but there was a tension pouring off him like sweat off skin.

"Rory," he said. "I love you. I can't ever leave you again, so I'm going to have to stay here. Shall I build a bachelor's shack down by the creek, or will you marry me?"

She could barely believe her ears. Yet she'd heard him right—no other words in the world could put that look of mingled triumph and fear in his eyes.

"I'll marry you," she said. "We've already cut down enough trees around here."

"Oh," he said, and began walking slowly toward her, "so it's the trees you're worried about."

"Only you, the red cedar. What has opened your heart, He-Stands-In-Lightning?"

"You. You have more power than lightning. You are Red Woman, The Fire, and you have burned your way into my very soul."

He took her into his strong, loving arms and held her close as his skin. So close and for so long that it seemed they'd stand just that way forever. Aurora closed her eyes, leaned her head against his broad chest, and drew in deep breaths of his smells of dust and horse and leather and . . . Cole.

*Now* she was home.

Dear Reader,

Sexy Scottish heroes, tantalizingly long nights spent mesmerizing a man, love stories that won't be forgotten...all this—and more—awaits you next month from Avon romance!

Linda Needham is fast becoming a rising star of romance, and her latest, *The Wedding Night*, is a wonderful, sensuous love story filled with all the power and passion of her earlier books. When a young woman is forced to marry a dark and dashing nobleman she expects to do her duty...but she never dreams she's also lost her heart to the one man capable of breaking it.

Lois Greiman's *Highland Brides* series is at the top of many readers' list of favorites. Her latest sweeping, sexy love story *Highland Enchantment* is sure to please anyone looking for a thrilling hero...and a powerful love story. If you haven't read the earlier books in the series, don't worry! This title is supremely entertaining romance for you, too.

Susan Sizemore is a name many of you recognize, and her Avon debut, *The Price of Innocence* is filled with the lush sensuality and powerful emotion that her fans have come to expect. When Sherry Hamilton looks across a crowded ballroom, she never expects to meet the eyes of the man who once took away her innocence. Can she now face a man she has never stopped hating—and loving?

Mary Alice Kruesi's *Second Star to the Right* is a must read for lovers of contemporary romance. It's tender, poignant, and one of the most magical love stories I've read in years. A single mother comes to London to escape her past, and finds her heart stolen by a man who makes her once again believe that dreams can come true.

It's all here at Avon romance! Enjoy,

*Lucia Macro*

Lucia Macro
Senior Editor

AEL 0499

## *Avon Romances—*
## *the best in exceptional authors*
## *and unforgettable novels!*

ENCHANTED BY YOU       by Kathleen Harrington
79894-8/ $5.99 US/ $7.99 Can

PROMISED TO A STRANGER       by Linda O'Brien
80206-6/ $5.99 US/ $7.99 Can

THE BELOVED ONE       by Danelle Harmon
79263-X/ $5.99 US/ $7.99 Can

THE MEN OF PRIDE COUTNY:       by Rosalyn West
THE REBEL       80301-1/ $5.99 US/ $7.99 Can

THE MACKENZIES: PETER       by Ana Leigh
79338-5/ $5.99 US/ $7.99 Can

KISSING A STRANGER       by Margaret Evans Porter
79559-0/ $5.99 US/ $7.99 Can

THE DARKEST KNIGHT       by Gayle Callen
80493-X/ $5.99 US/ $7.99 Can

ONCE A MISTRESS       by Debra Mullins
80444-1/ $5.99 US/ $7.99 Can

THE FORBIDDEN LORD       by Sabrina Jeffries
79748-8/ $5.99 US/ $7.99 Can

UNTAMED HEART       by Maureen McKade
80284-8/ $5.99 US/ $7.99 Can